Publisher: Published! A Village Voices Affiliate
Address: 1010 10th Avenue West, Bradenton, Fl 34205

ISBN-13: 978-0-984682751
ISBN-10: 0984682759

Manufactured in the United States

Publisher's note:
Blue Canyon first came onto the scene of writing erotic
fiction in the anthology – The Cougar Book, published
by Logical-Lust Publications in 2010.
Edited by Jolie du Pré, the book quickly became a
major hit among readers of erotica.
Available at all fine book-selling establishments.

Songs in the Key of Goth

Books I & II

I would like to thank the many women I've known in my life, for teaching me how to love and how to make love. To them I owe a debt of gratitude that transcends the mere moment of orgasm. To them I owe the teachings of near-spiritual elevation.

Oh God! Oh God! I'm...

Taste the Night

By:
Blue Canyon

wake!

    I waken to the hazy blue glow of the moon filling my heart with yearning, calling me to rise. I reach up—reaching, pushing through, climbing out. Looking down, brushing off the dirt clinging to me—stuck to my tattered clothes, in my mouth and ears. The creatures crawling in the Earth sung to me and I could hear them. Even now.

    My mind is as a clean slate, devoid of subject or focus. I can find no point of reference from which to plot my existence. Questions pound at the door of my brain, demanding attention to their needs, each having a singular purpose. Try as I might, I cannot fathom even the slightest memory of who I am or whence I came.

    The night is my domain. I know this without being told. I can feel its comfort around me like a blanket—protecting me against the grave cold. The grave—now empty behind me, I step into the shadows struggling to remember how I came to be here.

Rustling leaves startle me and my reflexes move with amazing quickness, but only an insect scurries nearby. Has my hearing grown so acute? Can I as easily hear something at a great distance?

As I make an attempt to focus I find it difficult to distinguish any single tone from the din. And what of my other senses? Looking back at the insect, I focus on it—bringing it closer to me with just my eyes—but nothing happens. Yet I feel as though something greater awaits me. However, I can ponder these possibilities only briefly.

Horses—I can hear them snorting, chewing. I remember horses. Perhaps my memory shall return. Other nuances begin to return and I can feel an almost complete picture. I smell their dung and the sourness of damp alfalfa hay juxtaposing the sweet molasses that's mixed in the grain. Drawn to the sound as I am, I feel as the wolf called to the scent of meat. But I am reminded how that very meat smell can lead the animal to be trapped. Does such a trap await me?

Hesitation slows my feet. Lumbering, searching, I am unable to find any evidence of civilization. Where am I? Where are these horses? Surely my hearing has not become so keen that I hear even gentle sounds so far beyond eyeshot. Would that I could be blessed with such great power. Imagine the uses such a power might afford me.

For have we not seen what the mighty can do? The muscles of the strong man at the circus, the sharpness of the Gypsy mind—these things lend awe to the common onlooker. Such a power could bring men to their knees and women to my bedchamber—if only I could remember where it is. The greatest opportunities, such as this one, come seldom in the life of an ordinary man.

Yet, I am not so ordinary as I may have once been—or perceive myself to have been. A prominence has been thrust upon me. Whatever I used to be, I am no more. I feel that for certain. Far be it from me to question such a gift, lest it be snatched from me in the blink of an eye. I would not belabor so over a trifling matter, but this is true uniqueness. I am, therefore, unique. The man who would be heralded as king. Meet...

Unaware as I am of the life I led only moments before, so too is the name I once bore lost unto me. The road ahead beckons and I know I must travel it. No life is truly alive if it remains stagnant. All beings must move forward—accepting or forsaking all that has been. Leaving behind decisions past and days lived. And youth grown away.

But what of my life before? Is there no significance to the roots from which I sprang? Must I discard all memory of that time for the sake of a gift from an unknown origin—that I know not how long I will possess? Nor even its true magnitude? One cannot know what to do with such a gift, particularly if one has no memory. Power corrupts and I feel the seed of corruption already planted deep within me. I would use such power for the good of mankind, but the call of

11

darkness is strong and sweet. Rather I would be not so blest. Can the gift be given back? Dare I look this 'gift horse' in the mouth?

The horses—I still hear them call, baying, trying to tell me something I am unable to fathom. I must seek them out, heed their council. They have much to tell me. I'm not sure how I know this, but I take with me the wariness of a bird in a cathouse or that wolf with the scent of meat in his snout. Until I regain the complete awareness of whom and what I am, danger lurks behind every shadow—even the darkest shadows that offer their odd comfort to my tense body.

Waking with tension would suggest restless sleep. Perhaps some tortured dream tormented my slumber, leaving me exhausted—having distorted senses. However, although my senses seem out of sorts, I do not feel exhausted. Quite the contrary, I feel great power welling within my body. I believe I could easily tear the head clean off one of those calling horses and gladly devour the meat inside.

Disgust sweeps past me but is quickly replaced by the churning in my stomach singing the song of hunger. Would my strange appetite actually be satisfied by the crude meat of such a majestic beast? Again I growl as an animal—answering my rhetorical question with a resounding affirmative.

I am suddenly shaken as the spit of an image flashes through my head. Although brief, I could see clearly and remember vividly. Shaking the blinding light from my eyes, I draw the image forward to examine it and find myself startled and perhaps a little frightened. Where I thought answers might lie, I find only more questions.

***

A dark street, cobblestone surface, small puddles have gathered from a recent shower. In them I see a hundred tiny reflections of the gas street lamps. The air carries a musty, yet intriguing scent as the moisture is quickly absorbed into the needy ground beneath. Somewhere in the distance—perhaps only a few streets away—I can hear the clopping of horse hooves casually striking the street.

I am coming from…someplace I cannot remember—but I am formally dressed. Therefore I deduce that I have come from a party or social gathering of some distinction. My own heels add to the noises that shatter the evening stillness as they strike the pavement with the determination of a man not entirely sure he wants to get home.

Something of light color draws my eye to an alleyway. Unafraid, I turn and enter the darkness within. My eyes adjust quickly and I can see her. A seductress. Her wiles are in full bloom and her smile still holds the sweetness of youth. Her top fallen, allowing her breasts to be exposed, offer a twinge of lust to my loins.

Approaching her, I dig in my pocket for the two pence a woman of her stature would require, but she

13

stays my hand with a gentle caress. Confused, I drop the coin back with the others in my possession and place my empty hand on her exposed flesh, feeling the rush of deviant pleasure from her hardened nipple. She is much shorter than I and I must lean far to kiss her pristine neck. The woman offers me all of herself by laying her head back against the wall behind.

I could have taken her then and there had I wanted—pushed her against the wall, lifted her petticoat, and had my way with her. As I said, I was not a man eager to return home. So it pleased me to move slowly, taking time to enjoy each moment, each new scent, every inch of her body.

The full moon—the only light available—washed over her as I drank in the beauty of her young flesh. When she leaned forward and I saw her face, I started. Even though her breasts were full and her scent strong, she looked as a child, showing dimples in her smile, and lashes—long and curled—brushing against her cheeks as she shyly batted them.

Taken slightly aback, I hesitated, staying my hand from the child flesh I'd been seduced by. Feeling fortunate I'd taken to moving slowly this night, I offered my apologies and turned to leave. She held me back with but a word.

"Sir?"

The music in her tones held me fast. A carnal part of me wanted her more than life itself, but my morals shouted into my ears saying the words of decency and caution—reminding me of the right thing to do by asking the simple question: "How would I feel if it were my daughter out on the street?"

But the loins spoke louder, calling me back to her budding womanhood, seeking the procreative urges that fester within us all. My hesitation told her all the answer she needed to hear. Her hand—resting on my sleeve—now slid down, off my cuff, away from my hand, exploring other places. I stiffened but did not push her away.

My entire body now tensed with apprehension, but I knew I would not turn from her again this night. I would enjoy her touch and her scent until the wee hours of the morning—morals be damned. I reached to embrace her.

She accepted my advance willingly, sliding her hands onto my back and resting her head on my shoulder. The night swam in my head and I could feel very little save her touch. The scent of womanhood again rose up wafting through my nose like a powerful uppercut, and my eyes rolled back, closed.

Suddenly the pain struck me. My neck stung, urging my hand to rise and swat whatever insect dared intrude on this romantic, though morally perverse interlude. I would not have such a creature interfere with the delights this girl could show me. My hand came quickly but contacted only the back of her head, lying against my neck.

Had she trapped the insect against my neck? Was it inside her mouth? Perhaps she risked the biting creature as well. Was she unaware or did she do it to eliminate the tiny beast because she, too, wanted the evening to remain uninterrupted? I felt about with my fingers, seeking understanding without sight. Her mouth indeed pressed tightly against my throat. From beneath, something wet trickled down—I assumed the girl's saliva as a womanly lust overtook her.

Verily, understanding eluded me until she pulled her head back to once again look into my eyes. Her petticoat had fallen to her ankles and she now stood completely naked before me, and yet I could barely look away from her face—from her mouth. Elongated teeth smiled at me through the dark liquid dripping off down her chin and onto her firm breasts.

Blood, my blood, she drank the very life essence that flowed through my veins. I cowered but my strength ebbed, pressing my hand tightly against my neck. Stumbling several times, I finally collapsed only a few feet away from her, not nearly far enough for anyone to see me from the street and offer assistance. Fear swam in my head even as her lusty scent had moments before. Her laughter hurt my ears and her hands-on-hips pose suggested brazen apathy. I glanced around for anything I could grasp and perhaps throw at the demon girl, but my hand found no purchase—no object. Hopelessness replaced my fear as my head sank to the hard ground. I could smell the dirt.

And then, blackness.

otor cars rushing by offer the only breeze available on a hot summer evening. With the air still and the heat high, I could certainly imagine a more tepid climate in a quieter town with great longing. Yet I have settled in Florida. Brushing off the memory of the woman/girl who sired me, I wonder about my choices past and present.

Air movement thrust upon me by passing automobiles carries a pungent odor that bears no resemblance to the fragrant flowers and fruits in some of the tropical places I've enjoyed so much. So why would someone like me live in a place like this, you might ask. I would be hard pressed to explain properly without divulging my true nature to you.

For it is indeed my dark spirit that has me squandering my nights away in this hellish land. Without war, there has never been a place on Earth that offers so much death—murder, elderly, suicide, random acts of violence—all these and more would serve me,

17

allowing me to feed without drawing attention. Here, I eat well.

The putrid scents of tar and oil mix, rising from the street in heat-infected waves, blown about by swift-moving vehicles with passengers happy to add to the olfactory nightmare by tossing out garbage, old food, and lit cigarettes along the way. And the resulting stench settles on my clothes and skin. I am not sure I can be comfortable in this time—this era. I feel I've been in this place the longest—trapped.

Why does it appear as though 2009 will never depart? Has the world become so afraid of the fresh winds of change that it would impair its own progress intentionally? Fate was never something to be feared but rather a companion, joining us on the journey of life, along for the trip but acting as guide when we strayed.

In the last hundred years—give or take a few—I have travelled the many lands of this planet, mostly in search of others like me. But my kind is not easily found. They hide in shadows, surviving, endeavoring to remain unknown, endearing themselves only upon those who would be made victim. Verily there were a few, mostly in Romania and Bulgaria—and that one in Czechoslovakia.

I roamed, searching, inquiring, being careful not to bring attention to myself. One such as I cannot simply enter a tavern and ask outright if any vampires live in the area. After they finished laughing I would be tortured and hung, and then locked up for an eternity—

or perhaps two. In my condition that would be a very long time.

After seeing how poorly people treat each other, I worked my way to America and discovered a true home—for nowhere else in the world is there so much death and so little compassion. Among these states, Florida excels, stands out, ranks high if not number one on the violence rating scale. In violence, I have become a true expert. To me violence is like chamber music, soothing. I often stop to listen. Sometimes, I prefer to play a tune, myself—becoming the musician of mayhem, the conductor of chaos.

All in all, over my hundred plus years of life, I have seen very little real progress in people outside their music. Oh technology has truly progressed to almost miracle status, but people are the dregs of the Earth. They alone prey on their own kind and laugh about it. They destroy lives—even those of their own children and loved ones—more efficiently, thanks to the technology, but with little care. Thusly they bring about a structure for reason, giving each murderous mind the chance to explain their heinous actions in a logical manner.

Over time, the courts have become disordered and less efficient. Many criminals are released, free to commit again, while many more suffer significant penalties for insignificant crimes. But it is not for me or any of my kind to become involved with the laws of mortals for they are foolish and breathe not life into my being. Let them tear each other down as one might an old building. It just means more for us to feed on.

Walking down Cortez Avenue, many is the time I can hear several arguments, a car accident or two, breaking glass, a multitude of the signature noises belonging to the heart of violence. Violence is inherent in the species and yet the purveyors come together in groups, seeking each other, desiring competition. I am befuddled. Were I to pursue such a life, I would surely choose a place where no other like me has already set roots, thereby giving me more opportunity and less attention.

The avenue, under my feet once again— although truly it never left, often reminds me of those cobblestone streets where I first met Millicent Continay, she who took away my life once that I might live anew. I often called her the Duchess of Continence because of her peculiar habit of peeing herself whenever her laughter got out of control. This singularly human weakness gave us all reason to laugh uncontrollably. She grew rather cross when I would speak that special nickname in public.

Tonight, as most, I search for someone to feed on. I search for the next unwary yet self-destructive victim to simply throw herself on my fangs. There are times when I feel I could simply lie back with my mouth open, so bent they are on ending their most beautiful miracle. They disgust me. Pity other sources of nutrition cannot sustain my life. I have tried. None satisfy my need. So I seek a quick end to my search for satiation that I might enjoy at least a part of the disappearing evening, as I often do, in solitude.

The club I frequent offers an odd mixture of tones sometimes referred to as *Techno*, though I would give it another name. Of all the musics I find today, this one offends me the least—even so, in my vast experience, I've discovered they all exceed comfortable volume limits. Despite my repeated suggestions to the management, none have ever accommodated my gentler palate, while my supersensitive ears continue to suffer the agony of resonance. It might be less disturbing were I not afflicted in such a manner, if one would call my heightened senses an affliction.

But vampire blood has run in my veins for a hundred years and I doubt that it could simply be removed. And yet the news broadcast I saw barely a fortnight ago suggested that very thing. Doctors claim to have discovered a means to filter elements out of the blood—any particular set of elements they choose. This could mean the end of many dreadful diseases.

Is vampirism a disease? They offer a cure for that which is not wrong with me. Another healthcare/get-rich-quick gimmick to separate money from the little people, or a deadly weapon to be used in the destruction and annihilation of the vampire race— either way, I'm not buying.

There have been many products on the market over years past that I have given more than ample attention. Unfortunately, few of them lived up to (or even came close to) their advertised promises. I see no reason to believe any blood filter can truly perform to the standards claimed, even if it meant becoming mortal again.

One particular such folly involved a product claiming to whiten teeth overnight. Of course, as you might well imagine, discoloration can be a problem for vampires. Blood stains. So I ordered. I didn't know it simply coated your teeth with a synthetic polymer. Normally this would not present itself as a problem. As I may have already mentioned, I am not normal.

When my fangs grew out of my mouth, the polymer cracked and the tips poked through the covering, making them look like they'd just hatched from two tiny eggs. But I must add, whatever the company used as adhesive lived up to its pledge. For days I could not brush or scrape off the horror that my smile had become.

I didn't eat during that time. Oh, not because of pain or embarrassment, but rather since I could not lure my victims to privacy. The greatest power a vampire can have is his lure. A vampire cannot simply bite someone in the middle of a crowded room. Therefore, he must project a sensual, confident image, one that potential victims will feel compelled to join, much as a fitness trainer who is out of shape will attract very few customers.

In this way Millicent Continay had such difficulty. Taken at the ripe age of fifteen, she had the most difficult time of anyone I'd ever seen. She didn't age. Her youth attracted very few—morals, of course, being her greatest enemy. In the end she resorted to trickery. My brief glance in her direction told me nothing of her age, although truly she'd been a vampire for eighty years when she took me. She used shadow and subterfuge to lure me. Exposed breasts stealing my attention, I saw only too late her little girl face. Then I was dead and buried, rising up that very night from the Earth.

Some things about vampires are so difficult to understand and impossible to explain. While Millicent remained fifteen, her breasts grew. I handled those breasts many times after I became a vampire, but the image of that night in the alley can still arouse me more than other memories of her.

The night has taken on an unusual deadness, as if all the moisture had suddenly been sucked out of the air. It draws my mind back to the present night in Florida. Dry air can be such a problem for vampires. Without any circulation, our skin is not constantly moisturized like mortals. Moisture in the air can help keep our skin pliable and give the appearance of life. In time the dry air would begin to cause pain and flaking skin would turn to decaying flesh. But that time is far away and Florida has normally high humidity—another great reason for living here.

The club—I'm nearly there, now—will have air conditioning which will dry my skin even further. But the threat of having to leave early is premature. As always, I have little intention of staying until dawn. The music can cause such pain after only a short time, not to mention the pesky sunlight that continues to come around every morning.

When I turn and see the club, I'm pleased the line is short. Overcrowding offers some interesting opportunities, but I've never been comfortable with too many people. Too much constriction, no room to move freely, if I had to make a quick exit, I might be hindered—unable. It is a situation I would prefer to avoid.

"Mr. Negrand," the doorman says, recognizing me. "Always a pleasure. We've missed you."

"Thank you, Randy."

He waves me in with genuine pleasure. I suppose I've earned a reputation for being a good tipper. It hardly seems like much to me, as money carries little meaning except when dealing with humans. But they worship the vile currency so and I earn favors by flaunting it. Of course, living more than one lifetime, I've managed to accumulate quite a large sum.

He says he missed me. In these tough economic times, he probably doesn't see many people who leave any tip at all, let alone a large one. But I find it peculiar since I've been gone merely three days, and it's not the first time I've taken leave of my regular schedule.

On the contrary, it is my habit to occasionally take time away for several reasons. Chief among them is the need to remain unpredictable. Too much habit can make one easier to corner. I don't need anyone associating even one particularly gruesome death to my presence. Also, a long time ago I learned about the many benefits of meditation. Taught to me by the Dalai Lama, himself—just before I drank his blood—I've learned ways to focus my mind and further influence those I would feed on. I suppose that gives me an advantage over many other vampires.

I make no excuses for my comings and goings. Randy and the others will just have to learn how to survive when I'm not around. Imagine how they would react if they knew what I really am. Mostly, I care not for their petty concerns. If they found out, I would feed on them. I have never exposed what I am except to those I already had my hands on, nor am I likely to begin such a dangerous habit.

Once targeted for lunch, as Millicent would say, then all bets are off. They can see your fangs or the blaze of your eyes. By then it's too late to scream, too late to run. That would happen tonight. I'd found nothing along the road to satisfy my hunger. I would have to feed on a patron of the club. Because a body could be traced back to me, I usually refrained from taking my meals where I frequented. On occasion, it became necessary.

Right now my first choice would be Randy. I don't take kindly to being monitored and my absences are my own business. He'd been warned before about becoming too inquisitive. He called it friendly. I called it imposing and dangerous. My smaller frame didn't intimidate him in the least, but he backed down—no doubt out of a sense of duty to the customer, and for no other reason. No matter, in the end his discretion would be in his best interest.

Inside, as always, the music accosts me, beating into my bones, disturbing my calm, scratching at the very fabric of my being. Even on a weeknight the place has a good crowd, and the music is at full volume. I wonder, not for the first time, why anyone would be so concerned about my measly contributions with so many patrons.

My nose crinkles as smoke, body odor, cologne, and pheromones combined to hit me at the same time as the music. Beneath it I smell the blood of the living, drawing me, calling. Wandering a room full of people can be distracting as the smell of blood and physical desire sweeps in from all directions. I force my stomach to stop growling even though no one could hear above the sound system that probably cost more than a person's life.

While almost anyone might make a satisfactory meal, I never found anything wrong with seeking out the more delectable, the fresher, the preferred flavor du jour. After all, no one is in the mood for the same food every day, and there's more difference between two humans than any mere mortals could possibly guess. Unless you've tasted it, you can't know the subtle nuances from A+ to AB-, or the bitter bouquet of the Os. If a man has never tasted the delicate flavors of a fine filet mignon, listen to him ramble on about the succulent nature of a common hamburger.

Perhaps my enhanced taste buds have something to do with the subtle distinction. But one scent this evening has pulled my nose away from the direction it wanted several times. I'm not sure what has caused my fascination, nor can I ferret it out. Each turn finds another couple bumping me aside for the sake of their near-sexual interactions—all without being removed from the club for lewd behavior. The only stipulation for this, it seems, is to remain clothed. Almost anything else is accepted or ignored.

When my nose finally locked on to its target, I confront a vision of youth and beauty, rivaling my beloved Millicent's. Her eyes catch mine. When I can get close enough, the music no longer bothers me—fading, at least temporarily. I hear none. Her heavy breathing, the pounding of her heart, the coursing of blood, these are the musics that invade my ears. And then, the whisper of her sweet voice.

"I'm Tina."

"Collin," I return. "May I have this dance?"

Traveling through Italy, one dark, fall evening in the late teenage years of the nineteen hundreds, I spied a raven-haired beauty eyeing me a little more than casually. Her eyes sparkled in my direction and I felt something peculiar from her—though nothing I could precisely put my finger on.

Her curls bounced around her shoulders and breasts, lending an air of youth to her—an air that the scent reaching my nose belied. The colorful dress and white frilly top she wore spoke more of Spain than Italy, and she spun it around with practiced grace. I could not help but be drawn to her.

The scent of flowers in the air became nondescript under the overwhelming aroma of this woman. Her lips pursed when she smiled. Sultry and seductive, she looked directly into me, through me, all over me. I felt uncomfortable for the first time in my life— fidgeting slightly under her wanton scrutiny.

"Bellissimo, Señorina. Le a molto bella!"

"Grazie, Señore."

"What is it about you that draws me to you so?"

"It may be hard to believe, but I am a vampire."
She spoke in brazen tones, making dangerous
admissions in public to a total stranger.

"Indeed." I felt surprised. I can usually spot
another of my kind from many yards away, but this
lady had me baffled. "And what is your name?"

"Ana. Ana Fiorelli."

"How long have you been a vampire?"

"Several years. Who keeps track of such
things?"

"I'd never known a vampire who didn't know
precisely how long ago they'd been changed."

"Look at that, tomorrow you won't be able to
say the same thing." She smiled.

"Yes." I felt skeptical. But why should she lie
to me? I could imagine no gain from such a fable and
yet I doubted her word. She just didn't *smell* like a
vampire. I would never be so rude as to say such a
thing. "Well, I too am a vampire."

"I know. I felt an attraction to you instantly.
Are you planning on living here?"

"No. I seek a place—something different."
Looking around, I knew I would stand behind my
words. "This will not do, at all."

"It's a nice place. You could be happy here."
"Oh?"

"I would like a friend like you living around
here."

"You don't even know me."

"We are kindred."

"That does not make us compatible."

"We could try. I would like that."

"I may be more than you can handle," I offered. I still felt hesitation at accepting her word about being a vampire. However, I found her enchanting and disquietingly beautiful. It had been so long since I'd touched a woman—other than to feed, even the hint of an evening together brought a tingle to my loins.

"I doubt that," she challenged.

"Perhaps," I looked around, "we could go somewhere more private? Do you know such a place nearby?"

"I do, as a matter of fact. We could spend some time getting to know each other and then discuss your future in more depth."

"Spending time with such a beauty would be an honor, my dear. As for the other, we shall see. Can you accept such a limitation?"

"I can live with it, if you will consider my proposal."

I nodded, gentlemanly.

She held out her hand to guide. "Shall we?"

"Grazie."

The woman actually brought me to her flat which was quite spacious and tastefully furnished. I made no effort to hide my casual look around as she offered some excuse to leave the room and change her clothes for comfort. *She may not be a vampire but she has managed her money remarkably well.*

Returning to the main room, she wore a gentle and sheer one piece shortie—the kind of garment not used for anything save sleeping and seduction, I would imagine. Clearly, I did not feel at all like sleeping. Rather hoping she felt the same, I awkwardly approached her, knowing full well that my arousal showed for her to see. A man is often disquieted by signs of weakness and yet we frequently succumb to the lure of a woman's power—given her simply by the possession of female genitalia.

The disarray of my trousers proved me no more or less than a man, if indeed I could still be called such a thing since I'd been dead for almost twenty years. In the case of a vampire, dead does not mean 'things' do not work. And working they most certainly were at that moment. When confronted by rare and striking beauty—as I was then—composure can be fleeting.

As my hand slipped around her I discovered a waist thicker than I had originally perceived. This did little to deter the wanting I felt and in fact heightened my arousal for some reason I could not fathom. Although many men claim to enjoy larger women, I myself prefer one who is slender and demure. But this was no ordinary woman. She boasted of being a vampire while smelling of humanity. Though my doubts remained, something about this enchantress kept me interested for more than the time it would take to bite her.

That is how I have come to measure such things. If my curiosity lasts longer than 'bite time', I consider it a love affair. This woman continued to excite me, despite my familiarity with only the briefest encounters in the past. With very few exceptions, the women I loved were not worth the time beyond biting them. *In fact,* I would often quip, *some of them should have been bitten years ago. It would have been best for the world if they'd been taken out sooner. Perhaps vampirism would improve their intelligence. Perhaps, if I just killed them outright, it would at least reduce the population of lower minds.*

I chose not to make any of them into vampires. The truth is; I didn't want to tarnish our name. Oh, people call us dark, they call us demons, but we are the elite—Gods among the helpless, wolves in the fold. I could not risk polluting the bloodline with the insufferable pipsqueaks that inhabit the planet. I would rather the entire race wither away and die.

As Ana's hands explore me, I am drawn away from thoughts of such grandiose. Her touch brings thoughts of Millicent and I am pulled away from the joy of the present to the curious and sometimes intrusive memories of the past. A past I often longed to be rid of, a past filled with more emotions than just joy, a past I would rather forget. My mind, on the other hand, has a will of its own and travels where it will, much to my sadness.

***

Millicent stood before me, hands squeezing her own breasts, calling me with her eyes. The scent of her adolescent arousal filled the air. I always felt its intoxicating effects very quickly, almost as if her scent had been engineered specifically for my palate.

Early in my vampire life, barely a decade after the turn of the century, I spent nearly every waking moment with her. She became my focus, my song. If it were possible for a vampire to love, I would have pledged my life to her in eternal sacrament. I might have even dared set foot inside a church.

Closing the gap between us, we embraced— nothing in the middle now, not even clothes to keep our skin from making contact. The youth of her face that I found so disconcerting on the night we met, now only enhanced the arousal she felt growing between my legs. Her body, forever firm and tight, quickly shifted position and I found myself staring at the wall as she knelt before me—using her mouth, kissing me intimately, scraping her vampire teeth along my skin there as that part of me fit perfectly between them. I could not help but reward her.

But such a night with her would hardly be over. To her, this action was only a prelude to greater things. Vampires have great stamina, but hers knew few bounds. She would often lie back, swinging her feet up and laying her knees back on either side of her head, allowing for quite a view. Then she would instruct me to stand over her and plunge in with all my might. I would often be reminded of one of those drilling rigs, but it wasn't oil I would find at the bottom of this well.

My feelings for her flood over me, cascading, like standing beneath a waterfall. I'd never believed in love, even when I was alive. But as a vampire I thought it impossible. My time with Millicent seemed like pure joy and I never wanted it to end. But the consideration of love, even with my head in the clouds, never occurred to me…at the time. Now, looking back, well, who is to say what is or is not? And it makes little difference.

Once done with the lovemaking, she and I would venture out and have someone to eat. She liked to play with her prey, a cat toying with her mouse. I, on the other hand, retained some respect for the living and offered them a simple, quick, respectful demise. I believed that sparing them the fear would be about as humane as I could offer without denying myself the luxury of ever eating another meal. I would save them their despair and the horror of death by exsanguination.

At the beginning of our relationship, Millicent and I would go out and eat first, then return to our lair and have sex all night and into the day, sometimes. After a time, however, I became—shall we say— disenchanted with the antics she played as she fed. There were times it would be difficult for me to perform or even become aroused. I could see this hurt her but I had no control, and she would not stop her child-like habit. So we agreed to work in reverse.

While this put a damper on the limitless lovemaking sessions—we had to make sure we got to eat before sun up—it nevertheless allowed us to do both without complication. Although there were times when I would have forgone food for sake of making love to her longer and longer—my Eve, my Juliette, the only sunshine I could bask in without searing the flesh from my bones, thought only that I did not find her attractive anymore.

Even though this could not have been any further from the truth, my protests fell on deaf ears and she carried her hurt all the time—with her, like a trusted purse. This night, as most, our session of love needed to be timed and I did my best to find oil at the bottom of that well. Discovery came, as did we. Then we fed.

***

Almost any time of day or night one can smell tomatoes and vegetables cooking as the women like to simmer their foods for days. The flavors of human food still had some appeal and could bring about a pang of hunger as easily in a vampire as it did in a living person. But Italy was full of one thing that never sat well with vampires.

Garlic.

I managed to ignore its unique and pungent odor and, having no memory of a time when I loved the tiny herb with the giant taste, concentrated on the beauty in my arms. Ana had backed away and removed her petticoat. When she lay on the bed, her legs went up and her knees fell beside her head, arching her back in a familiar manner.

A shiver shot through me as the memory of Millicent flooded back in brief flashes. My arousal intensified at the uncommon positioning and Ana smiled her approval. While the memory of Millicent's immature woman scent could still attract my loins, I could not tell if that memory had done it this time or the scent of the aroused woman in my current company. Ana smelled divine. I could not resist. I tasted.

This position offered more than fond memories of a time long ago. Easy access to her most intimate parts gave a man the feeling of power—though most men were completely under the spell of the vagina and wielded no real power of their own. Vaginas were the true demon on Earth. They could hold mortal men at bay, draw them closer, seduce them to do unspeakable things, turn them away from their family, bear false witness, steal, and become secularly seduced. While I wanted to enjoy this wanton beauty for many hours, I knew I could turn away at any moment I chose, simply because I wanted as much.

I drank deeply, her favors—longing to enter her, driving harder toward the end of one thing, leading to the next. Enthusiasm taking control of me, I sped toward one crescendo after another, knowing she would not soon forget the name Collin Negrand. Then, as she lay nearly exhausted from the attentions I provided, I stood and began to drill—pounding to depths previously unknown. Her bed was particularly noisy.

Her moans escaped in soft, guttural growls. If I expected her to have the stamina I did, she disappointed me. I kept going until I felt satisfied, but at some point during it all, she'd managed to become nearly comatose. This might offer some men a boost to their ego, but as for myself, I could only question further her statement that she was indeed a vampire.

Once sated, I dismounted and settled beside her—her legs falling back to the bed. I allowed my eyes to close. Further dreams of Millicent swam into my mind but few of them were as enjoyable as the brief flash of lovemaking I'd remembered earlier. These images, from what little I could remember, were from a time when sadness ruled and torture came in many forms. By the look of our coverings when I woke, I must have slept in motion, tying myself up in the top blanket, pulled up against a cold that did not exist at this time of year.

Next to me, an empty space in the bed offered many thoughts—betrayal, abandonment, and danger chief among them. I jumped to my feet, still naked with my manhood swaying, and looked around the room for would-be vampire hunters. I saw none. Tiny noises drew me out to the main room.

The day had worn on and the afternoon sun sank in the distance. I saw Ana sitting at a table eating. While I did not recognize the dish, my nose could not so easily be fooled. Along with a myriad of odors coming from her food, rosemary and basil among them, I could instinctively pick out the garlic. To most it will simply ward off the advance of one such as me—if it is laying around loosely. But to ingest it, the stories say the vampire body will burn from the inside out. And it will burn until nothing is left.

These stories may or may not all be true, but many come from gypsies and other vampires who do not speak falsely. This burning from the inside is told to take several hours, beginning much like heartburn and increasing beyond the pain of a burst appendix— which I'm told is minor by comparison. In the end, the painful burning overtakes your entire body and the outer skin deteriorates, falling away like flakes of cheese when grating it.

Ana, I now became convinced, was not a vampire. Her ruse brought me here when I might otherwise not have done so. Although I felt no disappointment with our sexual encounter, lying seemed so childish. Once again these thoughts returned my mind to the fifteen year old blonde who first seduced me in an alley twenty years before.

I fought to stay in the present, to deal with the quandary of Ana and what I should do about her. Leaving behind a mortal who knew who and what I am was a risk I didn't feel comfortable taking. And yet, she'd been so open and kind, and a good partner. And her dark beauty was beyond compare. I stepped into the room.

She stood quickly and looked at me. She'd neglected to dress and her glory displayed perfectly for me to admire. She bounced toward me and I struggled with the appropriate reaction. Before I could decide, she'd arrived and began kissing me around my chest and neck—leaving little burn marks where her garlic-laced lips touched. And the pain felt so good.

"Let me clean you off." She knelt before me as Millicent used to do, taking me in her mouth and showing me her love. With my more delicate skin burning slightly, I still managed to become aroused and soon she brought me to a new release, making sure to 'clean up' as she'd promised. In that moment I decided that no matter what I chose to do with her, killing her would be out of the question.

odern Florida, as I call it, holds little of the quaint romance that Italy did over eighty years ago. While I generally traveled abroad in those days, I'd be willing to wager that Florida may have been rather quaint many years before, as well. Now it's a thriving metropolis with barely any distinction between where one town ends and another begins.

Far be it from me to hinder the advancement of mankind in its progress toward whatever Utopia awaits it, but sometimes I can't help but long for simpler days. I draw these conclusions frequently when I've become inundated by the buzz of electronics. Beeping sensors and humming circuit boards all ring into my hearing range, bringing on another of the few human weaknesses vampires can be susceptible to. Headaches. I don't dare even walk into a computer store.

Dancing with Tina brought me a small amount of entertainment, then the music intruded again as if it had reign to return at will. I'm sure I should feel fortunate to have received any relief at all, but disappointment still fills my heart. As I try not to look directly at the girl, knowing my eyes would give away my discomfort, the intuition afforded her gender does her proud.

"What's wrong?"

"Sorry. A headache. The music is so loud in these places."

"Yeah, great, isn't it?"

"Not particularly."

"Huh? I didn't hear you."

"I said," trying to speak a little louder. "Would you like to get out of here?"

"Don't waste much time, do you?"

"Would you prefer that I did?"

She looked introspective and quickly replied. "No, I think not." She eyed my full stature admiringly. "I'd rather you get right down to business," she added, pointing down.

I thought, perhaps, she meant something to do with her shoes. I looked at them—a handsome pair of shiny black strap-ons with heels that were tall and fat. *High heels with balance, hmmm.* Very nice, but I saw no connection to her comment or the 'dirty girl' smile I saw on her face. Rather than appear ignorant, I decided to answer the girl with a knowing glance and some vague 'uh-huh' kind of response. She smiled immediately.

Her smile looked much like Ana's and I briefly wandered to that memory once again. Ana had been human, as I'd suspected. She admitted, after much persuasion, she desired to have sex with vampires. This urge overwhelmed her frequently. As lovers, she concluded, we were far superior to mortal males. After the swelling in my pride went down, I reminded her of the dangers.

"What can they do, kill me?"

"Or even worse," I replied. "They could make you like them, a vampire."

"That would be great."

Excuse me? Though I recoiled, I'd heard correctly. She *wanted* to be a vampire. In the modern world, she would be referred to as a 'wannabe'. If she wants to be a vampire, who am I to refuse. *Besides, then I don't have to worry about a mortal knowing the true identity of a vampire. It all works out.*

"Am I the first vampire you've been with?"

"No. I've had many."

"And none would turn you?"

Her cheeks flared red and she averted her eyes. "Until now, I never got up the nerve to ask."

"Still, none killed you."

"Obviously," she shot back.

I admired her brevity, and her bravery. "I wonder why not."

Well, the entire situation gave me the creeps just a little. I know that's odd, a vampire creeping out over anything so mortal. Something about the honesty of the girl touched me. I've met so many people and I can't help appreciate a genuine soul when I meet one.

Fortunately for my generous attitude, there haven't been too many.

"Would you like me to turn you into a vampire?"

"Would you? Really? You'd do that for me?"

"Are you sure it's what you *really* want? You must be sure."

"Oh, I've been sure for a long time."

"I'll make you a deal. You must listen to me tell you about how my life is from day to day. Once you are a vampire you cannot take it back simply because you decide you don't like something about it. Before you answer, I must warn you. I am no yarn spinner. I will instructionally list the many aspects of life as a vampire that differ most significantly from being a mortal. Some are good and some are not nearly so—not so good, indeed. You must decide for yourself."

"And if, after all that, I still want to become a vampire?"

"I will grant your wish."

"My own personal genie," she giggled, touching me intimately.

I could not help but smile at her lightheartedness and charm—two of the first things she would most likely lose when she changed. *Truly a sad loss.* But for now, the challenge was mine. And where to begin?

"You can go outside day or night. I cannot expose myself to direct sunlight."

"Well, I've never been one for tanning."

"I cannot eat garlic." I offered this, confident it would deter her.

"That's a loss I'll have to deal with. What else?"

"My senses are heightened. I can smell and hear things you cannot. My taste and sight are equally enhanced. This can be difficult when I'm around too much noise or odors that are distasteful."

"That sounds wonderful."

"Anything you know that represents purity can cause trouble. Silver, religious symbols, running water, all these are potentially injurious and perhaps fatal."

"Lots of things can kill us mortals. Some of those things don't even give vampires a rash."

"True. You know something of us. Perhaps you would like to ask some questions?"

"Can you die from a wooden stake through your heart?" she asked, carefully.

"But of course. Can't you?"

"Oh, yeah. I never thought of that. How about decapitation?"

"Again just as you."

"But bullets can't harm you." She said this as a statement rather than a question.

"Not unless they're made of silver or they've been blessed."

"Do you sleep in a coffin and all that?"

I laughed. "I sleep in a bed, as do you."

"It doesn't sound like we're much different."

"My weaknesses can be deadly. You cannot say that. You cannot be killed by something as healthy as the sun."

"No, but you can't be killed by bullets. You can't suffocate."

"That is true. But I cannot save a child by giving mouth-to-mouth."

"Do you want to?"

"To what?"

"Save people?"

"I am not a heartless beast," I reassured her.

"No, but you possess a tireless beast."

I caught the object of her attention and smiled, dismissing her brevity as far too casual for the seriousness of the situation.

"Must you feed every night?"

"As with many animals, I can sustain on one feeding for several weeks at a time. This I can supplement with regular human food—particularly the red meats. Pork is not much fun since it must be fully cooked for humans, but beef offers a great many savory flavors. It can be a most enjoyable treat."

"Can you catch diseases from someone's blood?" she continued.

"To the best of my knowledge, I cannot." I sighed. "But there are so many new illnesses now. Who is to say?"

"Can you turn into animals, like wolves and bats?"

I couldn't hold a little chuckle. "I don't think I've ever tried that one. Why would I want to?"

"That's about it for me. What else have you got?"

I gave her a stern look. "There is no manual. You could touch something deadly to vampires, never having heard a warning about it. Perhaps other vampires don't even know. And since our bodies turn quickly to dust, we may not learn, even after you die from it."

"And yet you live."

"I could no more change being a vampire than you can change being a woman."

"And there's no manual about being one of those, I assure you. But I've managed so far."

"Yes, and very well, I might add."

"Then you'll do it?"

"Your argument is convincing. Yet I still have reservations."

"So," she finally said. "What else is there to discuss?"

***

While I might normally take my dinner anywhere along the road, something about Tina made me want more. I wanted to have sex with her before I ate. So I accompanied her all the way back to her apartment, ignoring many dark places along the way where I could have fed and simply been done with her.

Her small living space felt homey and smelled of stir-fry, although I distinctly noticed MSG and corn oil. Humans could be so quaint about issues of health. Oriental food didn't bother me much though I could hardly be called a vegetarian. However, I noticed in the last twenty or so years, Asian's began adding garlic in their food almost as much as the Italians. Hers didn't smell that way and I suspect she made the dish herself.

"Very nice," I complimented her apartment.

"It works." Then she added, "For now."

Her blouse came off and I noticed one of those new bras women wear that allow them to show through an unbuttoned front. When she turned I caught my breath. Her ample chest struggled against the material she still wore. I hadn't paid proper homage to her figure at the club.

She smiled, offering a full view by holding her arms out to her side and turning slightly left and right. I could do nothing but smile and nod. She only meant to ask if I thought they were nice. I answered in the best manner I could, under the circumstances. My grunt could hardly be distinguished from a canine belch.

Somehow she managed to find it complimentary. She reached behind herself. When she sprung her breasts loose, I could feel the pain of the red welts flaring up on the skin caused by the too-tight undergarment of torture. Her large, pale nipples looked at me sadly. Obviously they weren't happy about being trapped in that terrible device all day, either. After her pants fell, I enjoyed another tight-fitting garment. Her

47

thong fit right in where it was designed to go. I couldn't help but admire the round shape of her derriere as she walked toward the bed, leading me with nothing more than hip-sway.

I followed, removing my clothing.

Unlike Ana, this girl had stamina and a very creative mind. Twisting into contortionist positions, I found myself ducking a swinging foot or clamoring to re-enter her, having fallen out during her antics. On the rather more positive side, I will say this. I had an exceptional time with her. Possibly, I had a better time than with anyone else before. How odd, now that the time to bite her is nigh, I should feel no remorse, no hesitation, and I know I'll have no regrets later.

Peculiar the way feelings work after one has become a vampire. I should think very highly of this young Tina for the time she gave me in bed. But I do not. All I think at this moment is how, among other things, her blood will also probably taste very well.

She lay on her back, breathing as if exhausted, making no effort to cover her voluptuous, naked body. I leaned in and rested my head on her shoulder. The smell of her blood only a few inches away, aroused me even more than her bare breasts. The time for hesitation had passed. I stretched out my teeth and leaned forward.

When I feel the pressure of my fangs against the outer layer of someone's neck skin, it's much like having the head of my penis just touching a woman's outer labia. Anticipation still exists, but all doubt is now gone. There is no more wondering *IF* you will become intimate. It is now a foregone conclusion. I felt much the same at that moment. I tightened my neck muscles, making ready for the final thrust that would take me inside her.

A nice little snap of my head, rather like a sneeze, and my fangs slipped in almost as easily as that penis entering the vagina. Lubrication was totally irrelevant. Her body spasmed much the way it felt when she orgasmed. Her hands pushed against my arms in one last, vain effort to push me away and stop the pain. Her strength was no match for me.

With my senses so acute, I could feel every layer of skin I passed through. Even my teeth could feel the difference, nearing the warmth, anticipating the flavor. When finally the tips of my fangs emerged on the other side and poked into the blood vessel located right there, I quickly withdrew them and began sucking the life-giving elixir through the holes I'd made.

The flavor of salt and beef warmed over my tongue, thick and heady like a wine roux. As I swallowed, I could feel the tinge of iron feeding my needy body. But it felt shallow, like she may have been iron deficient. I craved more as I continued to drink. I sucked at her neck like a college boy trying to give her the best hickey he could—marking his territory. Even after the last drops came to my wanting mouth, I continued to suck, trying to draw out any remaining morsels.

Of course any resistance had ceased several minutes before and I held her lifeless body up, hugging her closer, sucking harder, feeling her dead breasts pressing against me, growing cold even as I kept searching for more. But she was empty. With a curse, I tossed her useless body back to the bed, disgusted that she offered so little satisfaction when she'd been such a good lover.

After I drink, there is usually a feeling of the blood working its way into my body, sustaining my life. Warm tingles spread over me and I feel euphoric, like taking some of the drugs I've been offered. In the last few decades, the use of hallucinogenic drugs has increased. Many are the times I've been going to have sex and the woman handed me something to supposedly enhance the experience.

The only problem is, like most poisons and chemicals and medicines, they have no effect on vampires. I enjoyed what I enjoyed because they did. And because, as most men, I needed the release. With it, I could feel sated once again, if only for a short time. But euphoria, I understood. I'd been euphoric from champagne back when I was mortal. And I could certainly see what Ecstasy did for my partner.

Of course, I felt euphoric every time I drank the blood of someone living, as I did right then. I could feel the strength returning to my body. My breathing grew deeper and my penis stood up. I wanted to throw my fists in the air and roar. But I did not. That's just the way I always felt. No sense asking for curiosity seekers by making a great deal of noise.

Feeling the strength surge through me so quickly often had an exhausting effect. I allowed myself to fall next to Tina's body on the bed. I knew I wouldn't sleep so I could take some time to rest. Of course, if I slept and the sun came up, I would be trapped. This girl could have a roommate or a relative coming to visit. There might be no way out.

Since the energy of her blood kept my body full of tingling life, I knew I could not close my eyes for long. Like a runner after a race, I felt far too energized with my metabolic rate up, to get any sleep. Yet I felt exhaustion. So I lay there, enjoying the view of her naked body next to me, as it began turning ashen.

Of course the morning would bring with it questions. I, long ago, discovered a way to avoid all that. I always take the body with me. With increased strength, it is not difficult to carry a body around all night. And then I could dispose of it in some more secluded location. I have a regular spot.

I dressed and picked her up. With her body over my shoulder—she weighed less for lack of blood—I headed for the window. Naked, with her buttocks in the air, her privates were completely exposed. Somehow, I didn't think she'd mind anymore. At this stage of her life, all her cares and woes—including embarrassment—were released and she would toil no more. *I perform a public service. If not for me, this young lady would live another sixty or seventy years struggling to survive, feeling agony and disappointment. I delivered her from all that. I truly am a God.*

Out the window, up the fire escape to the roof, a couple buildings away and I returned to the ground. Making my way through shadows, I soon found myself away from eyes that might see; I meandered back to my sanctuary—remembering to dispose of the body along the way.

Another night, I'll live.

A s I fulfilled Ana's wish, feeling her warm blood coursing down my throat, her naked body pressed against mine, I thought of my own time of changing. I'd been dragged unwillingly into a life I could not understand and did not want. I accepted what I became because I had little choice. Ana made that choice before I met her.

Once I'd taken most of her blood, I offered her some of mine. Of course it would not be so satisfying for her as for me. With the nail of my right index finger, I cut my left wrist and allowed the blood to flow freely for as long as it could. Vampires heal quickly. To her credit, Ana drank obediently…and deeply.

Soon, when her strength returned, she rose. Unsteady and not completely herself, she came to me, full of death and in the thralls of the first rush of senses. She brought with her a need to have sex and a need to eat. Both are quite common when a vampire first wakes. I had no one to explain this to me when I first emerged from a grave.

"Ana, my love, you are awake."

"Yes."

"You feel hungry."

"Yes."

"You must not go out yet. Allow me to bring something back for you."

"Yes."

I knew her mind would return and she would again act as normal. But for now, she remained in the throes of disorientation. I slipped out and grabbed a young man right off his bicycle. When I entered the room with him, Ana groaned deeply. The young man, obviously scared out of his wits, noticed her nude form as she approached and he relaxed a little.

She came closer. I held the boy. She touched him intimately. He relaxed. Then she lunged at his neck and drank deeply. When it was over, I watched as her body tingled. Her nipples grew harder than ever and her womanly juices flowed. The smell of sex filled the room like smoke from an unwatched dinner.

I attacked her with animal desire. She opened herself and took me deeply. Our sex lasted for hours. The sun rose and still we coupled. Her windows had been well covered since before I first arrived. Perhaps she planned to become a vampire. Or, more likely, she just had trouble sleeping once the sun rose. Either way, her room remained safe long after the world had turned into a sacrificial shower of molten light that would burn our skin completely away in a matter of seconds if we dared venture out.

Insatiable, she drew my attention over and over, even when I tried to rest between times of exertion. I'd been with vampires before her; none were as she in bed. Most had limits even as mortal women do—a point beyond which they tire or become dry and sore. I could deduce no cause for the incredible stamina she displayed save her Italian blood which now soared through my own veins as well—even though she'd shown little sign of such stamina before I bit her.

Although mine would be a temporary effect, I could feel the deeper drive as she pulled me inside many times. Even after I thought I might collapse from exhaustion, she managed to urge me to further performances, milking me completely each time. I amazed even myself. This is hardly a time for boasting, but I dare say I was like a juggernaut.

Before the effects could wear off I asked if we might go out and find some other partners to enjoy my new-found stamina with. Her angelic (demonic?) face lit up with the light of the rising moon. *Had we made love all day?* At any rate, I knew her answer was an enthusiastic affirmative. Besides that, we had to dispose of the bicyclist's body.

Out in the early evening, we saw many eligible prospects to have fun with. Although Ana and I were hardly a couple, we decided to play 'swap' to give the appearance of normality. Several couples that fit our tastes appeared willing. The first couldn't come tonight but asked for another date. The second, I can't quite explain. I could detect an odor that didn't set well. Ana seemed not to notice. I suspect one of them may have had a blood disorder.

By the third, we'd made a match for the evening. The man, a thin, muscular type who looked like a long-distance bike rider, had unruly dark hair that kept poking him in his left eye. Ana giggled. The girl stood lithe and petite. A tight unitard clung to her like another skin. Her proportions, although slight, caressed my eye with gentleness and seductive desire.

Ana's loft seemed most appropriate since I had no place in town and the couple owned a small cottage, but too far to the north. We retired to her spacious hovel with all due haste—my lust growing within and without. On several occasions as we made the half-hour trek back to her place, the girl, Claudia, found her way to 'accidentally' caress certain parts of my anatomy. The gentleman inside me found this vulgar and inappropriate for public display. The aroused vampire wanted to bend her over every trash receptacle and planter we passed along the way, just to taste her body over and again.

From the occasional glances I offered Ana and her new friend, Marcus, they were faring little better. I could smell Ana's sex, although it mingled with the heady scent of Claudia's desires. The evening offered promise and I intended to take full advantage of this serendipitous opportunity. *What good fortune that we might stumble across such a pair on a night like this when it suits us best of all.*

We agreed to all be in the same room so we might enjoy opportunities to swap or work two on one. Thoughts of these deviant practices only drove my desires to further heights, causing a slight dizziness in my head. Anticipation and a touch of fear had me falling to the floor as I raced to pull my pant leg from my foot—which seemed to have grown suddenly three times too large to fit through.

Claudia had no trouble slipping out of her one-piece jump suit. She wore nothing beneath as I'd suspected. There were no lines from undergarments. Marcus and Ana paralleled our actions, stripping and pulling each other. I managed to remove everything with only a few bruises to show for my clumsy effort. When I felt Claudia's lithe body inside my circled arms, my desire grew even further. I felt awkward but she appeared to enjoy the feeling of my manhood between us.

We explored each other's bodies, touching and tasting, hardly noticing that our partners did similar things right next to us on Ana's large bed. The room filled with the aromas of lust as each of us hit several climaxes, then changed position, and began again. Claudia, though petite, had great muscle control and stamina—for a mortal. While I began gently so not to hurt her, she urged me to further energies and I complied by pounding harder and faster. She took everything I gave her and wanted more.

When I did glance toward Ana, she and Marcus were twisted into a lovemaking pretzel that I could barely decipher. His sizable manhood slipped into Ana from several directions and in different openings. Not one to be outdone, I grabbed Claudia up in my arms and threw her back to the bed on her belly. With little ceremony, I entered her anus with my fully erect penis, and buried myself to the hilt.

Her moans suggested it might have hurt but also that she wasn't a virgin there, either. She gripped the tousled bed coverings in both fists, holding on for dear life, pushing against my every thrust, milking me once again beyond my ability to understand why I didn't dehydrate. Even as we both collapsed she touched me, suggesting after a brief respite—that *she* would generously offer—we could have another go. I sighed with as much enthusiasm as I could muster.

Soon Claudia began to moan even though I still lay next to her, searching for missing breath—it should be mentioned here that despite the fact vampires don't breathe, we need to ventilate our bodies when we've exerted too much—much like a dog that pants to control his body temperature.

Soft moaning sounds escaped Claudia's lips. I could not fathom what brought them on. *Could Marcus be revitalized so quickly and paying attention to her while Ana and I are still exhausted? How can this be? They do not smell like anything other than mortal. Not even a hint of vampire—or anything else, for that matter.*

I lifted my head with my tired neck muscles and glanced down between Claudia's legs as best I could from my angle. There, working on what appeared to be all the appropriate buttons, was Ana. I could only see the top of her head which bobbed almost completely out of sight. She worked Claudia into a new frenzy, stopping for nothing. My shock subsided quickly in my exhaustion, even as a new tingle began to grow in my loins. I let my head flop back down. *It would seem deviant pleasures abound on this night. I find myself rather liking them.*

And soon all heads rose again. I struggled at first to find my strength and balance, but it returned quickly, like the old saying about riding a bicycle. I found myself, once again, wrapped in Claudia's arms and enraptured by her scent. In the end, as I rose to check the time, I found it difficult not to fall back into her calls for me to fill her again—coercion and weak knees conspired to push me inside her once more. She lay back, open, knowing her vagina could speak volumes to the weakened male libido.

Determined—stumbling into the main room that had less opaque curtains, I realized that sunrise would arrive soon. While our guests might be able to leave, Ana and I would have a hard time getting out of an offer for breakfast or some other casual venture. I felt it necessary to inform her. *We must end our little fracas for the evening and see our guests out.*

Suddenly I heard a scream that could curdle blood. I'd never thought about that saying before but now it sent shivers through my body. The thought that blood might curdle brought forth a gag reflex. But my feet already took off toward the source of all the noise, which did not subside but only weakened a bit.

As I turned and entered the boudoir I'd been in almost constantly for two days, I saw the scene of horror and Claudia's fear-filled eyes nearly popping out of her head. Ana, feeling no need to be delicate or discrete, had bitten Marcus and was too busy sucking every last drop from him to notice the girl's scream—or my arrival. Blood spurted over his belly as Ana sucked from the vein in his penis, most accessible as he lay erect.

"What are you doing?" I growled, pulling her off the young man.

"I got hungry."

"These were nice people. They could have served as sexual partners for years. There are millions of others we could feed on that would not sate us so."

"They're just humans," she tried to sound sure of her resolve.

"Aren't they all," came my only response.

In Ana, understanding began to dawn. "I-I didn't…"

Nothing could be done at this time. I looked at Claudia. Her screams instantly became whimpers. She curled up with her knees in front of her face. Her exposed pudendum had me feeling regret that I would have to destroy this sensual beauty. Her stamina, her grace, her scent, all reminded me of the lust that came with a mortal as they passed over to undead.

I approached her. She withdrew. I hesitated. Something— spark of intelligence, perhaps—shone in her eyes. I waited. The fleeting glance could not be confirmed and still I hesitated. *Could this be someone that will be able to deal with what I can offer? Perhaps a welcome addition?*

"Listen. Can you understand me?"

Claudia nodded, her odd noises subsiding to almost nothing.

"Obviously we are vampires. I never meant for your boyfriend to be killed."

She whimpered a bit louder, then it faded completely.

"We cannot allow you to tell others about us. I wish to offer you a choice. I could kill you or I could make you a vampire. Now you must decide. Life as a vampire is not quite as romantic as it might seem, but it is life. Either way, everything you knew, will be gone."

"But…but she…," Claudia stuttered, pointing at Ana. "…still has her flat."

"Yes. She only became a vampire last night. That is why she acted so impetuously a moment ago. She may live here undetected for some time, but eventually, her true nature will be known and she will be forced to move on—leaving behind everything and everyone. Is that a sacrifice you are willing to make?"

Claudia hesitated.

"Please, take your time. Think about the consequences of life as I know it. If you knew all, death would not seem so frightening. You have until dawn. That's just over an hour. I wish you to wait in the other room with me so you don't have to look at...that." I glanced in the direction of a cowering Ana and her dead play toy.

Claudia's bulging eyes blinked and watered, trying so hard not to look at the other woman. She nodded ever so slightly as she stood and walked, zombie-like, into the main room just behind me. I helped her sit in a place far enough away from the door that I might reach her before she escaped. I could see understanding in her. I backed away and began to pace. I always abhorred being forced into something. It often led to mistakes, mistakes that could lead to capture and death. I never sought these things and made every effort to avoid them.

Painful thoughts ran through my head as I listened to the sound of Ana ravaging the body of Marcus. Though I would rue making Claudia into a creature of the night, she would most likely choose that path over death. I would oblige. I didn't have to wait long. Only about fifteen minutes later she called to me.

"Collin?"

Odd how her fear gave her an accent, rather Australian, I would think. The sound appealed to me in a humorous sort of way. While I doubted she intended to entertain, I nevertheless enjoyed the beautiful tone of her voice. She mistook my hesitation for distraction and repeated herself.

"Collin?"

"Yes?"

"Will it hurt?"

"I promise you, except for the prick of my teeth entering your neck, you will feel nothing."

"Surely there is fear?"

"None of my victims have shown any. They peacefully fall asleep, and then…it's over."

"I meant, is there pain in becoming a vampire?"

"You wake up hungry."

"I always do."

"Then there will be little difference. Except for your choice of food, tomorrow will be much like any other. But you will no longer have opportunity to work on your tan."

A tickle of near-hysterical laughter escaped Claudia's lips as she sat up with determination. A strong-willed woman, she would meet this new challenge face-to-face. I admired her. Even with her matted hair and red, swollen eyes she looked beautiful. And her thin, muscled body kept me on edge the entire time. Of course we were all still naked.

"I would choose to become as you are."

"Each decision has its own unique consequences. Be sure you understand and accept the one you make now, for once done, it cannot be undone."

"Will I be aware of any regret?"

"Not that anyone has ever told me of."

"Then let it be done."

"Ana!" I called.

She bounced a bit as she sprinted into the room with curiosity on her face. "Collin? Is everything all right?"

"Yes. Claudia has decided to join us. Please make sure you've taken care of everything in there. Clean up your mess. You remember how you felt after you ate."

"I sure do." Her bare breasts jiggled as she laughed. Then she turned and disappeared, hopefully to get rid of the body as I'd hinted.

"Are you ready, Claudia?"

"What will she do with Marcus?"

"She's going to take care of him. Don't worry. After you change it wouldn't bother you to lay right next to him."

Claudia shivered.

"As I said, there are unique consequences. Would you like to reconsider?"

"No," she said with resolve.

"Then let's proceed, shall we?"

"Yes, while I still have the strength to make my own choice."

I approached her slowly, gently, like a lover, pushing her knees apart. I touched her gently and caressed the skin that had given me such pleasure before. I gave her a kiss and pushed my way inside her again, hoping that arousal would distract her from her fears. She reluctantly returned my kiss but did not react to my entry—even as I began to slide in and out. I felt no animosity but I'd hoped to make it more pleasurable for her. I failed. She feared what was coming and I could not help her avoid it. No one could blame her for being afraid.

"You will feel two pin pricks. It will only hurt for a second."

"You would know."

I leaned in closer and she sucked in her breath.

ampires seek little beyond continuing to participate in what passes for life. There are few forms of entertainment—other than the hunt—that amuse us for very long. Even the hunt can become quite mundane. This, above all else, has led to the demise of many of my kind—even to the point of near extinction. Despite my being sire to three and they, in turn, siring their own, our numbers remained small.

Oh, we do not die of boredom. But after a hundred years, or two, life can become rather boring and quite bothersome. Getting up one evening after the next can be ever so grueling and draw away even the deepest convictions to stay alive. Self-confidence and superiority complexes mean little after a couple centuries.

Of the many pleasures we partake, sex probably ranks the highest. While we cannot procreate, the pleasure derived rivals that of human males. In this way, we become like cattle, corralled in fences and driven whichever way the vagina patrol wishes us to go. And as with our human counterparts, little can tear us away once the scent takes hold.

At least a mortal man can have morals or religious convictions. A vampire with religious convictions wouldn't last very long. Religious men are not allowed to kill and often bear purified symbols. Centuries of hunger can be quite overwhelming. Insanity would surely be inevitable. And, as it happens, I'd rather enjoy a good meal whenever I like.

The prime rib of the vampire buffet is the blood of virgins. Untainted by human intimacy, they taste far superior in every way. A pudendum that has never been forced apart by a man's brutal entry is the sweetest meat. But that's only the beginning. A young lithe body can offer a multitude of delights. Once the preliminaries are out of the way, the blood calls.

Virgin blood is potent—creating a caustic reaction going down the throat, like drinking a carbonated beverage too quickly. But the energy that comes afterward is much like sitting in a microwave. Waves of pain shoot out from every pore and all the muscles of the body spasm. But it is temper by fire, for when it is over, a stronger vampire emerges.

Many of my less-than-intelligent brethren know not of this. As we have conversed, they've told of virgin blood tasting no different. Their foolish ways have them coupling with the young woman before biting her since trying to do it afterward is not very appealing and can be so anticlimactic. But they, in turn, must surely taint the meat before they get to enjoy it. And so they never learn. *C'est la Vie!*

I, quite to the contrary, had the opportunity to have sex with a virgin only once. At the time I was but human. The niece of my dear brother would have caused me much embarrassment and unnecessary self-loathing—not to mention probably a good beating. And it would surely have raised quite a stir in the family if not the entire community. I cared not for such judgments.

Sarah flaunted herself to me on more than one occasion and I resisted as long as humanly possible. As a vampire, I would have devoured her in an instant. My mortal self struggled with erection problems and moral dilemmas as she danced in thin nighties while in my charge. My brother, you see, owned a mining business and worked many hours of the night. His niece by marriage had come under his care after the untimely death of his wife's sister and brother-in-law. When my brother's wife took ill and finally passed, he carried the burden alone—calling upon his unmarried brother, his only living relative, for help.

The unfortunate girl flowered into a sad beauty, blossoming far beyond her years, offering men what they desired most while still unable to understand any of the meaning. Of course her upbringing didn't allow her any such depravity. And yet she enjoyed my reaction as she teased. But came the night.

Most times she would dance from her bath to her bedchamber within my sight, hardly covering herself with a sheer nightshirt that clung to her still-wet body or half-wrapped towel, exposing her behind. Little was left to my imagination. However, one time she dared approach. Sitting on the sofa near me, Sarah boasted of knowledge that belied her youth.

Would that she only spoke of such things the night might have ended different. Talk can be quite arousing and yet more easily resisted. But the touch of a gentle hand is so much more difficult to ignore. When she casually leaned over to kiss me goodnight and her hand perchance fell in my lap, I knew the relationship I had with her up to that point, would forever change.

She played innocent but the hand aimed so perfectly. And her kiss didn't end with a peck as it should have. My own hands betrayed me, seeking the tender chest flesh of a young girl barely held in by the sheer fabric. I sought a distraction that I might save my dignity. By this time Sarah had other ideas.

Dropping her gown and exposing herself was probably one of the bravest things she'd ever done. How could I disappoint her? How could I break down the effort she'd made to grow up by rejecting her so abruptly? Spurning her then would have been detrimental. For the sake of her natural growth and emotional stability I had to place my hands on her budding breasts.

Her nipples grew into my palms and she breathed deeply, but she did not pull away. If she did not know what came next, she faked confidence very well. Perhaps she'd witnessed someone in their intimacy. Or maybe she'd just heard some school kids talking. Either way, she performed admirably, and for hours, until we heard the bolt on the front door slide back and knew her adoptive father had returned for the night.

I merely had to slip across the hall with my clothes and emerge minutes later. But my conscience tugged at my soul. I barely slept for many nights afterward. I gave my confession to a head of cabbage, the only 'living' thing I could trust with such knowledge. And four nights a week I would lay with her in her bed, and enjoy the delights of a woman-in-training. The other three nights her father managed to stay at home and I would use all the self-satisfaction techniques I could imagine while picturing her lithe form coming to me—beneath me, on top of me, beside me, around me, with me—touching me, gripping me, tasting me. As I tasted her.

I fought with myself. The right thing is easy to see when someone else must pay the price. I knew fear would never allow me to admit my deeds. I participated in carnal knowledge with Sarah for months, giving little thought to anything as pointless as consequences. Who cared for such drivel when physical satisfaction could so easily be attained?

Unlike many of these stories, I managed to get away with what I'd done. My months of carnal bliss ended in a dark alley one night with another young girl who turned out to be ancient. Once bitten, I found

70

myself wandering for some time. An instinct lured me back to the girl I'd violated so many times before.

But I did not return to violate her further. Sarah told me on the last night that she was with child. Even as a vampire I reasoned that such a thing could not be allowed. An abomination of God and man—oh well. Who cares for such trifles? My only concern at the time was not to be chased—as a fanged, blood-sucking monster or a soulless child molester.

Sarah and her baby—my baby—had to die.

wo-thousand ten rang in like a shot…or rather a cough—from an old rifle with bullets made of dust. The century had been kind to me but boredom began to show me hatred. I hated life. I couldn't bear the weight of yet another year, and then another. I needed some kind of hobby besides chasing virgins and having sex often.

I'd been alone for too long. Ana ran off with a Brit named Henry without ever looking back—leaving me alone with an emptiness I could neither explain nor eliminate. Henry claimed to be a Prince. My doubts were inconsequential next to Ana's desire. Millicent—my sweet, sweet Millicent—smile like a summer day, often the only reason I would rise every night. But she'd been a vampire for so long. Even as young as she looked, she could not bear any more eternity. Sadness filled my eyes and I struggled harder for a solution to my boredom.

Almost from the beginning I've known the dangers of leading anything other than a careful, hidden life. Belonging to any group increased the chances of exposure. After a time, almost anyone might pick up on my lack of aging or some other minute distinction. I could not afford such risks. Life may have become boring, but death by an angry mob held no favor with me, either.

Nevertheless, the dreariness of the day that I could no longer enjoy kept me from feeling happiness. Indeed, it showed me the how the fruitless weeks and months could accumulate into something called eternity—a decidedly dreadful word. While in Hungary I met a vampire who was over five-hundred-years old. Five Hundred Years! And I would complain about a mere one hundred.

Hans Belchik, born of displaced Hungarian peasants, living in northern Italy, I'd met him as he journeyed to see his homeland. Hans had peculiar eyes. Perhaps the weight of all those years put pressure on his face. Heavy semi-circles of sagging skin hung from under each eye socket. He'd been turned at twenty-two years of age, yet he showed signs of growing older. And Hans was not the only one. How had Millicent grown her breasts so large?

I only met perhaps a dozen vampires in all my days, but many of them had actually 'aged' in some manner—and not always entirely kindly. In fact, most deteriorated in less-than-attractive ways. Of course they developed their skills of seduction to compensate. Only in this way could they continue to survive.

In each of them, I remember hearing stories of boredom. I often saw signs of demented thinking and distorted views. As a hermit might become detached from the real world, so did my brethren. They sought only to feed. Nothing more. I would occupy my mind in such a manner so as not to lose touch with reality.

Of course, I could take up knitting and become the laughing stock of the entire vampire world—which could very well be less than a hundred worldwide. Besides that, I'd tried knitting. Talk about boring! Puzzles, plastic models, ping-pong, even reading, all became like bathing in holy water after a few decades. *But is a killer all that I am to be? Can I not aspire?*

I'm not sure what brought on the memory of Sarah, but showering together had become one of our favorite things to do—although there was still no holy water involved. Even as a mortal man under such circumstances, I probably would have burst into flames at its touch. Thankfully, I never tried.

The bedside of a vampire often holds strange things. By my side I keep slippers, although I never use them; a bathrobe, even though I sleep and walk around in the nude; a pair of eyeglasses, although vampires have incredible eyesight; and a couple packets of blood, just in case I get hungry. I need no alarm as I hardly sleep and the call of night can be so incredibly loud when your ears are tuned to it.

Rising, as I often do, before the set of the sun, I can do little but stretch and brew a pot of coffee, as any further activity might take me too close to a window. To this day, coffee remains my one human weakness— besides sex. Over the years I've eliminated the need for sugar or cream. I've done this mostly because I move often, and keeping such things only adds to the turmoil of my already twisted life.

As I await the brew, listening to the groaning, gurgling of the pot, I am again taken to places long past yet still vivid. Perhaps my pastime is simply to nightdream about events from my past, like an aging athlete trying to relive his glory days with his few remaining friends—hoping to tell yet another worn out story in a new, refreshing way and keep their interest. Yet even those insignificant human beings would hope for a new chance at their old game. I, on the other hand, have lost even that hope. So I continue to dance through past images. I do so little else these nights, perhaps I just long for a time when I still enjoyed being alive for another day. In the end, the one important difference, I have no desire to return to days gone by. Nevertheless, my mind travels there.

Czechoslovakia, the collapse of the Habsburg monarchy, I travelled through the newly-formed country, keeping mostly to wooded areas. I worked my way north from Bratislava to Gottwaldov, keeping close to the Morava River. Finally heading to Olomouc and on to Ostrava where I met Teresie Masaryková. She claimed to be a relative of the great Tomáš Garrigue

Masaryk, who became the first president and founder of the then Czech Republic. As she bore the same name as President Masaryk's mother, I thought the relationship entirely possible.

But political affiliations did little to impress me. I joined Teresie for purely physical reasons. We tramped through much of the countryside, often times she would insist we run through fields without clothing. She said she felt so close to nature that way. Under the darkness of night and in secluded areas I would agree. Then we would roll in the grass and make love for hours.

The months flew by and the onset of hostilities that eventually led to World War II fell upon the land. I was forced to leave—never to return to her arms. In all, quite probably the most romantic situation I ever found myself in. And in the end, she never discovered my true nature. By some innocence or trust, she believed every story I told her to excuse myself from daytime liaisons.

Odd that memory should take me to her now. Bearing no reference to modern troubles, I see no interest other than the tingling in my loins at the thought of her embrace. Teresie was a good girl, giving pride to her family name, but she had such wanton thoughts. Many occasions she shared her vivid dreams with me. Many would excite me to pounce on her and enter the love nest she offered so freely.

A few times her stories shocked me. She talked of such things as I'd never heard before. Being a vampire and having lived as long as I had, I'd managed to hear many rather outrageous things. Never had anyone spoke thus before me, let alone from such a delicate creature as Teresie. Her words seemed as appropriate as sunshine from a rock or water from a horse's ear. Had her father known, she would have been locked away until her fiftieth birthday. Released only then with a cast iron chastity belt in place and her father possessing the sole key.

Evening skies smiled down upon us as we lay exhausted after sex, spread out on the grass. The stars completely ignored her tales. I envied them. Just as I thought her stories of wishing to have sex with animals were fallacy, she would insert some tidbit about her poodle, Csilla. Apparently, Csilla had a taste for Teresie's womanly parts—*all* her parts.

At times when she spoke of sneaking off to Rome and participating in orgies she claimed they still practiced, it actually came as a relief from the other more outrageous stories—appearing almost normal by comparison. I sometimes wonder what I saw in her. Then my memory draws an image of her eyes and her breasts, and I remember the way she felt on the inside. After a moment or two, I wonder no longer.

Would that I could wallow in her memory for the rest of the evening, but hunger calls. Who am I to refuse the lustful calling of my stomach, for it would surely rise up against me at a most inconvenient time, bringing forth some horrible display. After making sure the evening's darkness fully blanketed the sky, I dressed and went out.

With memories of a quieter time in the Czech Republic still floating around in my head, I decided not to go by the club. I knew the noise there would have me reeling in agony. Besides, Tuesday is always ladies night and the place is packed…with guys. Even though blood is blood, I'd rather have a woman. And with Fourteenth Street just a few extra steps, and since vampire legs hardly ever tire, I decided on the different direction.

This area offered a smorgasbord of tastes from which to choose, and little danger of being caught since violence lived on this street. I could easily blend in with the surroundings and slip away before anyone knew. It occurred to me that turning into an animal might truly come in handy at such times. I wonder, not for the first time, what made Ana even suggest such a thing.

As I approached a particularly dark area frequented by some of the dregs of society, the smell of alcohol-and-drug tainted blood accosted my nose. I frowned on reflex, but in truth I'd drank from winos and such. Just as if I'd taken the drug myself, they have no effect on a vampire—and sometimes the exotic flavors offered a tasty treat.

To the side of an abandoned building I saw a woman standing, waiting for a pick-up—a professional. She hawked me in her usual manner and I turned. As I got close, my nose alerted me once again. But she didn't smell only like alcohol. Her blood carried something with it—a disorder, disease, deformity. I knew not what dangers lay there and chose discretion. Her display of disappointment was nearly convincing.

Further down I noticed a crowd of people. They were quiet enough to not be looking for trouble, although I had nothing to fear from mortals. Several men and women of Spanish decent stood talking about which evening activity they would choose.

Occasionally a voice called out an idea in English, and another would dismiss it saying something about how recently they'd done that. If not for my own sadness, I might have found it amusing. I cursed the day Millicent changed me. Then I gathered my resolve and put on my best seductive lure.

Someone would notice me. Someone always did.

redictability is probably the deadliest part of an extended lifetime. If the days would change, or people would change, interest might return. But one day looked much like the rest and people would never change.

Each generation thinks they're unique, the only intelligent group who can make the significant changes to improve this planet more than all the others have in the past or ever will in the future. Each generation believed itself to be the chosen one. Such a sad commentary.

And, of course, predictability lends way to discovery and danger for one such as I. Any pattern that can be followed by another, can lead the authorities to my doorstep. A number of bodies could be linked back to me if they were discovered. It's not difficult to see the complications from following too rigid a pattern.

As I earlier predicted, someone did follow me. Two someones. A petite, adorable Chica swayed right up to me bold as brass. Behind her by only a few steps came another Hispanic woman of the larger variety. Fat women hold no interest for me. I would quickly dismiss her and focus my attentions at the little one.

Then the two girls kissed and the night air got warmer. *I could definitely go for some Mexican food tonight.* So maybe a change of pace would add the interest I sought and a fat girl still has all the right parts—particularly the blood. I allowed them to get closer. Since I spoke so little Spanish, I could only hope to convince them of my intentions by some other means. I spread my arms to group hug them, allowing each hand to casually brush the side of their breasts before travelling under their arms and around their backs. Neither girl flinched at my advance.

Behind them, the tiny crowd they'd belonged to grew agitated. I didn't understand most of what they said but it became increasingly clear they didn't like losing their dates. Most times I would say it didn't matter and make a hasty retreat before someone got a good look at my face and could identify me later. Somehow, as I saw a knife blade flash, I didn't think retreat would be the best option.

Discretion, it seems, is not always the better part of valor. Sometimes confrontation becomes necessary when forced upon you by an angry adversary. I moved the girls behind me, placing myself closest to the three men coming at me. From the corner of my eye I saw two more guys coming from a little shop around the other side of the building. At risk of exposing myself for something other than human, I would have to eliminate this problem quickly before the situation attracted any more attention than it already had.

I stepped in and swept the switchblade away with a hard backhand. Then I knocked out the guy who wielded it. Stunned, the other two attacked me in unison. I allowed them to come within reach and clapped my hands together—with their heads in between. With three unconscious bodies lying at my feet, the other two men hesitated. They looked at each other and decided to come ahead.

Marquis of Queensbury rules be damned. I kicked the first one in the testicles. That only left one. He produced a baseball bat. *Where did he have that hidden, I wonder?* Despite looking like he'd had a great deal to drink, he swung with fury and strength. And accuracy. The bat arced at me in great haste. I raised an arm, nothing fancy, just a block. It broke against my arm, splintering into at least three pieces.

That guy took the wise path and left, the loss of his baseball bat obviously giving him pause. Discretion became the better part of his vocabulary. When I turned, expecting to see empty sidewalk, surprise met my vision. The two girls remained—obviously enamored with my display of skill and fighting prowess. As I fought, I'd adapted a look of fury. Facing them, I forced my lure back on. No sense frightening the ladies…until I had to.

Even from a distance I could hear their hearts pounding as excitement filled them. The thrill of seeing the fight turned them on. While I thought such a display to be a senseless show, a head start with the ladies would certainly weigh in my favor. It would take less charm to get them in a compromising position. Each would cling to her own lust.

I wrapped my arms back around them and we began to walk. The girls giggled, making occasional small talk in Spanish. I simply enjoyed frequent gropes on each of them. But then rose the problem of where to go. My place was too far and they didn't seem to understand 'their' place, not matter how slowly I said the words.

We finally settled in an empty parking lot behind the 7-11. Hardly the romantic evening I would have preferred, but since I planned on eating these two, ceremony seemed much overrated. Why bother to woo them when they were already willing? Besides, behind the 7-11 was their suggestion. And who knew people could do so many things while in a standing position.

Whoever said an old dog can't learn new tricks obviously wasn't referring to old vampires. I have a new appreciation for fat women. Although I still find them aesthetically displeasing, the girl showed me a few new things. She couldn't be the contortionist Claudia had been, but where she lacked she made up in enthusiasm and talent. The petite girl, even though toned and fine, also could not contort beyond the normal range of motion. Hardly superior.

The most amazing part of the evening is that we were never caught. No one saw us even though a busy intersection and convenience store sat so close the lights washed us as we mated. I expected at least one interruption and a possible rousting by the *gendarmes*. None of that happened. If anyone saw, they quietly watched or turned away.

Watching a sex show and watching a vampire feed are two very different ends of the spectrum. When all three of us were sated, I readied to feed, first giving a listen in all directions for intruders and onlookers.

Behind me were the roaring sounds of occasional cars passing by and I could hear the electronic alarm telling storekeepers inside the 7-11 that the front door had opened. Further up the street, I could hear a couple arguing about money. The man offered to give his woman some bruises for a birthday present if she didn't shut up and the woman cried one berate after another about how little he cared for her anymore. According to her their relationship had been built solely on how amazing her pussy had been. The man suggested it wasn't that great to begin with and the woman collapsed into tears again.

In the distance in another direction, I could barely make out the slapping sound of a basketball being dribbled on a tar court. A school with an open playground lay down that road. The ball player probably wanted to get a few hoops in while the air remained cooler. Midday could be so draining for mortals. I didn't have to worry about that. Should I venture out when the sun shone it would drain me completely away.

Toward the South I could hear a multitude of television sets and radios all tuned to something different—overlapping, crashing in on each other—creating a din of nonsense. Thankful for the distance, I could hardly imagine living near all that. I looked back at the girls. They'd gotten dressed and were looking for new adventures.

I knew a goodbye kiss would not be out of order. I leaned in to the petite girl first, knowing the fat one couldn't run as fast once she saw what I did to her friend. Pushing my teeth through her muscled neck became something of a chore. Her surprisingly tough flesh finally gave way and I entered her in this different way. For a moment I thought she might manage a scream.

Difficulties come when noise is present. I can't remember who told me that. But fortune favored me and the girl remained silent as she collapsed to the ground. I turned to the other. Her mouth, on the other hand, flapped wildly and the noise that came from it couldn't easily be described in human terms. I reached for her, grabbing her by the throat, closing her windpipe, silencing the dreadful sound.

Surrounded by silence once again, I could clearly hear the footfalls of several running men. Apparently the big girl had been heard by more than I. Acting quickly—truly the only way I knew how—I stung her neck with my fangs using a sharp snap of my head, drinking all she had to offer in seconds. Then I made my way to the shadows, disappearing into the

85

night, but not before I glanced back and saw two men approach and heard more coming.

Those two bodies would be found—but they never saw me.

he newspaper reported on the deaths and added eyewitness testimony of a man who "picked the girls up on the street corner". I rather thought it made them sound like hookers. The eyewitness described the man as big and tall, Hispanic, with creepy eyes.

Well, I'm tall but not big. And who in their right mind would mistake me for Hispanic? I laughed.

Foolish as people were, they would find me around the turn of the century. The *next* century. With fears like that, who needs to worry? When I strolled into the club that night, I hardly had a care in the world. Then I saw the uniforms. Humans could, on occasion, be damnably clever.

Policemen sat in several key positions about the place, in search of someone—could it be me? In my years on this planet I've learned a thing or two about human nature. One of those lessons taught me the best way to confront a fear is head on. I walked directly up to the nearest officer and sat down next to him.

"Is there some kind of trouble, sir? Because I've had a real hard day at the office and I'd rather not deal with it."

"We're looking for a Hispanic man, comes in here sometimes. Do you come here a lot?"

"Not every night, but when work gets tough I stop by for a nightcap."

"Have you ever seen this man?" He produced one of those police sketches of a man's face.

I stared at it. "Well, no. Odd, though."

"What's that, sir?"

"It rather looks like me."

"You think so, do you?"

"Well, I'm not Hispanic. I'm French. My name's Negrand."

"You got an ID, Mr. Negrand?"

"Sure."

I reached out my hand with the appropriate card and passed it to the man. He looked everything over and handed it back.

"You live around here, Mr. Negrand?"

"Sawgrass Cove." I pointed, though it was probably an unnecessary gesture.

"Thank you. I don't expect any trouble tonight. But if it'll bother you, then going home might be best."

"I like to come here and unwind. I think I'll risk it for a little while."

"What kind of car do you drive?"

"I walked. No sense getting in an accident for such a short distance."

"That sounds wise." He gave me a deeply scrutinous look. "Thanks again for your time."

"Anytime, officer." Then to the bartender, "Whiskey, please?"

"How do you like it, pal?"

"Neat, thank you."

The music bombarded my reeling mind but I focused all my concentration on the policemen and their movements around the club. Mostly they spoke to patrons, producing copies of the picture for each to shake his or her head at. Some point in time during one of the few moments when I'd been distracted, they left without ceremony. Under circumstances like these I preferred to slink away and make as little noise as possible.

Since I hadn't eaten, I knew my night wasn't over. But I'd have to find someone elsewhere to pick up as a meal. If police were watching the club, they were too close. And it didn't take a degree in criminology to assume they were also swarming all over the area around the 7-11. I needed to look in a different direction.

I'd gotten careless. I knew leaving bodies would only raise suspicions, making people ask questions—questions I couldn't possibly answer. I gave all this great thought within the course of only a few seconds. Where else could I look for food? How long will the investigation last? Should they come calling on me again, could I produce adequate answers to their queries? How about an alibi? Perhaps I should move on.

Many other towns offered a great number of walking lunch boxes. I'd heard Miami had a high crime rate. To a man like me, it could be a destination of particular interest. But all that would have to wait, as my stomach reminded me of the basest of instincts known to man or beast. Hunger called my mind away from further thought.

I knew Joyland would offer the quickest choice and probably little more effort than my usual club—if I could only tolerate the music. Country and Western music often made my stomach do more summersaults than hunger did. Too many of those and eating would no longer be an option this night.

I hadn't come dressed for the venue, but I put on my lure to its maximum capabilities. Hopefully, no one would accost me for being 'different'. Believe me, nothing made me happier than remembering I am unlike most of them. I'm sure Mozart and some of the other great masters turn in their graves every time some cowpoke twangs another tune out on the radio about his dog dying. And can a grown man look any more foolish than with both thumbs stuck in his trousers behind a huge belt buckle?

Nevertheless, something to eat dominated my decisions at that moment. If I had to reduce my speech to that of a hillbilly child to get some, I would do so— ever so reluctantly. As it happens, a small crowd occupied the place and hardly an eye raised at my entrance. I scouted the room quickly, assessing each patron as a possible food choice.

Some deviant humor gland inside me decided to act out at that precise moment and I began naming each patron after a food. One young man, drunk nearly to the point of hanging upside-down off the barstool, could only be called *toasted 'possum*. The next guy watched me like a hawk. He looked like he might run away at any moment. What else could I call him but *chicken fried snake*. The next, a woman I aptly named *biscuits and gravy*, had attractive looking breasts the size of breakfast biscuits—a definite possibility. And I'd be sure to add the gravy. The last guy at the bar had a pock-marked face, his shirt untucked only on one side, and mismatched socks. *Mulligan stew* it is.

Biscuits and gravy, or Stacey Granger, as she quickly told me, had the sweetest little country accent you could ever vomit on. I forced myself to remember I wasn't there to count her remaining teeth, only to insert my own. Stacey seemed interested in spending some time with me. *New meat*, I suppose. I looked more tempting than any of the others she'd probably been with many times before.

With the however many drinks she had under her belt when I'd arrived along with the two I bought her, I decided she was probably pickled enough for me to take her right there at the bar. I turned to her and spoke softly.

"My place isn't far."

"Okay," she slurred. "Let's go." I fought to ignore her putrid breath.

The rest of the *meals* in the place turned but made no objections as Stacey and I exited. I hated being noticed leaving with someone, just as I hated bringing anyone to my place. Though certainly nothing to be embarrassed by, I saw no reason to attract attention by parading a number of 'guests' in and out of there. Worse yet, parading them in but NOT out. That would raise more than eyebrows. But I had little choice.

It amazes me that men can find fatty thighs, often called saddle bags, attractive. And why do all country women have to possess a pair? Stacey offered herself drunkenly, and I accepted with little enthusiasm. Her lovemaking abilities were probably poor even when she was sober. But in her inebriated condition, I would have had more fun with a London Broil.

Despite the number of disappointments, I managed to get the job done and then looked to her neck. She offered no resistance as she'd passed out at some point while I made love to her. Were I a sensitive man, I might have taken her casual unconsciousness as an affront to me, personally. From a woman sober, I never received a complaint, nor had any passed out from indifference. I'm sure this woman wouldn't complain, either—even if I left her unscathed. Since my stomach ruled my evening, leaving her in an unbitten state would not be an acceptable option. She probably wouldn't have remembered any of this night with all she drank.

All for the best, I say.

eeks passed with arrangements to be made. You'd be surprised how difficult it is to find movers who are willing to work at night. And my foolishness had me thinking they might actually *like* working in the cooler air without the scorching sun that burned even the living. Pardon me for not having a broader mind.

But in due order my things were packed and the five-hour trek to Lauderdale began. Fortunately I travel as I live—light. We arrived just before dawn. I gave the movers the appropriate address—a cozy, out-of-the-way place I'd arranged for in advance—and practically dove for the nearest motel and hid in a room until nightfall.

I ventured out at the soonest moment the yellow orb allowed. I found my new place and began the daunting task of exploring the nearby surroundings. A new town, new people, new places to eat, and new friends to make, I looked forward to it all—about as much as a root canal in one of my fangs. Which, I must say, sounded particularly dreadful—even though, to the best of my knowledge, vampires do not get cavities—unless, perhaps if they eat a lot of diabetics.

I had to get started and there's no time like the present, they say. Clichés be damned, I had to find someone to eat, and I couldn't afford to waste much time. My hunger burned within and the night would end far too soon. It certainly wouldn't be any better tomorrow night. At that thought the gurgling in my middle section increased, telling me to not even think about waiting that long.

Walking, I noticed the Earth had a different sound here. I focused my ears and waited. Despite the traffic I was able to determine the new sound didn't come from the ground at all. Small palm trees, called Palmettos, gave off the odd sound. To me, the high pitched screech sounded full of yearning and mixed tones, like real communication. I couldn't be sure, but I felt reasonably convinced the tree did not, of itself, make the sound, but rather something that lived within. Perhaps a lot of somethings.

Not far from North Andrews Avenue where my motel sat, I found a place called the Aruba Beach Café. It didn't sit on the beach so I thought it sounded like the kind of confused atmosphere that might dismiss someone like me when I walked in. The quaint interior offered me taped 'island' music with Goombay drums, fake palm and coconut tree decorations, bamboo wall coverings, and waitresses in grass skirts. When the skirts swished as they walked, I heard only the scratchy sound of plastic. Obviously fake. From the strain of my waitress's flowered shirt I deduced that grass and palm and coconuts weren't the only fake objects in the place—also made out of plastic, no doubt.

Nevertheless her face shone healthy and pretty when she smiled, asking to take my order. Her polite manner and bouncy voice got me thinking about more than just a meal. I ordered something to drink. She strutted away and I could not help but notice her perfectly round bottom. In fact, I did not see an ugly bottom waiting on any tables. *Perhaps it's a pre-employment requirement.*

As new patrons arrived and others rose to leave, I noticed a great deal of deliciously rounded bottoms and reconsidered my earlier thought about the waitresses. Obviously perfect bottoms were the status quo in Lauderdale. I focused hard on the drink sitting in front of me. A saying—old by human standards— swam through my mind. *I'd rather have a full bottle in front of me than a full frontal lobotomy.* I needed to calm my libido before some idiot with a vampire phobia lobotomized me with a ball-point pen made of silver.

Despite my growing hunger demanding more of my attention, I couldn't keep my mind from wandering down its deviant path. I gave in—just a little—to the desires of my loins. I allowed myself to smell the air for anything of interest, my waitress, perhaps. If it got too difficult for me, I would just back off. No problem.

96

Worst case, I could just leave. No law says I have to finish my drink.

My nose worked its magic. I could indeed smell my waitress. The seductive scent of her nether region caused me to spill a little of my drink as I tried to hide my face behind the raised glass. A few drops dribbled off my chin. Embarrassed, I pushed my chair back—drawing even more attention to my clumsy plight—and turned to leave, dropping three times enough money on the table.

Finding nothing along the way, I fell back to my still-packed apartment and curled onto my mattress, fighting back the pangs of hunger that wouldn't release me even long enough to fall asleep. Memories of my tragic life began to weigh heavy on my soul, if I indeed still have a soul.

I've never been a perfect man; I've crossed a few moral and legal lines in my day. But killing people can be so depressing. I never wanted to hurt anyone. Seeing deathly fear in the eyes of a victim just before I bite them is as disturbing as watching a loved one die in a hospital bed. Despite the advantages to my body, the hurt and regret eat at me always.

The consideration to terminate myself is not so new. Ideas have crossed my mind in the past decade or so. But how does one go about *doing it*? Do I fall on a stake? That would end me quickly. Sun or garlic would be agonizing, not a preferable way to go. I heard that Hans Belchik ate garlic. His screams ignited the horrific nightmares of local children for weeks afterward. That did not sound like something I wanted to do. After all, I'm brave—just not *that* brave.

My own dearest Millicent—somehow I just cannot seem to remove the pain from my memories of her—stood next to a window on a hot summer day and slapped her hand against the shade. To her dismay, it did not retract with a snap as they often did. She slapped it again with the same result. Determination gave her greater energy and she smashed her fist at it, breaking glass behind. The blind did not rise, but rather fell to the floor.

The result was the same. The sun rushed in the window like air into a vacuum. It enveloped her like a swarm of ants on a honey-covered tree. Her screams, although brief, haunted my dreams for…well, sometimes they *still* haunt my dreams. I never knew why she wanted me present while she performed such a ritual. I quickly pushed the vision out of my head and returned to the present.

The day wore on as I sat carefully, safely within my darkened apartment. There were only a few non-agonizing ways to take care of this problem. None of them appealed to me as I have never been the type of person to give up. Suicide—a dreadful thought in itself—I'd heard so many stories about disappointments of the afterlife for those who take their own life. Now that I think of it, I'm not sure the afterlife holds much promise for me anyway.

The aching inside me far surpasses the grumble of my stomach. My life has been filled with simply using others, and the future doesn't appear to offer much opportunity for change. What will I do with another hundred years? Even a self-imposed death seems to be a cheat. I need a way to redeem myself.

Perhaps night school—I could become a doctor, working in an emergency room at night when the most people get hurt. Of course that wouldn't do at all. Clean is one thing, antiseptic and sterile are dangers to a vampire. Almost anything pure and cleansing could put my existence at risk.

A conundrum assaults me. I don't want the purity of silver to take away my life and yet I consider suicide. Perhaps the hunger has my mind so distorted that logic escapes me. Why can't I fathom this out? Surely an answer can be found somewhere.

ightfall finds me wandering the unfamiliar streets once again. I can hear the sounds of people in all directions, but my preoccupied mind won't allow me to distinguish any one voice. Not that it matters, I care not for the babblings of a thousand mindless drones and the trivia they wish to debate endlessly as if one single bit would solve all the world's problems.

I need to find something to eat. Answers to my questions have not been forthcoming, leaving me alone with the only other urge burning around inside me, namely my hunger. A town so full of life and death could certainly offer up some delectable morsels for me to snack on while I decided my eternal fate.

At the next corner I noticed a convenience store. Looking at my surroundings, I discovered that I'd become lost…once again. But the smell of blood drew me ever closer—closer—closer, forgetting my own warnings from just a little over a hundred years ago about a wolf blindly walking directly into a trap because of the smell of meat.

The girl resembled, more than anything else, a street urchin. Her tattered clothes and dirty face said she hadn't bathed recently. But her hungry eyes told a deeper story. Her life had been taken, destroyed. She lived on the street but had no adult guidance. She made her own way in the world, as best she was able, and couldn't imagine how to get out of the rut she lived in.

"What is your name, child?"

"Stephanie."

"How old are you?"

"I don't remember. I think I'm nineteen, but I could be twenty."

"Are you telling me the truth?"

"Yes."

"People might be more likely to help a younger child."

"I know. No one wants to help me anymore because I'm too old." She began to cry.

"I could help you."

She managed a modicum of control. "You could? I mean, you would?"

"Come." I reached out my hand to this pathetic creature. Perhaps I would make her a vampire. Her life could be no worse.

I took her down another street where no lights interfered with the solitude I sought. She came willingly, knowing almost anything could happen to her. She'd probably been hooking since before she knew what the word meant. Nevertheless, I could smell the fear permeating through her skin.

She glanced at me from the corner of her eye, sizing me up. I did not present a threat and she relaxed. I held a gentle hand on her arm, leading her, as I would, to solitude. We found an empty lot and disappeared into the deeper shadows. Expecting the normal interaction, she began to take off her worn out clothing.

When her shirt fell I saw nothing under, probably nothing could be afforded. Her body had spots of grime smeared irregularly throughout. Her shame and determination shone through at the same time in her eyes. I would have seen those things in her even if I couldn't smell her feelings so strongly.

She stood half naked, awaiting my advances, willing to live up to my desires but still hating and frightened by the lifestyle she'd been forced into, of which there seemed no way out. I approached her, touching gently, intimately. She enjoyed the soft attention and I surmised she'd been handled roughly more often than not.

"You can tell me what you'd like," she offered, resigned. "I know how to do all kinds of things."

I felt a pang of sorrow for the tragic life the girl led. I knew I could proceed without concern and yet I hesitated. I'm not sure. Perhaps I felt guilt? Could I? I certainly did not cause her tragic life. And then, an epiphany. It occurred to me that while I hated my life, I felt compelled to offer its same burden to her, as if it were a gift or reward. I hadn't helped anyone, save those I killed outright. The others, the ones I turned, I cursed them. Even inasmuch as mine is, I turned their lives into something loathsome and valueless. And, unfortunately, timeless.

I looked at the girl through the eyes of revelation. Could it be that conformity would result in harmony? I considered all the possibilities and quickly saw another alternative. I lifted the girl's chin with the side of my finger.

"Can we talk, first?"

Her eyes shone bright, then quickly saddened. "No one wants to hear what I have to say. They only want to know about the other things I can do with my mouth."

"I wish to tell you something. And then I would hear your response."

Stephanie pulled her shirt back up, though she made no effort to return her modesty—if indeed she had any left, and sat on the ground where I offered. I sat next to her.

"I've got to tell you something and it may come as a shock. I ask that you try not to be afraid. Can you do that?"

"Very little can shock me, mister."

"Please call me Collin. And you were surprised a moment ago when I suggested we talk first."

The girl looked up sharply.

"So, perhaps you *can* try not to be afraid?"

"I can try."

"Very well, then. I am a vampire."

The girl stiffened and leaned away. I knew she would run if I didn't keep her attention.

"Please, wait."

She continued to move away.

"You cannot outrun me." I quickly jumped past in the mere blink of an eye and stood blocking her path

She froze.

"I only wish to speak with you."

Stephanie did not return to the spot where she'd sat next to me, but she settled into something that resembled relaxed.

"Perhaps we can help each other."

"H-How?"

"You need a change in your life and I need blood."

She stared at me.

"I could help you get away from all this if you would let me drink from you. I promise not to kill you."

"Can a vampire be trusted to keep his promise?"

"I do not know. But I assure you I mean what I say."

"How could you help me?"

"I can give you strength. I can offer a place to stay and food to eat. I can bring you out of the street."

"I'm not hungry." As if telling tales behind her back, her stomach growled emptily at me.

"I see. If I can be of no help, then I shall leave you. Here," I handed her money. "For your trouble."

As I walked away, I began to see a new path for my life to take. I felt a ray of hope inside as I considered all the burdens of such a choice—and all the benefits. If not Stephanie, then someone—a person down on their luck, searching for a chance to break out and become something close to their potential. By the time I reached the sidewalk, I *knew* it would work. Then I was stopped.

"Wait."

Her soft voice called from where she still sat. My ears heard as clearly as if she stood next to me. I turned back toward her but did not move otherwise.

"Maybe I could do what you ask."

Still I waited.

"You let me live and give me a chance, and in return I let you have some of my blood when you need it. Is that about right?"

"No."

She started, sucking in her breath.

"Although I need not feed nightly, I would need more than you alone could provide. You would not survive. The arrangement would be for me to feed on you tonight only."

"You mean, only once? You would help me for this and nothing more?"

"Perhaps sex?"

"Sex, I can do. I have no fear of sex. Death, on the other hand, even my life looks better than dying. Every night I live in fear of dying. You promise to help me?" she asked.

"I promise," I vowed. "Do you have any family you'd like to contact before…?"

She held up a hand. "I have no family that would care to be notified about anything to do with my life."

"For that I am truly sorry, my dear."

I took her hand and led her back to my apartment.

he blood of young Stephanie revived me more than I could ever have hoped from a single source. But I still needed to eat more often than her body could afford without risk. I pulled away from her neck reluctantly, leaving her weak but safe—as promised. Then I cut my wrist as I had in the past and bade her drink. But this time I restricted the amount.

"One drop, please, but only one. You mustn't drink more for risk of becoming as I am."

She did as instructed. Her strength returned quickly and her eyes sparkled. I saw the beauty that hid beneath the grime and despair. She stood and stretched. The smile she offered gave me hope. What she offered next lifted my spirits more than anything I'd ever experienced.

***

I needed others. I hunted at night, bringing Stephanie back things she needed for survival—human things. On occasion she bid me drink from her ample source, and often I partook of her body in other ways. With new life and hope for the future, her physical acts of love became interesting—even fun for her.

Stephanie became a full woman, happy and healthy. She found work and returned to school. Apparently no one noticed her intelligence before they abandoned her, tossing her aside like a useless puppy that won't stop relieving itself on the carpet. My heart leapt at the good I could do for another human being. I'd never imagined.

We lived together in this manner for two years until she graduated community college and got accepted at a full campus to pursue training for her career choice as a pediatric doctor. In a short time, I'd become fond of her and felt a deep seated pride swell within me as I watched her walk up the platform to collect her parchment.

As a thank you gift the night before she left, she rode me all night long. Normally I would have tried to participate but she insisted on giving me a treat for all I'd done. Even though I tried to reassure her it was hardly worth mentioning, she would hear nothing more on the subject. In the end, I lay back and let her do what she'd become so good at. To this day I am not sure which of us felt more satisfied.

***

Months passed, I would feed off someone, but only enough to survive. And always I gave more in return, insuring no reports to anyone about me. Then I would move on. Despite adding to the complication of my life, this worked out for the best. No one found a body and no one came looking for me. And most times my help would be in the form of money or assistance. Very few needed my blood, which is fortunate. A sudden wave of people mysteriously and suddenly becoming healthy and resisting persistent diseases could attract as much attention as dead bodies.

Despite my earlier misgivings, I managed a job at the local hospital—as an orderly. I also went back to school for nursing. While I could stay away from the more dangerous implements of the trade, I could still be involved with the sick and downtrodden. On many occasions I would taint the medicine for a patient with a small drop of my blood. Their recovery would hardly be miraculous, but steady and positive nonetheless.

During my service there, I also discovered the blood bank. While the blood would serve me well, I had only little access. Nevertheless I could get 'bottled' blood on occasion and have no need to bite a person. Also, given the right circumstances, the morgue offered some alternate eating options, although this would be infrequent as the body needed to be particularly fresh for me to feed from it.

After my shift I still walk, in search of food and people to help. Since they would be one in the same, I often travel the streets where the underprivileged could be found. The world offered an abundance of such people. But occasionally I wanted something different, someone with a little class. Someone...*clean*. Sometimes I just needed a break from my toils, chosen or otherwise.

Lost in deep thought and still wondering if I'd found my calling, there were still so many hours of the night when I had little to do. I know that would surprise anyone seeing the wretched and discarded members of society. If generosity had become my new standard of living, it might appear I'd have my work cut out for me for many years to come. But even a vampire could not work twenty-four hours a day. We all need some form of recreation.

So I walk for a while, trying in vain to clear my head and focus on what I could do. At some point in time this night, a red glow washed over my path and illuminated my shoes. Distracted, I did not see it until I'd nearly passed. When I finally looked up I saw a sign. *Plato's*. Completely ignorant but very curious, I approached the door and knocked.

A man, bouncer by the look, greeted me in a friendly manner that did not seem intrusive. This man looked as though he would handle his business without noticing the face of the person he spoke to, under any circumstances. *It sounds like my kind of place.* After I inquired further I discovered what sort of business hid behind the heavy front doors. I could hardly believe what he told me.

The man generously allowed me a brief look inside where I saw a number of things instantly. Besides a considerable number of people lounging about drinking and conversing, I saw two couples engaged in brazen sexual activities in public view, a man with two women who looked on the verge of doing something erotic, and a woman slapping a nude man with a whip as he struggled against the chains that bound him. Try as I might I could not keep the smile from twisting my mouth up at the edges.

Definitely, my kind of place.

OH, TO BE YOUNG AGAIN!

By:
Blue Canyon

The corporate building gleamed like a mirror. Inside, men and women in business attire hustled from one point to another with a sense of purpose that would escape any casual observer.

Coming down an escalator stood two prominent men, dressed for success, chatting with each other. Being friends for quite some time, they were unconcerned with their age difference.

The older man, one Martin Kernicky, admonished the younger for not stopping to enjoy life. The other man, Mr. Kent McDaniels, worked day and night to make it to the top of the corporate world.

"You have to rest sometime, Kent. Smell the roses. It's not good for your health to keep up this pace."

"I'll rest when I'm up where you are, Marty."

"You certainly will. A very long rest. Eternal rest."

"Yeah, you're just afraid of the competition."

"I am serious, Kent. What are you doing this weekend?"

"I thought you and your wife were taking a cruise."

"We are. But I asked what YOU have planned."

"Oh. Well, I've got some papers to correct and the Edison account has to be…"

"So you are going to work the entire weekend," Martin said, not exactly as a question.

"Well, yes."

"Here." The shiny object flew gracefully through the air making a perfect arch.

"What's this?"

"The keys to my summer cabin by the lake. Do you remember where it is?"

"Yes, but..."

"You shouldn't argue. I'm a man of great power."

"Yeah," Kent chuckled.

They walked outside. Martin met a beautiful, younger woman, dressed in a tight mini dress and a thong that showed when she reached up to hug him. They got into his car and left with barely a glance back.

The younger man stood there with his mouth open and parts of him tingling. He gathered himself back together and got into his own car, a 1983 Maserati, fully restored, and drove off, putting his bundle of papers and a laptop on the empty passenger seat.

As he drove, he wondered about the cabin. It might be a great change of pace to unwind and he could still do his work. There just didn't seem to be a good reason not to go. So when he came upon the turn-off, he took it.

The longer drive didn't seem very appealing so he settled in to the conforming seats and stepped on the gas. Before long, as the sun sank in the distance, his car began to act oddly. The engine sputtered and he lost power. He maneuvered onto a dirt road to turn around but the road was too narrow and the car had other ideas.

With no warning, he lost control. The car lurched forward and limped ahead until it finally stalled, as if out of gas. He looked at the gauge and it read well over half way. But his limited mechanical prowess left him with only confusion. So, resigned, he got out of the car and raised the hood with almost no idea what look for.

As darkness fell on him like a shroud over his head at the gallows, he looked at his surroundings. Mostly he searched for houses. Scanning the barren horizon, he found none, with the exception of a broken down stone building. It resembled an old castle more than anything else, but he had little choice.

He approached the vine-covered structure that was almost completely obscured by a fog that didn't seem to exist anywhere else. Rising moonlight filtered through, giving off an eerie effect, but Kent didn't hesitate as he approached the large wooden door.

The huge brass knocker lifted easier than he thought it would. When it came down, the sound echoed throughout the interior of the building and back out from in between the stones.

In the foggy evening darkness, the sound came from everywhere and Kent felt a chill race through his bones. The massive door made no creaking sound as it moved back and a dim, flickering light sprinkled through. The silhouette standing there looked small and frail, unlike the traditional image of a lurking butler with a deep, almost lethargic voice.

A voice, as frail as the shadow that shone out through the door, spoke to him and he almost didn't hear. He stepped forward and leaned down to hear better and be less threatening. She spoke again and there was no fear in her voice.

"Can I help you?"

"Yes, my car has broken down. Can I use your phone?"

"I'm sorry, young man. I have no phone."

Kent looked at her with confusion. She was decidedly old—ancient, one might say. She had sparkly eyes and her smile seemed warm and motherly. She waited patiently for him to speak further.

"Is there somewhere I can go where there's a phone around here?"

"No," she said cryptically. "Why don't you come in? I have some tea on the stove and you can warm yourself by my fire."

Kent noticed the chill in the air for the second time and decided waiting inside had to be better than outside. He stepped in, trying to look as non-menacing as possible. But when he reached out a hand as an introduction, she did not withdraw. Though he meant her no harm, he puzzled over her fearlessness.

"Kent McDaniels."

"Martha Bickery."

"A pleasure, ma'am."

"Please call me Martha."

"Only if you call me Kent."

"Well, that sounds right proper," she answered, with a sharp nod of her head.

They sat near the fire and drank tea at a huge wooden table that looked Victorian. They talked of many things and Kent found her enchanting. But all the while his eye caught a large painting on the wall to his right. A woman in it sat in a tall-backed chair and smiled gently, inviting.

The eyes in the portrait were so alive and Kent admired the artist who painted her. But something familiar about the model drew his focus, even though Kent felt sure he'd never seen her or the old woman, nor the stone building in which she lived, for that matter.

Finally it dawned on him, the old woman's eyes looked the same. He turned from her to the painting and back again. The similarity was haunting. The woman in the painting had a striking beauty and Kent felt sure the old woman, in her day, did as well.

"Is that an ancestor or a descendant?"

"Neither."

"But her eyes are so much like yours. She must be a relative."

"You could say that. It's me, silly man."

"That was you? My God. You were beautiful."

"Thank you, very much. How would you like to meet her?"

"That would have been wonderful."

"You could still meet her."

Kent found it difficult to form words. "What?"

"Do not fear. I have powers. I am a witch."

"What?!?" Kent sounded almost silly, as he repeated himself, but the fear could still be heard.

"No need to worry, my young friend. No harm will come to you."

"Then, what are you talking about?"

"I wish to be with a man again."

"You mean…sex?"

"I do."

"But is that possible?"

"I can do it."

"But why would you?"

"As I said, to lay with a man…perhaps for the last time."

"What?" Kent said, running his finger around his now-sweaty shirt collar. He swallowed loudly.

"I'm very old, good sir."

"And this would be the last time? Why?"

"I won't be making myself young again."

"But you don't even know me."

"I don't want to marry you, just to have a night or two."

"A night or two?"

"I won't be able to maintain the illusion for any longer than that."

"You won't?"

"I won't be able to keep it up. I don't have that kind of power anymore."

"You mean you are too weak? Could you be hurt?"

"No. I just can't maintain it any longer than that."

"So, why would you want to do this with me?" His voice sounded more frightened than before.

"I don't think you understand. I just want to have the chance to lay with a man one last time. No one would lay with me, as old as I am. But her," the old woman pointed at the painting again, "she had suitors coming from everywhere."

"So, you want to use your powers to make yourself young again, and sleep with me for as long as it lasts?"

"Yes."

"And that's all?"

"Yes."

"Have you done this before?"

"Oh yes, many times. Does that make you think poorly of me?"

"No, not at all. I'm just a little nervous…and flattered."

"Look at the painting, my young man."

Kent looked deeply into the eyes of the striking woman, layered onto the canvas.

"Would you lay with her? Tell me it's not what you were thinking as you looked at it before."

"It is true. She had my full attention for a while."

Martha smiled sweetly again. She had used it often that night, and Kent felt warmed by it. He felt very close to her in a "chemistry" kind of way. It's the

121

kind of thing that only happens when two people can become as one with just conversation and a stare.

"I want you to relax. Lay down on the bear skins and open your shirt. Allow your eyes to close, and fall asleep if it is within you to do so. I will be back in a while, just remember what the girl in the picture looked like."

"Where are you going?"

"It takes time to prepare," she said in a comforting tone. "I will return soon."

Kent, surprised to be tired, rested his head down. His eyes drooped and he drifted peacefully off to a comfortable, though light sleep. If he dreamed, he didn't remember any of it later. He woke when her hand touched his arm. He always slept alone and he'd become unaccustomed to being touched by anyone else.

As his eyes opened against the stickiness that had come in such a short time, he managed to focus with some ease in the dim light from the fire. An image formed in front of him. An image that became beauty incarnate.

The woman from the painting stood before him. Her beauty radiated from her like heat from the fire. He basked in it for a moment and stared deeply into the eyes that so captivated him earlier. He recanted his first impression of the painter's talent. Her eyes in the painting weren't nearly a tenth as miraculous as in real life.

Her smile became somehow even warmer, perhaps just from the anticipation of what lay ahead.

122

He looked down her length and, for the first time, noticed her clothing. She wore his shirt. He didn't even remember taking it off, but it looked so much better on her.

She didn't bother to button it and it opened down the front enough to show without giving away any sensual secrets. As far as he could tell, she wore no pants of any kind. In fact, the shirt—all she wore—covered very little.

She leaned closer to him. Her body had an odor that Kent could not identify. It smelled musty and arousing in a primal way. If he'd wanted to resist her, he didn't think he could. Her smile and her eyes could draw in most any man. But her breasts hanging in front of his face and his head spinning from that odor, he knew her enchantment overwhelmed him. Perhaps her witchcraft had infected him.

Somehow, he thought it to be a ludicrous idea and he dismissed it. But as her lips finally touched his, the fear of a hex re-entered his mind and would not leave until...

Her fingers touched his chest and all thoughts became lost. The only thing left—his only desire—to be with her, in her, a part of her. He wanted to give it all to her and he started with…

Time felt lost as he entered her again and again. Their lovemaking went on through the night and into the early morning. He lost all sense and he passed exhaustion many hours before they showed signs of stopping.

His orgasms couldn't easily be counted. He felt himself drain into her even as his desire rose again and his passion drove him to further levels of stamina and he pounded into her, working toward another peak. She had begun to sweat and lose consciousness as the sun rose and colored the eastern sky.

He finally lay back and allowed her to fall next to him. They rested there, quickly losing any ability to stay awake, and imagined they saw the sun rise. In truth, neither of them managed to have their eyes open for more than a few seconds after they stopped.

The day wore on and they slept together through it. No one lived there except her. No one visited there except him. They lay naked upon the sheets and cuddled happily until they woke and began to excite one another all over again.

This time they made love for almost an hour before they stopped. Being very hungry, they got up for something to eat. Neither of them bothered to dress or make any gesture of modesty.

Once sated, they returned to the bed chamber and began their carnal ritual once again. The room smelled of sex…and…something else. Kent felt, once again, momentarily distracted by the disquietingly unknown odor. It was like jasmine and something bitter. Although it was overpowered with the additional smell of sex.

Once again his juices filled her and she moaned with delight. She thrilled at the touch of a man—such a virile man. He certainly made her heart race. She wanted it to last forever, despite her limitations. She tried to focus any remaining power she might have on extending her "visit" to youth, but she just didn't have anything left.

She quickly went back to the pleasure of the moment and allowed herself to orgasm once again, as Kent pushed his manhood into her from yet another angle. Her head spun and her eyes shut from a kind of satisfaction/exhaustion that would not be defined. And all she could think, for her last time to be young and with a man again, was that she had chosen wisely.

She did not know how long she would live, but she would never again have the strength to make herself young and be with a man. He would be her last. The man was a dynamo and again their sex lasted for hours. But this night, somewhere around 3 A.M. they fell fast asleep and slept well into the next day.

Kent woke up first and looked over at his lover, laying there on her back with the covers pulled up only to her waist allowing her breasts to remain exposed to his view. He moved enough to disturb the bed…and her. She woke and looked at him with some concern, but after a moment she relaxed into something that resembled resignation mixed with deep sorrow.

She'd seen the reaction on his face before. Not on *his* face, but the same reaction on others. She looked down and saw two very old and sagging breasts, covered in wrinkles and hair, and nipples that looked as though they'd been used to carry buckets of water.

Sadness overwhelmed her and she excused herself from the room as gracefully as she could. Kent made no move to discourage her. When she came back, she had dressed and he finished tying his last shoelace. She spoke with as much dignity as she could muster.

"You must leave now. There is nothing left here for you."

"But…?"

"You know I am right," she said, holding up a hand to stop what he would regret saying to her. "You have a job and a life. And this is what I truly look like. I am ever so much older than you."

"How old could you be? 80?" He tried to sound convincing.

"I am 126. Magic has extended my life a little."

His entire being sagged. He stared at the floor and tried to discover the pattern to the wood grain as if that, in itself, would provide answers to such perplexing questions as: what to do next.

"I'm not sure what a proper goodbye would be under such circumstances." Kent felt foolish, inept.

"Just say goodbye and accept my gratitude."

"I, too, am grateful."

"Then we should leave it at that, don't you think?"

The old woman would speak no more, as she walked with him to the door he'd entered so recently.

She gently rested one feeble hand on his shoulder and pressed him outside as much as she could. A sullen sadness entered those perfect eyes—a sorrow that would never have the opportunity to leave again.

As the darkness within fell upon her like a blanket, her body sagged down in depression. She pushed at the door with just the briefest of glances in his direction. He wished he hadn't seen it. Kent recognized the same depression that had begun within him only moments before. The door closed with a fatal *clack*, finalizing the encounter.

Outside, he walked to the road and toward where his car waited faithfully for him to return. When he turned back to look at the broken stone building, another startling image accosted his eyes.

It was gone. In its place stood a more modern home with windows and a driveway. Power lines going overhead and down into a main panel suggested they would have a telephone. He turned and walked back the way he came and yet to a different destination and wondered where the old castle had gone.

Could it all have been his imagination? Or could she shroud the entire area with her magic? And when her magic grew too weak, what then? He derived none of the answers to these questions until the door opened and a woman stood before him.

She looked very different from the old (and young) woman in the castle that moments ago had stood on this very spot. And yet, something about her eyes seemed familiar to Kent and he caught himself staring.

"I'm sorry to bother you, but my car broke down out here on the road. I was wondering, could I possibly use your telephone?"

"Coming back from a weekend at the lake, Mr. uh?"

"It's McDaniels. Kent McDaniels. And no, I was…" his voice trailed off for a brief moment. "Are you saying its Monday morning?"

"Yes, Mr. McDaniels. It most certainly is. Did you lose the entire weekend?"

"I-I'm not sure?" Again his voice trailed into some oblivion that was nowhere near where the woman now stood at her door.

"Mr. McDaniels?"

"Yes, I'm sorry. It's the weirdest thing," he said, scratching his head and looking around for…something. Finally, he regained his composure. "I could use that tow truck, ma'am."

"The name's Bikery. Margaret Bikery. Please come in, sir. The telephone is right here on the kitchen wall."

He entered the modest home and was accosted by a familiar odor. Kent tried not to notice but it held a recent memory. And then it hit him. The old lady had the same scent in her house.

"Pardon me, ma'am, but what is that smell?"

"It's a very old recipe, Mr. McDaniels. I'm told it's been handed down for at least a half dozen generations. I use it for potpourri. Would you like to know a secret?" She leaned into him as if someone would hear, but no one else was there.

"Sure," Kent said, casually.

"I'm told my great-great-great-great grandmother used it as an aphrodisiac," she said, giggling with a bit of embarrassment.

"Did people back then even use aphrodisiacs?"

"Doesn't seem likely, does it?"

"Oh, I don't know," Kent offered. "I think people back then were regular people just like us, Ms. Bikery."

"Please, call me Margaret." Her smile warmed and the sparkle in her eye caught his.

"I'd like that," he returned her smile. "And you must call me Kent."

"Well, that sounds right proper," she answered, with a sharp nod of her head.

*   *   *

The toilet stood proud, not as lonely anymore. Most mornings it had the company of the woman—too old to argue with uncomfortable bodily functions. She hugged the cool bowl and allowed the tiny amount of partially digested food left inside her stomach to evacuate the hard way.

She spent this morning as she did most of them these days—wracked in pain, begging for mercy, and wondering what her future held as her ancient body rejected almost everything happening to it.

She already lived in an unnatural state, being well over 126, having sustained her life through artificial means. But this? This would almost certainly be her undoing. She looked up again at the small white stick with the bright blue dot and sighed with disbelief.

One lonely tear rolled down her coarse cheek, expressing the isolation she felt inside better than any words—as a new life grew within her ancient womb.

the flavor of life

By:
Blue Canyon

I reach for her in the night
as darkness falls around us like rain
she barely stirs as the sleep, like death, overtakes her
and I am forced to fend for myself, once again.

Still the pull of her scent calls me, stronger than thirst
I've tasted her blood and can still hear her heartbeat
I want her more than ever
as I throw the blankets down by her feet.

A simple T and lacy thong lay before my lustful eye
my hands I barely can contain
Till the dawn comes, when she must leave, she is mine
I thrust forward through the pain

Her silken panties slide off her legs
each foot withdraws as if helping
then I dive between them and extend my tongue
from within her sleep comes a small sound, yelping.

With consciousness still lost and darkness reigning
I taste that which I desire most
until that time when I am ready to mount
my sleeping, almost willing host.

Eruptions of pain and pleasure strike at my very soul
and rend me to the quick
while wolves howl and the moon hides
I withdraw my penis, slick.

She turns, suddenly awake, only to glare into my eyes
and says she can love me, never
my anger flares and I strike at her neck
to drink her life's blood, forever.

At the window, I turn to admire the beauty I'd just slain
my eyes come to rest on the honey pot where I'd lain
I wonder if this curse will never see an end
as claws come out, fangs protrude; my flesh to rend.

The night answers, solemn and dark
Nothing precious or sweet do I hark
All life, it says, will one day go by
Yours is not life. You will end in horror and pain. You
will burst into flame. Until the end…when you will
taste death, to finally die.

America, The Beautiful

By:
Blue Canyon

The hospital room, dark and nearly quiet save for the persistent beeping and barely audible breathing—air weighing heavily—all who entered found it difficult to breathe and instinctively spoke with softer voices. But it made little difference. No one would disturb the sleeping beauty lying just beneath a sheet and a thin, cotton gown, even if they shouted at the top of their lungs.

Even though the girl lacked any real covering, the room remained quite frigid. The woman, older, with heavy bags beneath her eyes, standing at the edge of the bed, looked down at the occupant and wondered—not for the first time—how we could be taught going out in the cold without a jacket would make us sick and yet the staff maintained this temperature in a place meant to heal.

"Who is she?"

The tiny voice startled the woman. She turned and saw, standing back by the door, a petite candy striper who looked far too young to work in such a place. *Surely she doesn't have any real responsibility around here.*

"She is everyone…and no one," the older woman answered, cryptically.

"I'm sorry, what?"

"She is just a regular person, like all other regular people. She has no health care, but she still needs."

"She looks like a movie star."

"Her beauty often leads people to think she's famous—that maybe they'd seen her somewhere before."

"Regular people deserve quality health care as well as anyone else," the young girl said, deadpan.

The woman suspected this was a pre-rehearsed line required from all hospital staff, rather than any real compassion. "Let's hope the administrators feel the same way."

"Are you her mother?"

"I am," she said, managing to sound both indignant and gracious at the same time. *Do I look so old?*

"I can see the resemblance. You have the same beautiful eyes."

"You're too kind. Unfortunately hers are not open…as are mine. Mine hardly seem to close anymore. Perhaps I'm making up for her." Her voice trailed off, nearly masking a sob. "Most unfortunate," she added, staring longingly at the coma patient. A tear moved down her cheek in jerky motions, getting caught on the dry skin, then finding a path once again, until it reached her chin.

"I'm sorry I intruded." With little else to say, the candy striper turned and left the room.

***

Outside, at the floor station, she dared ask. "What happened to her?" She cocked a thumb over her shoulder in the direction of room 314.

138

"You never heard the story?" the older, duty nurse asked. "My how things have changed since I was a young CNA like yourself."

"What is it, required reading or something?"

"It's a pretty amazing tale…if you believe in that sort of thing."

"*Believe?* Believe what? She got some kind of injury and now she's in a coma."

"The girl's name is America. Despite her exceptional looks, she is no one special. A common girl from a common family. I guess you'd call her an average person."

"America. Isn't that a Spanish name?"

"Usually."

"But she doesn't look Hispanic."

"She's not. Actually, judging by their last name, I'd say they're French."

"Then why the Spanish name?"

"I have no idea. People name their kids oddly, these days. I heard one guy called his daughter Chelsea."

"That's terrible. He must be some kind of loser. So what happened to that poor girl in 314?"

"One night, she went to a carnival and got her fortune told."

"You mean those silly, gypsy side-show tents?"

"Yeah. But maybe not so silly. According to the story, the woman foretold a horrible death at a young age. Of course America was distraught. She went to other fortune tellers and psychics to disprove the prophecy."

"So she believed it."

"Oh, she most certainly did. And, as you might imagine, she was rather scared about it, too. She desperately sought a solution—a cure, or at least when to turn right, not left. Instead she discovered a terrible truth. Apparently the first gypsy hadn't *foretold* the tragedy, she *created* it."

"What? What does that mean?"

"She cursed the girl."

"Come on, that's crazy. Do you know what century this is?"

The older woman shrugged. "That's the story."

"But you said 'horrible death'. What did you mean by that?"

"Ah, and therein begins the twisted part of this tale."

"More twisted than what you already said?"

"Way worse."

"Oh my, I think I need a cup of coffee."

The RN, Bonnie, laughed heartily. "I know how you feel. Give me a second to file this last report and I'll join you. I'll continue the story as we go. I'd like to see if you can finish your coffee once you've heard the frightening truth."

"Is that supposed to be some kind of challenge?"

"Not really. But it's a sordid tale and it doesn't sit well on everyone's stomach. You may wish you hadn't asked."

"I can hardly wait to hear more."

"You'll get more than you bargained for, I promise."

"Then coffee and horror stories it is. And I'll see how strong my stomach is."

As they walked to the pot, Bonnie spoke softly. She animated her words with odd voice inflections and generous hand gestures while the younger aide asked questions and hung on every word, barely containing herself.

"Sarah," she spoke to the younger girl, "it's time you realized the world isn't always what it seems."

"So you believe in this supernatural stuff, too?" she said, pouring coffee for both of them.

"Let's just say, when you've lived as long as I have, you see a great many things that can't easily be explained."

"Like what?"

"Oh, you don't want to hear an old woman's follies. Let's talk about room 314."

They 'sword-played' with two spoons as they both reached for the sugar and powdered creamer at the same time. After a moment, Sarah nearly spilled her coffee and they both calmed down—neither wanting to clean up any more mess than necessary.

"This is kind of like a slumber party," Sarah offered.

"Sure, but these aren't exactly pajamas. I'd be more comfortable in starched burlap."

"Ouch."

"Well, not all experiences are fun."

Sarah looked at the other woman with doubtful curiosity. Finally she shook her head. "Okay. So you said the one gypsy cursed her with a horrible death and yet she's still alive."

"You noticed that all by yourself, did you? You must be some kind of health care professional." Bonnie took a sip of her coffee, slurping over her lips to avoid a burn.

"Very funny," Sarah scoffed. "I've got a piece of paper."

"I've got a whole roll of the same stuff in my bathroom."

"Does it have my name written all over it?"

"Would you prefer that it did? I don't exactly hang it on the wall."

"Neither did I. So tell me about the girl and this silly curse story.

"It all began—according to the lore, if you believe it—," Bonnie spoke softly now, nearly a whisper, "—with an old gypsy who'd been beautiful in her youth. But a terrible accident, caused by the man she was to marry, left her horribly disfigured." She leaned in closer so she could speak even softer, adding to the eeriness.

"Oh, she managed for a time," Bonnie chuckled as she rocked back in the chair and then rested her

142

elbows on the table to get close to the young girl again. "But people turned from her—scorned her. Her scarred face frightened children. Her fiancée died in the accident and no other men would call on her. She sat in her home, night after endless night, wishing for company of any kind. She found none. In time she became very bitter, as you can imagine."

"They could have done plastic surgery, couldn't they? Or a skin graph?"

"Not in those days," Bonnie said, noticing with some satisfaction that the younger girl had goose bumps on her arms.

"What days? We've had successful cosmetic surgeries for more than fifty years. The girl in 314 is only—what—twenty?"

"Sweetie, that girl's been in this hospital— unconscious—for nearly ten years."

"Right." Sarah rolled her eyes. "If she's a day over twenty-five, I'll eat my own underwear."

"While watching you do that would bring me a great deal of joy—more than you could know—I feel compelled to tell you the truth."

"A-ha! You lied."

"No, I didn't lie. The truth is, she doesn't age."

"She…what?"

"She hasn't aged a day since they brought her in—back in '95. By now she'd be mid-thirties, going on forty."

Suddenly the girl sounded smaller. "Are you sure?"

"I was here when she came in. Every new nurse looks at the records because they don't believe."

"People look at her records? Isn't that a breach of confidentiality?"

"Back then, *every* nurse did. Except Shirley."

"Shirley?"

"She doesn't work here anymore."

"Why didn't Shirley check her out? Wasn't she curious like the rest of you?"

"Oh she was curious, all right. In a different way—if you know what I mean."

"Really?"

"And she tried to check her out."

Sarah sucked in a deep breath. "Are you serious? While she was unconscious?"

"Well, I guess she couldn't exactly resist, could she?"

"I know, but really. If I wanted someone to just lie there, I'd get a man."

"Honey, my man is *very* active in the bedroom...for about five seconds."

Sarah chuckled. "Sounds romantic."

"Hey," Bonnie said, raising both her hands up as if being arrested. "I've got two other lovers that treat me just right."

"Is that why you're always smiling?"

"That's it. And if I need something different, I'm sure any one of these bed-ridden gentlemen would be glad to accommodate."

"You're so bad."

"Me and Michael Jackson."

"You and anyone, it seems."

"Well, no women."

"Never?" Sarah asked, innocently.

"Well…"

"What? Tell me."

"I kissed another woman, once," Bonnie admitted.

"So why didn't she die?"

"*I…beg…your…pardon.*"

"Hello, girl? Horrible death? Room 314?"

"Oh, oh, oh. *Her.*" She said the last word as if she were singing it.

"Yes, *her,*" Sarah mimicked the song Bonnie started. "Why didn't she die?"

"Well of course there's a lot more to the story, and I'm sure some stuff we don't even know, but as I said earlier, America went to other fortune tellers."

"Did they all say the same thing?"

"Pretty much, you know. The charlatans only painted pictures of flowers and sunny days—bright futures and bliss, that sort of crap. But anyone with genuine sight told her the same story—or some variation of it."

"She must have been terribly frightened."

"I would imagine so. But the tale takes an unusual turn here. At some point America spoke to another gypsy."

"Did she say the same thing?"

"Yes, but she said a lot more. And it gets worse."

"Worse? How can that be?"

"This gypsy knew the other one. She told America the story about the accident and how this was actually a curse. The old woman, Georgina Shrub, had great power. According to legend, she cast this death spell on many pretty young girls. The last gypsy, Barbara Omaba, tried to undo the curse."

"Let me guess, she didn't have enough power."

"Right. The best she could do was put her to sleep. There was an investigation and Omaba's ethnicity came into question. There was also speculation about whether or not her parents had been married when she was conceived."

"They didn't know if she was a real gypsy or not?"

"Like it really mattered. Apparently they think she could have been the one who did something to the girl. She never produced a birth certificate. And after all, no one can prove the first Gypsy even existed."

"They couldn't find her?"

"She disappeared—fell right off the face of the Earth. Poof. Just like that," Bonnie concluded with a snap of the fingers on her right hand.

"And the only other way to find out if it's a real curse or not," Sarah said, pointedly, "is to let people die?"

"Some would have preferred it—or they didn't care. At least they would have the proof they so desperately sought."

"Ridiculous."

"You know how people can be."

"What about the others?"

"Other whats?"

"People she cursed."

"I assume they died."

"And nobody can do anything?"

"Only Madame Omaba. She did something."

"Sure, but does that beautiful young girl have to sleep forever?"

"The story says there will be a stimulus, something special that will happen to awaken her."

"You mean like a special kiss?"

"Something similar to that I guess, but I suspect it won't be as romantic."

"Won't she get old?"

"According to the story, when she wakes she'll be good as new—still only twenty-two—and she'll accomplish great things."

"*When* she wakes. You mean *if* she wakes."

"The story maintains that she *will* awaken."

"But when? She's been comatose for more than a decade. How much longer does she have to sleep?"

"I'm sure her mother asks the same question, over and over and over. But I'm not the one to ask. Perhaps one of the doctors has a clue, but I wouldn't hold my breath for that. They seem as baffled as the rest of us."

"So, all this happened just because someone named Bush said so?"

"Shrub," Bonnie corrected. "And yes, that seems to be the general consensus."

"So what's the special what-zit that'll wake her?"

"How would I know?" Bonnie retorted.

"Well don't the stories say something? Doesn't her mother know?"

"It all seems to be pretty mysterious, Sarah. I don't think these kinds of things come with an instruction manual."

"Well maybe she needs a kiss on her *other* lips."

"That's what Shirley thought. But she got caught before she could get to it."

"I'll just have to be more careful than she was. Ninja!" Sarah held out her hands as if seeking balance, although she stood still.

"And you're willing to do that, huh?"

"Be a ninja? That'd be cool."

"No, silly. Kiss that girl down there."

"To her? Oh yeah. I'd go there even if I *didn't* like girls so much. She's so beautiful."

"Why do you like girls that way?" Bonnie's eye muscle twinged.

"I like guys, too."

"Yes, but why girls at all?"

"Girls are more sensitive to my needs."

"But they don't have anything—you know—to put *in* you."

148

"That's why I have such a large collection of toys," Sarah rocked her eyebrows up and down a couple times.

"I have a toy," Bonnie admitted with pride.

"Good for you." Sarah thought for a moment. "You have *used* it, haven't you?"

"Of course, silly girl."

"And? Was it good?"

"Delightful."

"See? They're fun with a friend and great by yourself."

"You make me almost want to try being with a woman."

"I could turn you on to some web sites. Maybe you'd like to go to a club with me, sometime."

"On a date?" she winced.

"No. But I could introduce you around, show you the scene."

Bonnie smiled. "I'll give it some thought. In the meantime, don't go burying your tongue in that girl in 314. There's just something wrong about that, her being unconscious and all."

"I wouldn't bother. I like a girl that moves."

"Hmm." Bonnie didn't say anything further, but something about the younger nurse's eyes said she wasn't quite as turned off by the sleeping beauty as she let on.

At that precise moment America's mom walked out of the room looking more dejected than usual. Sarah's heart went out to her.

"You should have seen," Bonnie began. "She used to bring in a couple men a week to try and break the spell. Don't ask me where she picked them up, or what they did once inside that room, but she brought in some real hunks. Lord only knows what she's giving them in return for the favor."

"Bonnie! You shouldn't say such things."

"Well, they all came willingly, that's all I'm saying."

"Maybe they came because America is so beautiful."

"But they didn't know that 'till they got here."

"You have a twisted mind."

"That don't make me a bad person."

Sarah chuckled. "No it doesn't. Since only normal people frighten me, I guess you're safe."

"Thanks. I feel so much better now that I have your approval." Bonnie poked a finger at her and smiled. The finger just barely touched Sarah's shoulder.

"Sexual harassment!" she mock-cried.

"I just touched your shoulder, silly girl."

"Well, aim better next time. My tits are a little lower."

"And you say I have the twisted mind. Ha!"

Sarah smiled, genuinely. "That's right."

"Get out of here before someone notices you've been fondling all the patients."

"I have not. Only the good looking ones."

"Yeah, right."

"And only the women."

"Lesbian slut."

"I always appreciate public recognition. Can I get a trophy?"

"I'd get you one that looks like a pussy but we'd never get your face out of it."

Although amused, Sarah felt the serious weight of what America's mother believed about a curse, as if it rested on her own shoulders. Could such a thing actually exist in the twenty-first century? And if so, what would it take to break it? So many men came and none had succeeded yet. Could it be? Did the sleeping girl really need something from another woman?

Sarah struggled with the idea that a 'true love' kiss might need to be somewhere other than her mouth. Of course the entire thing reeked of absurdity. How could a simple kiss, on *any* lips, wake a comatose patient? And hadn't that other nurse gone there and tried? *Bonnie said she didn't get all the way. Could it be?* And really, who believed in curses in this modern day and age, anyway? *Then again, it could be fun to try.*

***

"Come, sit down, my pretty," she rasped. "I am Madam Georgina."

America fought the urge to run away. The winter carnival beckoned. The world had just rung in the New Year and 1992 all-but-begged to be explored,

151

like a previously undiscovered cavern in a series of caves.

Something about the old woman disturbed America more than she liked to admit. Maybe it was just her voice, or maybe something other-worldly. Perhaps America had a special sensitivity to the eeriness of the centuries that swam through the air in the old woman's tent. In the end, she overcame the urge and sat.

"My, what a beauty you are. A beauty, indeed," she rambled, rocking a little in her chair. "Let me see your hands, child."

America extended her hands and the old woman grasped them with a firmness that belied her age. The woman studied America's palms—gripping tightly— keeping her from pulling back like she wanted. As the old gypsy stared, she remained mostly silent, only allowing an occasional 'hmm' to escape her mouth. America wondered what Madam Georgina found so fascinating.

"You have an interesting twist in your life line."

"What kind of twist?"

The old woman glanced away, eyes searching.

"Tell me," America insisted. Even though she hardly believed in such things, she felt the supernatural vibrations from the room all converge within her, momentarily, and then they just as quickly swept past. *Could that be an omen?*

"I'm afraid it's not good news."

"Okay." She sat uncomfortably in the chair, shifting her weight from one thigh to the other. "I have to know."

"It looks as though your life comes to an abrupt end in your twenty-second year."

"That's only three years away. It can't be that I'll die so young. It's not fair!" Despite her doubts about such psychic drivel, America believed Madam Georgina, and she could not be sure why.

"There's nothing you can do to change it."

"Can you tell me how it happens?"

"It seems unclear, but there is water boiling, steaming, as if from a teapot."

"Am I to be burned to death by scalding water?"

The woman released a deep breath and slumped forward. "I can see no more."

America stood and dropped some money on the table. She didn't look at how much, she just wanted to escape. She backed away apprehensively, somehow feeling that something might try and jump her from behind. Just when she felt the edge of the tent against her back and she thought she might get clean away unharmed, the old woman sat straight up.

"Wait!"

America nearly ran, but something held her legs tight. She froze.

"You've given me too much money."

"Huh?"

"What do you think this is a government operation? It's two dollars. Everyone that comes in pays two dollars, no more, no less."

America tried to focus on the money. She could see several bills and at least one twenty. She walked back and settled, giving the woman three. "A tip."

"Thank you, my dear. Enjoy what life you have left."

America shuddered and left quickly. Even as skeptical as she felt, America *knew* something would happen when she turned twenty-two. Maybe not death—these circus jerks always erred toward the dramatic—but probably something bad. Perhaps she would lose her parents, or be horribly disfigured. At any rate, without knowing anything further she could do so very little about it.

As time passed, America became more than a bit curious about psychics and fortune tellers. She longed to find out as much as she could in hopes of avoiding some disaster before it befell her. Many disappointed her. Some merely reaffirmed Madam Georgina's prophecy.

After the first of the year she spoke with one at a local Mardi Gras festival. Although she felt no psychic vibrations this time, the woman appeared more genuine than many others. Her kind face invited America in even before the words came out.

"Come in, Deary." Her voice sounded grandmotherly—soothing and old, but ancient with knowledge. "Why would a lovely young child, such as yourself, need the services of Madam Barbara?"

Barbara? What a peculiar name for a gypsy. "I got my fortune told recently. The woman told me awful things. I just wanted to…"

"You just hoped someone could disprove that fortune? Or perhaps you wish to know all so you can avoid the prophecy? I assure you, my child, you can do neither. If it is to be so, it will be so. If what you say is true, I will charge you nothing." She held out her hands for America's.

America had been to so many she knew how it all worked even before the woman asked. Odd how they all performed much the same rituals. *Did that mean they're all real or they've all seen the same television shows?*

The woman offered the familiar 'hmm' as she rubbed her thumbs across America's palms. Suddenly a shocked look swept across her face. Her thumbs rubbed harder. She leaned closer to get a better look. Finally she spoke.

"It is as you say. There is a tragedy to befall you. But it is not natural."

"What does that mean?"

"Someone has hexed you, my child. This is not the natural order. Your life should not end at this time."

"You mean someone is going to kill me? But who?"

"It is a different way of taking a life. A curse."

155

"A *curse*? You've got to be joking." America nearly stood and left, but hesitation allowed her to hear further.

"Someone with great power gave you this curse. What is the name of the woman who told you the original fortune?"

"Madam Georgina."

"Oh, dear." Madam Barbara stood and paced about as if searching for something.

"Do you know her?"

"We are all sisters in Gaia, my dear. Even Georgina. But she is not as we are."

"How do you mean?"

"Georgina was born such a beauty. Adored by everyone, men courted her, kingdoms fell at her feet, she owned the world. When she turned twenty a rich and handsome man asked for her hand in marriage. Three months before the wedding was to take place, she fell victim to a horrible accident. Attacked on the street by a common thief, her face never could be returned to its original beauty. Her betrothed died trying to protect her from harm. Georgina became reclusive and her heart turned bitter, hating all mankind, particularly beauty. You are the very thing she envies most. You are her arch enemy."

America remained quiet.

"Does your mother know of this?"

"No. I've told no one."

"Why would you not seek the comfort of your own mother at such a time?"

"Come on, what would I say? Gypsy curses and death at twenty-two? She'd lock me away for sure."

The old woman shrugged and then shook her head. "No matter. Perhaps there is still time."

"Time? Time for what?" America leaned back in her chair as if trying to escape from the woman's words.

"Time to intervene. Time to undo that which should never have been done."

"Huh?"

"Time to save your life, my dear."

***

Sarah's finger snuck beneath the sheet but her eyes remained glued to the door, awaiting an interruption. The muscles in her arm stayed tense, ready to withdraw at lightning speed, if necessary. Surely, she did not want to get caught.

No hair grew where she headed. In fact, there'd been no hair growth anywhere in the last decade. The girl's body lived in great health, the skin pliable and smooth, hair shiny, fingernails pink and pretty. But no growth could be measured.

Sarah had to go past her goal to the bottom of the hospital gown, then she turned back up, drawing a line up the inside of an almost perfect thigh. When she touched the outer lips of her target, she shuddered. Of course she'd touched America in this manner before, to wash her, but this was different. She felt more intimate

157

and therefore more excited. Her own nipples grew hard while America's remained barely noticeable through the top of the gown.

She felt a bit like Arthur in the old tale. She approached the rock, knowing it shouldn't be her, yet expecting to be the one to withdraw the sword. If no one came, she could bend down and push her tongue inside the sleeping beauty. Sarah thought it would be *the* magic kiss.

Touching the woman's nether lips gave her more satisfaction than she'd thought possible. She liked a partner that moved, reacted, swaying with her advances—together, like a boat riding the ocean waves. But this woman's beauty and complete submissiveness drove Sarah to the brink of an orgasm without even touching herself.

She parted America's lips and inserted a finger. Some irrational thought suggested she would find the area cold and dry. She discovered, to her surprise, neither. *If the girl isn't dead, why should she be cold?* Somehow the warm sheath sent tingles over Sarah's hand, up her arm, and into her brain, pushing her all the way to that orgasm.

Sarah stood still, quivering, waiting for it to pass before continuing on with her deviant quest. Another glance at the door. *Was that a shadow moving out of the window as I looked up?* She hesitated a moment but became convinced no one approached. Hardly anyone else came around this late. The night nurse, Bonnie, didn't feel well and asked Sarah to keep an eye on things while she rested.

"No problem," she said, trying to control her enthusiasm. The thought of being with America consumed her from the night she'd first asked about the sleeping girl. And now she had the chance. She pushed the sheet back and admired the smooth vagina that engulfed her finger.

She couldn't tell if it was the most beautiful one she'd ever seen or if she'd been blinded by rapture. Either way, she bent her head closer. *Just for a closer look.* But a gentle smell wafted up and teased Sarah's nose, driving away any remaining inhibitions. She extended her tongue and planted it straight onto the sleeping girl's clitoris.

No reaction came from America, but Sarah felt reactions all over her body. Her mouth jumped for joy at the fresh taste, reminding her of one of those candy commercials on television. She explored deeper. *That other nurse, what's her name, Shirley, would have done most of the obvious things, if she'd had the chance. I have to do something different.*

Sarah thought about the usual things to do while you're there (*sounds like a travel brochure*), and couldn't remember a thing out of the ordinary. Every idea seemed like what anyone would do—insert your tongue, lick the lips, suck the clit—all common things seen in any adult movie.

Then it hit her. Anal. Sarah let her tongue slide down the rim of the vagina, touching into the hole

159

briefly, then proceeding further south. Finally she touched the object of her desire, expecting a sharp reaction from the girl. She stayed for a while, enjoying the feeling, but America didn't react in the slightest.

Sad. *Well, this doesn't have to be a complete loss.* Sarah slid her free hand into her own pants and found her own vagina, moist and ready to go again. In a swift motion she clamped her mouth over America's bare puss and enjoyed the aroma and flavor. For five minutes she rubbed herself into a frenzy and finally came so hard her knees gave out and she fell to the floor next to the bed. When her mouth pulled away from America's private place there was a loud sucking noise. After a few minutes, Sarah managed a look around expecting to see a witness. But no one heard as she'd fallen to the floor, and that was for the best.

She stood, pulling herself together and then reluctantly covered the sleeping beauty on the bed. She looked at the girl's peaceful face, hoping to see even a hint of smile. To her dismay, none shone through. *Good thing I don't have a delicate ego.* She bent down and kissed America on her mouth.

"Was it good for you, baby?" America, of course, said nothing. "I guess not." Sarah turned and headed for the door to make her rounds and check on Bonnie. At the door she turned back to look once again at America.

"You missed a hell of a time, girlfriend. We could have been great together."

160

She turned out to the hall, allowing the door to close itself behind her, and bumped directly into America's mom. The older woman looked at her with peculiar eyes, scrutinizing, judging. Sarah felt the color of guilt wash over her face, and probably her entire body. She averted her eyes, not knowing what to say. *Had she seen?*

The two women stood silently for what seemed like an eternity, when America's mom leaned forward. Sarah stiffened—wanting to run, but stood her ground. *Face the music and get it over with quickly,* Sarah's motto echoed through her head. *I guess I'll have to start looking for a new job.*

But the woman didn't strike. She kissed. She kissed Sarah full on the lips, a sensuous kiss that lasted far too long for a simple friendly gesture. Sarah felt her hands slide to the woman's back even as she noticed two hands come around her own waist. Their passionate embrace confused and excited Sarah. From the feeling, America's mom was getting excited, as well.

"Wha—?" Her breath taken, her fear muddied with desire, Sarah could barely form words. She stood away from the woman, but only by inches. They still embraced. She looked into the older, beautiful eyes.

"I wanted to thank you."

"Huh?"

"Thank you."

"For what?"

"Trying."

Sarah realized the woman saw the whole scene. Her embarrassment flared even brighter. This time, when she glanced away, she took her whole head with her. The older woman reached out a hand to the girl's chin and turned her back. She kissed again.

Swooning, Sarah barely wanted to break the spell that came over them while they embraced. Finally she opened her eyes and just stared. In time, she found her voice once more and sputtered out only three words.

"I…don't…understand."

"Anyone sensitive enough to care about her must be pretty special. You risked your job to try."

"Others have tried."

"I know."

"Did you sleep with all of them?"

"You'll be the first."

Sarah's heart pounded with anticipation. *She's actually going to sleep with me. I said it only as a joke, but she wants to. She's so beautiful, she could have anyone.* "Why me?"

"The way you paid attention to what you were doing, the way you tried different things, things I'd never seen before, not just the usual, this tells me you care about the person you're intimate with. It was quite a turn-on watching you, even if it was my own daughter you were with."

"I—I've never been with a mother *and* daughter before."

162

"There's a first time for everything. Meet me here, after your shift." She handed the girl a card.

Marsha Coutier
Interior Design

The simple business card included an address and phone number, but nothing more. Sarah thought that a little too minimalist for a designer, but she could hardly be called expert.

"I get off at 6:00 a.m. You really want me to knock on your door at that time of the morning?"

She kissed Sarah again. "Only if you want to."

***

Entry found in America Coutier's diary:

July 26th

I can't believe that woman frightened me so much.

She's just a carnival gypsy fortuneteller, hardly something for a rational person to concern themselves with. And yet I could barely breathe. When she foretold of my death, I nearly fell out of the chair. But such things can't be true. Can they? They never come to pass. Do they? And how can I avoid something I know so little about. She only said it would happen in my twenty-second year. That's pretty vague by itself.

But the other one, Madam Barbara, she was nice. She told me she'd help. She couldn't undo the evil spell Madam Georgina placed on me, but she could soften it. She said I would simply fall asleep. But I could sleep for a hundred years. And when the right person came along and touched me in a most provocative way, I would awaken.

Sometimes magic can sound so silly. Even though Georgina scared me, I have no fear of dying before my time. I assume most of this mumbo-jumbo is simply that. These carnival fortune tellers hype it up for show and I fell for it.

I hope Kent asks me to the dance today.

"I'm sorry, Mrs. Coutier. These kinds of people are nomads. Even if you wanted to believe in the silliness of their spirituality, finding them would be near impossible."

"I have to try, Sergeant. My daughter is lying in a hospital bed, in a coma."

"Well, the FBI has the case now. Their networks reach further than anything we've got. I suggest you take this diary to them. They may find it more interesting and perhaps useful. I'm sorry we can't help more."

"I understand," she said, standing, although clearly she did not understand. She stormed out of the station and immediately went home to her computer. *How many Madam Barbaras can there be?*

Only she found nothing. The internet had no listing for a Madam Barbara anywhere. A year went past and the pseudo-Mardi Gras came back to Ybor City. Marsha Coutier attended for the first time in her life.

Still being of firm body and pretty face, Mrs. Coutier acquired several strings of beads before she happened across Madam Barbara's tent. Fortunate to find it at all in the madding crowd, she entered without hesitation, just to make sure it didn't disappear right before her eyes like these things do in the movies.

"Madam Barbara?"

"Come closer. I've been expecting you."

"You have? But you don't even k—"

"Mrs. Coutier. A pleasure to finally meet you. I would ask to what I owe this honor, but I already know. You have come about your daughter, America— she of such beauty that men's breath be taken away at the mere sight of her smile."

She paused, stunned, but maintained her focus. "Do you know what is wrong with her?"

"Nothing is wrong with her—at least, nothing that could be understood by your doctors."

Now Marsha Coutier looked baffled.

"I know that sounds cryptic. But come, I will tell you all that I know. Please sit."

Marsha sat staring across the round table with peculiar markings around the periphery. They looked Greek to her.

"They are Romanian."

"What?"

"The markings you admire so much."

"How did you…?"

"I saw the curiosity on your face."

"Ah. I thought maybe you were reading my mind."

"I don't claim that I can do that. I'm a Democrat."

Marsha furrowed her brow. "So, tell me what you know about my daughter."

"A long time ago there were many gypsies like me, women who could foretell another's future. Sight is not common among my people, but more frequent than with any other people on Earth. As the years have passed and the world has become modern, many of our old ways have been forgotten—died out. Today there are only thirteen such as I."

"You mean fortunetellers?"

"Not just fortunetellers, Mrs. Coutier," she near-shouted. "Actual seers are a far cry from simply performing amusing parlor tricks. We live every day with a true insight into things we'd rather not see. And often we cannot avoid seeing them, although we might wish to do so. Do you understand, Mrs. Coutier? Sometimes they are terrible visions. Sometimes they are even worse. Only on the rarest occasion are we

166

blessed with a happy picture. On these days we rejoice, my sisters and I."

"And who is Georgina?"

"She is the one who has taken your daughter from you. It is her black soul that has cast your daughter from the light. Georgina so loathes the beauty of a young woman, because she lost her own attractiveness long ago, she would commit such an atrocity without any regret or fear of retribution."

"How can I find her?"

"You cannot."

"I'm sure the police can."

"They cannot help you, Mrs. Coutier. Only the touch from the right person may awaken your lovely daughter."

"You're joking. This is the twentieth century. Life just doesn't work this way."

"It is not the twentieth century for gypsies. Our powers are rooted in the past, long ago. You cannot bring them into modern light. Georgina has, in her madness, cast a spell upon your daughter that she might die. With all my power I could not undo such a spell. It is near impossible to affect the power of another. The best I could hope to do was weaken it—alter it—divert its power to something less deadly. All my effort and the best I could accomplish was that she sleep for a hundred years.

"But have heart, Mrs. Coutier. The right stimulus will awaken her and she will live a beautiful and full life afterward."

"And I have to sit around and wait for someone to wake her, and I can't even know how to do it? That is just unacceptable."

"It is all I have to offer, Mrs. Coutier. I am sorry."

Unable to fathom her assurances, Marsha Coutier turned her head to the side, looking at anything other than the old hag sitting before her. Despite her kind nature, she presented a most loathsome image. Perhaps it was only because she knew more about America than anyone else alive, except perhaps Georgina.

"What must I do?"

"I can only offer you the knowledge that she will have a chance for life. This—the best I could do—I have vowed. I could not sit by and see such a lovely creature destroyed in a heartbeat simply because Georgina cannot get laid. We all know it's easy to find lots of sex, just become a politician. But Georgina's face is so distorted; she will surely live out the rest of her days in abstinence."

Marsha backed away from the old woman.

"It's difficult to think while my daughter is lying in a hospital—unconscious, but I feel I owe you a debt of gratitude."

"You owe me nothing. I wish I could have done more, but age has driven away my true strength. I did what I did, for her. I could see the gentleness and purity of her heart. Although innocent, she showed great potential. The world could only be a better place with her in it."

"It's very kind of you to say that. Thank you," Marsha managed before leaving.

***

A quick glance at her watch told Sarah it took her twenty-one minutes to get to the Coutier residence. Although she had no concrete proof, she surmised Mrs. Coutier to be living alone. Of course, Mr. Coutier could simply travel a lot for work or some other simple explanation like that.

Either way, Sarah didn't care. The older woman really affected her by a simple touch. Sarah didn't hesitate. No way would she walk away from this opportunity. She reached up a fist and knocked firmly on the door. It swung open within a few seconds. *Maybe she's as enthusiastic as I am.*

Marsha Coutier looked statuesque in her satin robe and hair down. Sarah couldn't help but admire the older woman's obvious beauty. Her waist still looked thin enough to give her an hourglass figure. Her tits, probably braless at this time of morning, didn't sag. The ass she'd touched the night before through pants, felt round and enticing.

"I'm so glad you came."

"I haven't…yet."

Marsha smiled generously as Sarah stepped over the threshold and entered a world of luxury. Obviously the Coutiers were affluent. Faux marble pillars bracketed the foyer, standing guard over an enormous living room that sank two steps deeper into the floor. With a quick glance she saw a glimpse of a well laid kitchen and a hall leading the other way.

Different light sources emblazoned the room, washing shades of white up the walls and directly on furniture and paintings. Behind one large fern, standing in the corner, shone a swath of green light from something mounted on the floor. The room made Sarah feel warm. *Sometimes color schemes can do that.*

"This is beautiful."

"Thank you. Would you like something to drink?"

"Nothing alcoholic, please. I'll have to drive home, later."

"Not if you don't want to."

"What?"

"I checked your schedule at the hospital. I hope you don't mind. You're not on tonight. And it wouldn't hurt my feelings to lie around in bed all day with someone warm to snuggle against."

"Are you kidding?"

Marsha Coutier tilted her head to one side, shrugging her left shoulder. "I don't think I'm kidding."

Sarah looked around the room, drinking in the quality lifestyle. When she'd completed a full circle and once again faced the older woman, she smiled. "If it goes well, I could hang here. But I'll still pass on the alcohol. I worked last night. I'd hate to fall asleep and miss all the fun this morning."

Marsha smiled, knowingly. "Why don't you come into the kitchen with me? You can decide what you'd like."

The young girl bounced behind like a generation gap version of follow the leader. When Marsha finally turned toward her, they were in the kitchen. Sarah stood in awe. The most magnificent thing she'd ever seen.

"Wow."

"Yes." Marsha opened the refrigerator. "I have a variety of soda pop, if that's more appealing."

Sarah didn't answer, still staring at the wonderful kitchen.

"Juice, perhaps?"

Sarah was caught up in awe.

"I'm sorry," Marsha spoke again. "I've never *been* with a girl so young before. I'm not sure how your tastes run."

Sarah suddenly noticed she was being spoken to. "Oh, sorry. Do you have any Dew?"

Marsha handed the young girl a green can and a glass. Then her hand went to Sarah's hair. "You have such beautiful, auburn hair."

"Thank you," Sarah said, blushing a little. "Yours is gorgeous."

"Sandy Blonde. Some would call it 'dirty' blonde. Not exactly a flattering name—or color. I have to use special shampoo, rub in a body-enriching cream, and take vitamins to get my hair to look as good as it does. And it still pales next to the shine you have. The lights in the ceiling reflect off it in little sparkles."

Again Sarah felt her face blossom into full red. Marsha reached out and ran her finger down the younger girl's cheek as if to wipe away the embarrassment. "No need to be ashamed. You have the attributes of youth. Enjoy them, for surely, even as the sun rises and sets, they will fade."

"Well, I'd be happy to grow old as beautifully as you have."

Marsha leaned in and brushed her lips against Sarah's. The younger girl held her breath. Sarah's hand came up and moved the length of Marsha's arm, then touched her breast. It was Marsha's turn to hold her breath.

"Let's go into the other room, shall we?"

Sarah nodded and followed. A luxurious sofa, well over-stuffed, invited both asses to sit. Sarah sat first, near the middle, but leaving enough room for the other woman to have space if she preferred. Marsha sat very close, allowing her thigh and hip to slide against Sarah's all the way until she rested fully on the cushion. Sparks crackled in the air.

Although she'd been invited by Marsha, Sarah took the upper hand. She pressed her palm against the older woman's shoulder and guided her back so her head rested against the couch. Sarah's hand slid down Marsha's body and she rubbed between the older woman's legs. The robe had fallen aside when she sat and exposed a simple panty. The delicate material was hardly a barrier and Marsha began to feel a bit lightheaded.

Meanwhile, Sarah planted her mouth on Marsha's neck and ear, painting her with saliva, kissing and nibbling. Marsha's eyes rolled up in her head as she felt the first rush. She had a calm orgasm, no noise and very little body spasm, but Sarah knew immediately when the panty got wet.

"Are you always so quiet?" she whispered in Marsha's ear?

"Not always, but mostly. Is that okay?"

"I don't mind—as long as it's natural. But I tend to make lots of noise. Is that okay?"

"That's fine."

"No one will hear?"

"Let them."

Sarah smiled and moved her hand up to the sash that still managed to hold the robe more-or-less in place. One quick pull and it fell away as Sarah brushed it aside and admired the woman's exposed breast. She pressed her hand across it. The already firm nipple scratched at Sarah's palm like a lone fingernail. Sarah scratched back, running her nails across the ample breast and plucking the nipple like a guitar string.

"Mmmm," Marsha moaned.

Sarah let out a sound that resembled a cat purr. Then she bent and clamped her mouth over that nipple, sucking at it with as much force as she could muster. Again Marsha moaned and arched her back. While

Sarah pulled the nipple further into her mouth, her hand went back to Marsha's crotch, rubbing the panty once—twice—then dipping under the waistband. No hair slowed her motion.

She found the bare, smooth lips and immediately tensed. A part of her wondered if something would prevent her from actually getting this far. To this point she thought she could have misinterpreted the older woman's advances. Unlikely, yes. But entirely possible. And such had been her luck, lately. But this time, her concern was unfounded. She slipped her middle finger deep into the wet hole. Marsha sucked in her breath, but made no show of resistance.

Sarah, not one to waste much time, began kissing her way down Marsha's breast, onto her belly, and beyond. Finally getting near her point of true interest, she slid off the couch and positioned herself between Marsha's knees. She bent her head forward and stuck out her tongue.

Rubbing it up the crotch of the panty didn't do much for Sarah, but it nearly drove Marsha mad with passion. For the first time Sarah could see the fabric and saw her butt exposed through the thin thread that ran up between the cheeks in the back. *A thong! I didn't think older women wore them.* She dove in again with more enthusiasm.

Finally her hand came up and pulled the delicate cloth aside, allowing her tongue to make direct contact. The flavor didn't exactly appeal to Sarah. Perhaps it was just something in the woman's diet. But sex floated in the air and she wouldn't stop now. She pushed her face into the lips and began moving her tongue in and out.

When she pulled away, she allowed her tongue to slide up to the top and swirl around the clitoris. Marsha began to squirm. Sarah did a rapid-fire flicking with her tongue, pushing Marsha closer to her big finish. Then she stopped. Marsha's eyes came open quickly.

Sarah grabbed Marsha's thong and quickly, gracefully, pulled it down her hips and off her feet. No magician could have pulled a tablecloth any better. Then she quickly lifted Marsha's legs up and pushed the knees back against the older woman's chest. With the object of her desire now fully exposed, Sarah set to work. Her tongue explored everything, moistening the area to the point of dripping down onto the couch cushion.

The younger girl inserted a finger while she sucked on Marsha's love button. She wiggled the finger frantically. Then she withdrew it, dripping wet, and reinserted it into the woman's constricting anus. Marsha yelped. Sarah allowed her only the briefest moment to relax and then she began pumping that finger in and out of her ass, pounding her fist as hard and as fast as she could like a prize fighter hitting a bag. Sarah aimed the finger upward so it pushed against the thin membrane that separated anus and vagina, and she rubbed her fingertip against the G-spot behind the clitoris with every thrust. She continued to suck from the outside.

Marsha's hips came off the couch and she let out the most romantic moan Sarah ever heard. The young girl didn't stop for a moment. The older woman's orgasm seemed endless and Sarah wanted to give her the best ride she could.

Finally everything subsided and Marsha fell back to the couch with an unceremonious thump. Her exhausted breathing gave Sarah a thrill as she continued to lick the other woman clean, not missing a drop. Marsha simply lay there, allowing, resting, spinning.

"Oh, baby, I'd say you needed that," Sarah said, finally moving her head up to kiss the other woman.

"Damn," was all Marsha could manage.

Sarah hugged her and continued kissing around her face, neck, and breasts—all the while giving her a chance to get her breath back. Oddly, she continued to breath funny. But that just went to prove the night…er, day, wasn't over yet. Finally, at some point, Marsha sat up and began pulling at Sarah's shirt.

Sarah stood and undressed, quickly and yet laboriously—seductively, hoping to entice the woman further. But Marsha needed no enticement. Her hands brushed all over Sarah's body, helping push clothes, touching tender flesh.

Once nude, Sarah felt Marsha push her back to the couch where she fell into a complete reclining position with her legs wide open. She wanted them open, she would need that to allow Marsha inside, but she hadn't planned on getting them that way by falling. The entire motion felt much the same as rolling down a grassy hill.

Marsha put her face between Sarah's legs, but didn't touch. When the young girl glanced in that direction, she saw the older woman just looking— examining, checking out the goods. It was embarrassing and exciting all at once. Sarah left her legs open.

Then in one swift movement, Marsha's lips were kissing her, caressing her. Sarah felt the older woman's tongue come out and rub up her thigh and against her lips, finally pushing its way inside. Sarah couldn't help but moan. That's when Marsha began swirling her tongue around down there. She didn't seem focused, but she made up for it with enthusiasm. *Maybe she hasn't had that much experience with girls. Maybe she's NEVER been with a girl! Wow, I might be her first? But she came onto me so easily.*

"Ahhh!" The screams that Sarah knew would come, began earlier than she expected. But her head already spun aimlessly and the smell of her own sex coupled with the orgasm she'd given the other woman was beginning to drive her crazy. She knew she'd come soon. She also felt reasonably sure this wouldn't be the last one today. She gripped the cushions tightly and waited for the inevitable, hanging on like a person on a roller coaster as it starts its run.

A mere few seconds later she felt all her muscles lock as the woman's relentless tongue battered her pussy lips, and the tension in her body drained out through her vagina and into Marsha's waiting mouth. To her credit, Sarah noticed the older woman didn't spit. Even after Sarah began to relax, Marsha's tongue continued its brush strokes of love.

This is going to be some fun day together. And she wants me to hang here overnight and tomorrow. I could get used to this. It could even become a regular thing between us. Of course, that would just be terrible. Yeah, right.

Marsha rose up and kissed Sarah passionately. Sarah felt heady as the flavor of Marsha—still on her lips—mixed with her own taste now covering Marsha's face. Hands groped and Sarah's eyes rolled back. Marsha ground her hip into Sarah' crotch. *Oh, my God! I'm going to come again and she isn't even touching me.*

When Sarah sated for only a moment, Marsha leaned back and looked her in the eye. "I guess you needed something, too."

"That was incredible," Sarah admitted. "Still want me to spend the day?"

"And the night."

"Even though I don't work, I'm going to need some sleep. If we lounge around like this, I'll probably doze off at some point."

"That's okay. I'll just snuggle against you. Maybe I'll sleep as well."

"Damn, you're beautiful."

Marsha smiled and averted her eyes.

178

"Now who's embarrassed?"

"Huh? Oh, well I'm old and I'm not accustomed to anyone telling me I'm beautiful."

"Why not? Guys and girls should be lined up at your door just to have the chance to say so."

"I'm not so sure," Marsha said softly. "I had a short relationship with a woman once. She wouldn't even go out to shop with me, let alone dinner."

"Well, if you need to go out anywhere and you want some company, you just call me."

"That's flattering. But under the circumstances, I can't help thinking you're only saying that because you're lying here with me, naked. I'll continue to sleep with you even if you wouldn't be seen in public with me."

"Hey," Sarah said, sitting up and placing her hands on her hips. "I'm not a politician. When I make a promise, I'll at least *try* to keep it."

Marsha raised an eyebrow. After a moment she nodded her head. "I suppose you're right. I shouldn't be so cynical. After all these years, it's difficult to see the good in people."

"You've been alone for a long time?"

"My ex-husband is a Congressman. He left me for his twenty-year-old secretary. The day he left he said some things to me, awful things, ugly things. I guess I believed them."

"Those political types don't know how to build anything beautiful. They only know how to destroy. In the end, they're all self-serving. It's hardly a true

179

reflection of yourself. I mean, why would you let anyone else make the decision about who and what you are anyway?"

Marsha chuckled softly. "I guess I never knew how to judge myself. Maybe I just focus too hard on pleasing other people, at the expense of my own needs. I think that's why I was so attracted to you from the beginning. You seemed so intent on taking care of someone else's needs, even above your own."

"I've got to admit, that confuses me."

"How do you mean?"

"You caught me messing with your daughter. Shouldn't you be angry, or something?"

Marsha laughed. "I want my daughter back. I'm willing to do most anything to get that. How do we really know what will awaken her? Surely not a simple kiss." She leaned in and kissed Sarah. "And sometimes I feel so lonely. I know that sounds selfish when I should be focusing *only* on my daughter, but I'm not dead. And I don't even have her to talk to."

"Why did you name her America? You're not Spanish."

"No. But I wanted her to be the people, all people. I wasn't looking for *common*, but I wanted her to fit in."

"You're not originally from here?"

"No, we came over on the proverbial boat."

"But you hardly have any accent."

Marsha laughed. "Sometimes I do. When I'm angry, I guess. But I've worked hard at making it go away."

"Why?"

"New land, new language. This is America. I live here, now. I am American," she finished, proudly.

"You should have kept the accent. I like them."

Marsha laughed, weakly. "It all seems so trite now."

"Because of your daughter?"

"I don't think anyone can fully understand what it's like to lose a child, unless they've lost one of their own."

"Don't give up. She's not dead."

"She has no life. I can't help but despair."

"Well, I can't fix that for you, but perhaps I can make you feel a little better."

"How?"

Sarah once again took the upper hand and pushed the older woman down. The young girl went to work on helping her new friend forget all about her troubles. *Nothing like a good bang to get your motor running and your mind lost.*

***

Carnivals came and went like political promises, and even less committed to any one pattern than the weather. Gypsies, like Republicans, could be friendly as long as things went their way and you supported them. Cross them and there wouldn't be enough left of you to be identified.

Most carnival-goers roamed blissfully unaware of the mystique behind the culture. A close-knit religion, darker than voodoo and just as dangerous—safety remained *because* so few knew.

But Marsha Coutier knew. She'd felt the bite of the gypsy fang and the burn of the gypsy venom. And unlike so many others, she'd lived to tell about it, for it had not attacked her own person. Sadly, it struck at innocence and beauty.

Marsha wandered among the wooden trailers and beater cars with dark, hand-painted windows, looking for something she couldn't define—answers, perhaps. Surely nothing could be found walking the common paths where regular patrons trod. Any truth found would be discovered behind the caravan—in the wagons the gypsies used as living quarters.

Despite sparse but warm glows radiating from each wagon, a heavy dark shroud kept the light from reaching out too far. The darkness weighed the air down as though lead particles floated all about.

Marsha stepped into that darkness and immediately felt like a blanket had been thrown over her. She half expected hands to reach out and grab her, as if she were being abducted. Despite being prepared for something to happen, Marsha jumped when the young woman stepped out from the shadow behind the third wagon.

"Are you lost, perhaps?" The young woman rolled her 'R's, lending to the *Bela Lugosi* act.

Marsha couldn't decide whether to be frightened or aroused. The dark young woman exuded sexual prowess and un-tethered beauty. Her wild eyes shone brightly under a thin veil of jet black, silk hair. Marsha considered how to respond and chose discretion.

"I think I may have been looking for you," she added syrup to her voice as she stepped forward and brushed the dark girl's arm with her fingertips.

"I do not sleep with white women."

"I tan easily." She stepped even closer, intimately.

The gypsy girl scrutinized her, narrowing her eyes and dropping all remnants of a smile. She stepped quickly back to arm's length. "Darkness surrounds you."

"It's very dark back here."

"There is another darkness. Something deeper."

"I don't know what you mean," Marsha claimed, dropping her own smile.

"Why are you really here?"

"I told you," Marsha insisted.

"No! I do not know you. White people say gypsy pussy don't taste so good."

"I'd heard that. I wanted to find out for myself."

The girl shook her head. "There is something else. Tell me the truth. I will know otherwise."

"My daughter suffers a gypsy curse."

"Aha!" The girl recovered her stance now and strutted back and forth in front of Marsha. "And you wish revenge?"

"No. I seek only a solution—a cure."

"There is no cure for gypsy curse, foolish white woman. Go away. Be with your daughter while you still can. Go away or a curse may befall you, as well."

"The curse was put on by a gypsy calling herself Madam Georgina."

The girl froze, her eyes grew unbelievably wide. Her right hand rested on her chest above her heart and her left reached out to the wagon to steady herself. "You must come with me," she whispered, huskily.

Marsha followed.

One particular wagon sat apart from the others. A gentle mist escaped cracks near the roof. Marsha wondered but chose silence. The young girl led her straight for it. Marsha could see the distrusting eyes of men and women working around the encampment. They saw the young gypsy girl leading and said nothing.

Just outside the door, the young gypsy held up her hand. "Mama Luna is very old. She can tell you everything without you even speaking, so do not lie."

"I won't, I promise."

"You must go through the door. I cannot go with you."

Marsha reached out her hand, nervously.

"Before you go in, I have a question."

The older woman withdrew her hand and turned.

"You took a great risk. What would you have done if I'd said yes?"

"Yes to what? Oh, that." Marsha released the door handle and stepped down next to the girl. She kissed her full on the lips. The gypsy girl did not withdraw. "I would have made love to you."

"Gina," the young gypsy breathed.

"I would have made love to you, Gina. You are an uncommon beauty."

Gina sighed. "Perhaps when this business is dealt with you could come back."

"I'd like that, Gina. I'd like that very much." She glanced around at the hostile, mysterious surroundings. "I don't think I'm exactly welcome."

Gina waved a dismissive hand. "If I say you are welcome, you are welcome. That is my home, over there—the purple one. I sleep alone."

Marsha smiled and turned back to the door. When she glanced back, Gina could not be seen anywhere. *She disappeared?* From behind the cracked open door a weak voice floated out—trying to escape.

"Come in, my dear. Come in."

Inside Marsha discovered a thick fog of incense. *That explains the 'mist' coming out of the trailer.* Marsha gagged for air as she sat on the proffered couch when the ancient woman gestured.

The bent and frail lady walked over and extended her hand. Marsha put her hand in the wrinkled palm expecting the usual 'treatment'. The old woman simply shook it twice and dropped it. This was no ritual as the others had been.

"You have travelled far in search of your answers."

"There is a life at stake."

"Yes, your daughter's."

"How did you know?"

The old woman cackled a devious laugh—frightening, if not for her frailty. "I overheard as you told my great-granddaughter."

"Ah."

"And now you seek salvation."

"Only for her."

"Untrue!" the old woman's voice reverberated, evangelistically. "You seek for yourself, as well."

Marsha sighed, resigned. "How could I not? What mother wouldn't?"

"Tsk-tsk. I do not condemn, I observe."

"Can you tell me how to save my daughter?"

"I cannot tell you what you want to hear…"

Marsha visibly sagged.

"…I can only tell you what you *must* hear."

"In regards to my daughter?"

"Yes."

"Then you must tell it. Give me everything you know."

"Ha! *Everything*? That could take a while."

"Tell me what you can about my daughter and how I can help her," Marsha insisted.

"Be warned. The terrible truth I offer cannot be unheard."

"Unheard?"

"If the knowledge burns your eyes from their sockets, no power on Earth can extinguish the flames. You understand?"

"I don't know."

"For such knowledge there is often a price. What toll the Gods would extract—this you must pay in full. Once started, nothing can stop it."

"I don't have much left to give."

"Perhaps you don't see how much you truly possess. Perhaps your despair has clouded your vision."

"I have little choice. I cannot leave my America in such a state."

"One more thing, I have no control over what is said. If it is of use, so be it. If not, there is nothing else to be done"

"I'm not sure I understand."

"The knowledge of the ancients is not stored in my old head." She offered another weak cackle as she tapped her knuckles against the side of her head. "It would surely be lost in no time."

"Where does the knowledge come from?"

"The Gods—the powers that be—whatever you believe in. They are sometimes forgiving, which can be good, but they are always honest. What they say is for only you to hear."

"But you will be here as well."

"I am often unable to remember any words coming from my mouth as I speak. My mind is so taken by these forces, little of me is left. I am simply the vessel."

"When will I know what they ask in payment?"

"I cannot answer that. You will know when they are ready. More than that I do not know."

"I must risk it."

"I could see that much in your eyes from the moment you stepped into my home."

"How do we…begin?"

"Come. Sit here." Mama Luna gestured toward a broken, worn out desk, piled high with papers and clothes and trinkets.

Marsha stepped forward and sat in a simple wooden folding chair. Although Marsha was a thin woman, the chair creaked as her weight came to bear. She shifted uncomfortably, but did not get up. Mama Luna smiled gently, as if she knew something about the chair but was unwilling to tell and ruin the punch line of the joke.

"You must concentrate only on your daughter and her well-being. Do not allow yourself to be distracted by anything else. Sometimes I moan or scream as they take me over."

"Does it hurt?"

"Not as you know hurt. But there is a power that comes from outside our reality, entering me, taking me over."

"Are you at risk?"

188

"No more so than travelling to Pakistan."

"Perhaps you haven't noticed," Marsha said, "but that's become very dangerous these days."

The old woman only cackled again. Marsha cringed at the raspy sound. Then a dead silence fell around them. Marsha didn't think the air was any different but her skin had begun to crawl for no good reason she could fathom.

When the scream came from the old woman's mouth, she no longer sounded raspy. The demonic noise shook the strings of beads and flowing tapestries that hung from the walls. The chair under Marsha creaked with fear, even though she hadn't moved, being completely frozen with terror. Something…furry ran over Marsha's foot and she stood upright but moved no further.

"What is it you seek?" moaned a voice that came from everywhere.

"Don't you know?"

"Insolent! Shall we take our leave, then?"

"No! I'm sorry. I'll cooperate. I wish to know how to help my daughter."

"She slumbers."

"I wish her to awaken."

"This is a *human* condition and must be solved by *humans*. It can only be done with *humanity*." The voice screwed up the word every time it was said as if it were distasteful. "Someone of power must use her, treat her as they do all people."

"What does that mean?"

"Your world is such a violent place. Even those who would be friends think violent thoughts toward each other—and their neighbors. Your leaders think of you as chattel. They would sooner see her die than take a moment from helping themselves to offer a hand. Why should we do differently?"

"Does her death serve a greater purpose I'm not aware of?"

"No."

"Then why allow it?"

"Why interfere?"

"You sound just like the indifferent leaders of my world. Apathy serves no one."

After a moment of silence, Marsha thought they might not respond further. Then: "There will be a price."

"So I've been told. What is it?"

"You shall know when you know."

"That's rather cryptic."

When the voices did not respond, Marsha pushed forward.

"So what can you tell me about my daughter?"

"Let the world take her."

"What? What do you mean by that?"

"Your world can awaken her. When the injustice has reached the appropriate level, she will take up a stance of righteous indignation. She will live and her life will have great meaning for your world. She will become the sword of the people. But first she must be thrust upon by that very sword. Impaled to release the demonic curse."

"Excuse me. Are you saying she has to be stabbed to live?"

"It is what it is and cannot be altered. Cruelty surrounds your kind."

"Is there nothing else you can tell me? What will awaken her? Will I get to see her before I die? Can you explain how she'll live if she's stabbed by a sword?"

Dead silence. Marsha hadn't realized how loud she'd been yelling to the voices until the quiet returned. She looked about but saw no one. The old woman had vanished as her great-granddaughter did earlier.

"Thank you." Marsha threw a twenty on the table and left.

No one bothered her as she walked through the wagons, even though Gina had not returned to escort her. Could any of what was said truly be called an answer? Marsha struggled to understand some deeper meaning in the cryptic words, but failed at every attempt.

And what would be the cost for this apparently useless knowledge?

***

"Who might you be?" Bonnie asked with the authority of a security guard. Being the night nurse in charge of an entire wing could bring out the *Gestapo* in a person. She stood as if she could block his path. The truth is, his stature under the bulky military-type jacket suggested she would offer little or no resistance should he try to push past her.

"My name is George, ma'am. George Shrub. I'm the great-grandson of the gypsy woman who put the curse on a young girl you have here. Could you tell me what room she'd be in?"

"Now what would I want to go and do a damn fool thing like that for?" She firmed her position in his path.

"I've come to help."

"How do I know that? You could be here to finish what your grandmother started."

"*Great*-grandmother. She was a bitter woman. I guess she had her reasons, but that hardly gave her permission to do the things she did to so many people."

"You've got that right. What the hell could have happened that would make her feel she could do those things?"

"Hadn't you heard the story? I thought it was well known."

Bonnie simply shook her head as she placed her fists on her hips.

"No matter. It hardly excuses everything."

"Well, I'd like to hear it anyway."

The young man shrugged, resigned. "Okay, but I'm sure I don't know everything, just what's been handed down."

"I'm all ears."

"Hmm." He looked at her with a crooked smile. "Anyway, this took place a long time ago. My great-grandmother was said to be very old—older, in fact, than any person has been known to live.

"She—I'm named after her, by the way—fell deeply in love with a man named Roger Wallace. A Brit, or a Scot, or something, but anyway, one day he asked for her hand in marriage and the family forbid their relationship. Gypsies marry Gypsies, and that's final.

"So the two of them spent a great deal of time in secret rendezvous and clandestine communiqués. A most awkward way to build a relationship, for sure, but they managed. And they saw each other as often as they could. Despite the fear of being caught by the elders of the tribe, their love continued to grow.

"One particular evening in May, Wallace took her to a show. Rather lame by today's standards but quite a society gig in the day. She always felt so high class around him, and he treated her like royalty. On the way back from the show, he walked her as close to her home as he would dare. But they never parted ways. At least not the way they planned."

"But I was told he was responsible for the attack."

"I thought you didn't know this story."

"I hardly heard any of it. The only thing anybody can tell around here is that she was horribly disfigured in an accident caused by the man she loved. And that he died protecting her in that same instance."

"Actually, that's true, although really quite vague. Great-grandma, Georgina, didn't learn until later that he'd arranged for them to be attacked."

"Okay, I'm really confused now. Why exactly would he do such a thing? It sounds like she would have given him anything he asked for. So what was left to take?"

"I think you misunderstand. He didn't want anything from her. No one knew this. I only found out myself a couple years ago. I managed to speak with a descendant of the old man, one Adam Wallace, in a phone conversation. He told me the truth about the incident."

"And what truth is that?"

"Roger Wallace wanted to defend my Great-Grandmother from an attack."

"What? An attack he set up?"

The young man shook his head. "Don't you see? He did it on purpose to show the gypsy tribe he could protect her and that he loved her that much."

"Oh, I see." Bonnie looked away, thoughtfully. "So what went wrong?"

"I don't know if anyone knows. The two hired attackers got carried away, or they were unprepared for Wallace's defense, or some crazy accident, we just don't know."

"Wow that must have made for some unusual headlines."

"Every headline for weeks, it seemed. Even though there was a war going on, the newspapers had some twist on this story right there on the front page."

"Was this Wallace that important?"

"Not to my knowledge. I think the papers—or whoever controls them—just wanted to distract the public from thinking about the war for a little while. At that time, I hear it was going bad for our side. Not much hope, you know."

"What did they need to distract people for? Don't they have a right to know the truth?"

"Oh, no. They couldn't allow that. If people thought the war might be lost, they'd become saddened, horrified, frightened. The government couldn't allow that. People had to be kept complacent and even happy."

"Why would they need to do that?"

"So they'd spend money. As long as we think the way we do, the government thrives."

"The government thrives because I pay my taxes."

"The government thrives because *everybody* pays their taxes. When you spend your money, after taxes, the store you shopped at has to claim that same money as income. Then *they* pay taxes on it. Then they pay their employees, who in turn pay taxes on it. Then they go out and spend. Many of these steps can happen in the same day, even. That cycle continues until the money reaches the highest levels. Then the money finds its way into someone's pocket."

"You're not cynical or anything, are you, Mr. Shrub?"

"Only realistic, Ma'am."

"Well, let's get back to reality, shall we? Why are you here?"

"I told you, I want to help the girl."

"And do you know what it'll take to wake her?"

"I do not. But there's a testing process I can go through—several different ideas that might stimulate her."

"So you're going to experiment."

"I've got a plan. I'll run through the ideas I have and observe her reactions to each one."

"If there aren't any reactions?"

"There should be."

"You don't sound very convincing. Do you even *want* to revive her?"

"It's not about what I want. This is about my destiny."

"Your destiny, huh? Who told you that?" Bonnie asked in disbelief.

"My mother—a wise woman."

"She told you, you would revive the sleeping beauty that her own grandmother cursed with death? A curse, mind you, that was thwarted by another gypsy."

"Well…not exactly."

"What, exactly!" Once again the nurse made herself formidable in the man's path. She managed to stand taller—even in her nursing flats.

"I'm told, no matter what I do, there will be chaos. Tranquility must be disrupted if she is to awaken."

"Don't you be bringing no chaos to my ward."

"Now it's my turn to ask. You *do* want her to wake up, don't you?"

"Mister, don't twist my words around to mean something else, like you're the president or something."

"President?"

"You know, of the country."

"Even I don't lie *that* much."

"Maybe, but it sounds like you create turmoil as if you were one."

"Peace and quiet is all-well-and-good if you want to rest, but disruption may be the only way to make this work."

"How do you mean?"

"If you want to wake the person you're sleeping with, you don't tiptoe around. You make noise and shake them. I assume you've tried lots of other ideas— nice things—gentle things."

"Her mother has brought many people in."

"And what did they do?"

"I'm not really sure. I didn't go in the room with any of them."

"And nothing has worked.?"

"She's still asleep," Bonnie stated, matter-of-factly.

"Maybe I can change that."

"Does her mother know you're here?"

"No."

"Why not?"

"Because of who I am. I didn't think she would be too happy to have me come here."

"Then I can't let you in there. You'll have to bring her mother back with you."

"I told you she might not be happy to have me here."

"Not my problem."

"Do you realize who I am? I'm George Shrub."

"That doesn't carry much weight around here. There are some who would say you're the cause of all this."

"Me? I only came here to help out my mom."

"You helping your family only makes you sound more like a politician. Do you care even a little for that poor girl lying in there?" She waited a moment. When no response came, she spoke up a little louder. "I asked you a question, mister. Do you care about America?"

The man glanced at the floor. Bonnie noticed he shuffled his feet a little. *That's a sure sign he's not telling the truth.*

"I don't actually know the girl. To me she's nothing but an inconvenience. I could be home watching the football game. Dallas is playing."

"How touching. Bring her mother or don't come back."

He turned and shuffled off without further sound. Bonnie continued to stand there long after he'd disappeared into the elevator. She didn't notice the young candy-striper standing beside her.

"Whatcha doin'?"

"Huh?" Bonnie started. "Oh, there was some guy here that wanted to mess with America."

"Another gentleman caller?"

"This man isn't like the others. There's something peculiar about him."

"Did he go in? Why are you looking toward the elevators?"

"I sent him packing. I told him to find the mother and come back here."

"Mother?"

"The girl's mother. Marsha Coutier."

Sarah failed to completely stifle her chuckles.

"What's so damned funny?"

"He won't find her."

"Why not?"

"She stayed at my place tonight."

"What? Girl you are so bad."

"She keeps coming back so I think maybe I'm *good*."

Just then a low rumble sounded through the halls. The charge nurse desk trembled as if with fear. Bonnie's hand, resting on the desk, came off and she pulled it close with a jerk. She held it against her chest and cradled it with her other hand as if she'd been injured.

"Do you feel that?"

"Oh, yeah," Sarah replied. "The way she can move her tongue…"

"Not that, you silly slut. I'm talking about the vibrations."

"Vibrators?"

"On the desk, in the floor, can't you feel anything?"

Sarah simply shook her head.

"Girl," Bonnie said, suddenly sounding like an old black woman. "If you ain't coming, the Earth can't be moving. Is that about right?"

"Well, you know I'm only used to one kind of trembling. Somehow, you're not doing it for me, hon."

Before Bonnie could sufficiently reply, the lights went out and the building began to shake as if it had suddenly grown legs and was running a marathon. Bonnie and Sarah grabbed for the desk as the emergency lights blinked on. But the desk offered little security as the board on the front cracked and half of it splintered away. Both women fell to the floor that tilted at an erratic angle.

"Is this an Earthquake?" Sarah managed to yell over the thunder.

"We don't have Earthquakes around here, girl. You're not in Kansas anymore. See to the patients."

Sarah made her way down one hall while Bonnie headed in another direction. Neither tried to stand upright while the building continued to tremble. Within a few minutes, the longest Sarah ever experienced, she'd managed to check most of her patients and none had fallen out of bed or were in any danger. She couldn't imagine how the building could list so far and no one got hurt.

When finally all the dust settled and everything became quiet, she tried to focus through the clouds floating all around. Who knew that such a clean building like a hospital could have so much dust. Her ears rang from the sudden absence of noise, and her fingertips trembled. The roots of her hair tingled and she felt drained and shaky, the way a person feels when they have the flu.

She stood, tentatively, waving her arms out to the side for balance, though neither hand could reach anything for support. But the building remained stable and so did Sarah. She made it to a window and glanced down to ground level, and saw a sight.

There, on the grass, stood a young-ish man, putting things into a large duffel bag. When he'd finished, he turned and walked away into the parking lot. She noticed his olive drab jacket that fit rather bulky over his shoulders, and his not just faded but actually worn jeans. Then she made her way through the rest of her patients.

When she arrived back at the central nursing station, she approached Bonnie. "That guy," she began.

"What guy?"

"The one who left just before all this."

"What about him?"

"What did he look like?"

"Not particularly attractive. Short, curly hair. His eyes were set close together and he looked like…"

"No," Sarah interrupted. "What about his clothes?"

"His green jacket looked like something military. I thought it was kind of grungy, you know, not washed in a long while. And his jeans were wearing through around his thighs. He had on these black sneaker-like things that were probably the cleanest thing he wore. They didn't look too old."

"I just saw him."

"Where?"

"Outside, down on the lawn. He was doing something."

"Could you tell what?"

"No. When I saw him he was just finishing. I saw him putting stuff away in a duffel bag."

"You think he had something to do with this?"

"I don't know," Sarah screamed, just as the building began to shake once again. "But he looked rather suspicious."

Pieces of plaster, broken and loose from the first shock, came free and fell to the floor in a few spots. One overhead light fixture swung down like a pendulum blade from the old Poe story, missing everyone but still creating a hazard.

"Is this another Earthquake?"

"What do I look like?" Bonnie asked, "an encyclopedia?"

"I've never been through one before."

"Neither have I. Maybe this is what they call an aftershock."

Then it was quiet again. They began slowly cleaning up and making the proper phone calls. By 3 a.m. the place overran with technicians and supervisors. To add to the chaos, family members, alerted by some means Bonnie couldn't fathom, had come to check up on loved ones.

"Quiet," Bonnie observed, "is something we're not going to get tonight."

"Look at the bright side," Sarah added, just for the sound of her own voice. "You're not at risk of falling asleep on the job tonight, either."

"I never fall asleep, girl. But the patients, on the other hand, they'll be lucky if they get any sleep tonight."

"Well, I *have* to sleep when I'm here. Marsha doesn't let me have any when I'm home."

Bonnie chuckled and shook her head as she went back to work.

***

Friday night, 2 a.m., the ward was as quiet as could be. Few visitors came on Fridays, preferring to go out. But by two in the morning on any given day, the place would be quiet. The nurses made little noise and even the cognitive patients would be asleep.

When Sarah first started working there, she had trouble remaining awake. These days, with her love life on the upward swing, she actually found reserve energies she didn't know she had, despite what she'd told Bonnie a few days before. And, of course, she'd become accustomed to the night shift.

"I just heard the elevator motor. Care to guess it's for us?" Sarah asked.

"Two bucks," Bonnie said.

"I don't have two bucks."

"You can owe me," Bonnie offered, generously.

"Okay. Two bucks says it's for our floor," Sarah agreed.

"Wait. I was betting on it being for our floor."

Both women giggled until they heard the elevator 'ding' its arrival. They stopped abruptly and watched as Marsha Coutier stepped out, quickly followed by George Shrub.

"Well, he managed to find her, even in your special hiding place."

"I wasn't hiding her," Sarah said with indignation. "I just didn't want to share, that's all."

"I see. A rose by any other name…"

"Would stink," Sarah finished. "I hate roses."

Marsha approached. "Good evening, Ladies."

"Mrs. Coutier," Bonnie responded, nodding her head.

"I've brought a young man with me."

"Do you know who he is?" Sarah whispered.

"Yes, honey. I know. I appreciate your concern but I think he might help."

"But he's related to *her*."

"I know. But I *must* try, for the sake of America."

"I understand. Maybe someone should accompany him the entire time."

"I'll consider your advice." As she started to walk away, leading the young man behind her, Bonnie spoke out loud—loud enough for Marsha and George to hear.

"That was quite a ruckus the other night, don't you think?"

"What are you talking about?" George asked with a veil of innocence drawn over his face.

"The Earthquake."

"We don't have Earthquakes in this part of the country," Marsha confirmed.

"Not usually. But the other night we got hit with a pretty good one." Bonnie let that settle for a moment then rested her eyes on George. "You should remember. That's the night you were here."

"Me?"

"You're lucky you didn't get trapped in the elevator," she mocked concern.

"Uh, yes. I made it outside in time." George suddenly seemed nervous.

"Do you have any idea what would cause an Earthquake around here where we've never had one before?"

George seemed to be having a great deal of difficulty breathing and his feet must have hurt because he kept shuffling them and adjusting his weight on one then the other. "Uh, maybe it was global warming."

"There's no such thing," Sarah said. "I originally came from Alaska. Believe me, it's still pretty cold there."

"The news says it's global warming."

"Uh-huh."

Marsha must have considered the matter closed because she turned and began walking toward room 314. George turned sharply and fell in behind her, like a well-minded Cocker Spaniel. Sarah watched them walk, boring holes in their backs with her eyes.

"I don't trust that man."

"Neither do I," Bonnie responded. "But he couldn't have caused an Earthquake…could he?"

***

"What do you plan on doing?" Marsha asked, more than a little curious.

"First, I'd like to examine her condition."

"Are you a doctor?"

"No. But I must start somewhere."

Marsha offered a reluctant sigh, but nodded her ascent. The young man turned and began touching the girl, not intimately or in any way rough or inappropriate, but tactile contact with her face and arms, even her legs. After a few moments, he stood upright and faced the older woman.

"I understand her condition better. I still don't know what will wake her, but I'm going to begin with some simple herbs. These won't have any effect on you or I, Mrs. Coutier, so please don't be afraid."

"I'm only afraid she won't wake up."

"That fear is not unfounded as I've made no guarantees that any of this will work. But I've found papers left by my great-grandmother that offer hints. Unfortunately they leave too many hints in different directions. I'm not sure how to approach. The only comfort I can offer is that none seem dangerous"

"None *seem* dangerous?" Marsha chided.

"To the best of my knowledge, nothing I plan to do will cause further damage to your daughter. She will awaken, or she will remain the same."

"Oh, that's reassuring. What kind of papers did your great-grandmother leave you?"

"Mostly they're some kind of cryptic stuff."

"May I see them?"

"I didn't bring them with me. Let me try these herbs. I'll bring the papers by your place tomorrow."

"Not too early. I don't sleep well anymore and I like to get it when I can."

"I understand. Will noon be fine?"

Marsha just nodded and stood by, watching as he proceeded with his herbal potions. Although she felt a little ill at some of the noxious odors he produced, none of them had even the slightest effect on America.

***

Warm and cozy, that snuggly place in your bed when you're still asleep, the kind of place no one really wants to leave, Marsha squirmed against the silkiness. But this silk was not the sheets but skin—Sarah lay sleeping next to her, a cute, gentle snore escaping her sweet lips—Marsha admired her beauty without turning to look at her. And there was something so sensual about knowing that firm, young body cuddled against her like this. Why would she *ever* want to get up?

Then the knock on the door resounded through her home—and her head—once again, followed by a tirade of doorbell rings. She got up gracefully, smoothly, hoping to be quick and stop the noise but not wanting to wake her lover in her own haste. She slipped the heavy, comfortable robe over her own nude form and stepped out of the bedroom, closing the door quietly behind her.

Although she'd expected him, Marsha still started at the sight of George Shrub standing in her doorway. She glanced over at the clock, barely visible from the foyer and saw 11:59. *How did I manage to sleep so long? I shouldn't complain but I never get that much sleep anymore, not since…*

"Hello, Mrs. Coutier. May I come in?"

She considered what might happen if he found out a young girl—one of the nurses caring for her daughter—slept naked in the other room. In the end she decided there were no ethical issues to be concerned about. She waved the young man inside.

"Excuse me while I go put something more appropriate on."

"As you wish. It doesn't bother me either way."

"I'm sure. I'll be right back." While flattering, Marsha had no interest in becoming involved with someone so young. Then she realized Sarah was also that young. *But that's different. How?*, a voice asked. *Because it's a girl*, she replied in her head. *I don't want to get mixed up with any more* men, she confessed.

By the time she reached the bedroom door, she'd begun to walk faster and harder, feeling his eyes might be boring into the back side of her robe. She immediately regretted her anxiety when she closed the door a little too forcefully and the sleeping nurse tossed in the bed. Marsha stood still, waiting.

The beautiful young Sarah tossed once, twice, and finally settled on her back with one arm over her head. This position exposed one of her small breasts. Marsha became instantly aroused. She approached the bed, momentarily forgetting the guest in the other room. When she got close enough she saw something that shocked her.

Just to the right of that cute pink nipple sat an angry purple bruise. *Had we gotten that rough this morning?* Marsha tried to remember some of the things they'd done. She caught the image of a particularly delirious time when Sarah had begun kissing her feet and managed to get her pussy against Marsha's. The young girl rubbed frantically, like a person having a seizure, until Marsha could hardly see straight and drool slipped out of the corner of her mouth.

By the time images of a certain red toy inserted into her mind she became very wet. *Not now! Not now!* She managed to cover the young girl's bare breast without disturbing her further. Then she dropped her robe.

Her own nipples had grown hard and she could smell her own wetness—an odor she found very intoxicating and almost always leading to further debauchery. Forcing her hands away from her own body, she grabbed pants and shirt and quickly dressed without any undergarments. She bounced back into the living room and found George right where she'd left him. He sat on the love seat. She sat in a chair next to him.

Even though she felt uncomfortable beneath his stare, she also appreciated his obvious desire. *It never hurts to be admired, even though a young man like that would probably get hard over anything with a pussy if it bent in front of him.*

"Okay, George. What have you got?"

He managed to pull his eyes away from the front of her shirt and spread out about a dozen pieces of paper, different sized and shapes, all torn from full sheets in a haphazard manner. Scribble adorned each one, some long sentences and others just a few notes. One simply showed what appeared to be a chemical formula.

Marsha, feeling somehow empowered to determine something about each piece, didn't look at them for any length of time. Rather she waved a hand just above them, perhaps an inch or two, as if she were a gypsy herself, feeling for vibrations or something from one of them. When she finished, she obviously felt nothing.

"There doesn't seem to be anything here."

"Did you think you could identify something with a wave of your hand?"

"I thought—" She hesitated for a moment. Her eyes darted back from his direction to the table. Something had caught her attention. She glanced around with just her eyes, keeping her head still, rolling her eyes about in chaotic fashion. Finally she rested on something. George couldn't tell what.

"Is there something, Mrs. Coutier?"

"Yes…I think…" Her fading voice made George lean closer to hear. When his ear hung only a couple inches from her mouth she spoke again, rather loudly. "This one."

She grabbed one particular piece of paper from the table and handed it to him. He stared at it then at her and back at the paper again. He'd read it, of course, Marsha saw him do it. But confusion remained on his face. His brow furrowed.

"Why this one? What did you see?"

"I don't know. I…"

"Tell me what's going on, Mrs. Coutier."

"I…"

George reached out and grabbed both her shoulders and shook her. "Tell me!"

The loud noise got Marsha's attention. "Shhh. There's someone sleeping here."

George seemed genuinely apologetic. "I'm sorry. Please tell me what's going on."

"I went to see another gypsy, someone who might be able to take off the curse completely. I mean, I appreciate what Madam Omaba did, but I'd like America to wake up. So I went somewhere else."

"Okay. So?"

"She let me speak with the powers-that-be."

"No!"

"They told me some things about America. They hinted that I might be able to find how to wake her. I think they meant I'd be able to recognize it when I saw it."

"Recognize what?"

"The method to awaken her, of course."

"Did these powers also mention there'd be a price, a heavy price that could leave you crippled or worse?"

"There was some hint of that. Why? Do you know something?"

"Not about you, but about them. I've been witness to three people who have tempted the fates by asking favors such as you have. One man lost his manhood. It fell right off one day in the middle of our encampment."

"I have no *manhood* to offer, but I'd gladly give up any body parts for my daughter's sake."

"Even those beautiful boobs?"

Marsha looked down at herself, and in doing so inadvertently thrust her breasts out further. George pulled uncomfortably at his shirt collar. "Even those," she answered.

George yanked his eyes away with great effort. "The second, a woman," George continued, looking at the floor, "watched her only daughter die."

Marsha sat up quickly. "They wouldn't save my daughter and then take her, would they?"

"I don't think so, but one never knows with the powers. They can be so unpredictable and their reasons are not for us to understand. I'm sure they have a plan."

Marsha looked more concerned than before. Her eyes darted around the room as if searching for something solid to grasp. Finally she looked back at George. "You said there was a third?"

"Yes, a friend of mine. The man thought he could be smarter than the powers. He first protected himself from their wrath. Since he had no children and no living family, he felt sure he'd be safe."

"What happened?"

"The powers took his girlfriend."

"Are you sure it was them? How did she die?"

"Gunshot to the head."

"Murder? Suicide?"

"She couldn't have been murdered so far inside a gypsy camp with no one noticing anything. And she was a sweet girl, no one could hate her."

"Except Georgina."

"My great-grandmother was nowhere around."

"What about suicide?"

"This girl was as happy as could be. She'd fallen madly in love with my friend and they were like school children together."

"An accident, then."

"She was an expert marksman, like most gypsies. I assure you, this was no accident."

Marsha looked at George and then allowed her eyes to roll toward the bedroom door. *What if they come after Sarah?*

***

People tend to like clean places. They also prefer the company of intelligent people. And yet they've become uncomfortable in hospitals. This is mostly due to the mood. No one goes there because they are well, happy, looking forward to an entertaining evening, good food, or saving money.

This brought most people to the conclusion they hate hospitals and apprehension often accompanies anyone entering the front door, even if they're just coming to visit a friend who's going to be fine. Despite wearing that same anxiety like a cloak, Marsha Coutier entered and even stayed on an almost daily basis. She hoped, despite being a realist. She prayed, even though she couldn't be called religious. She examined and monitored, although she had no medical expertise.

She loved, above all else, because she held the title; mother. Her devotion remained undaunted despite years of sorrow and failure. She clung to all that she had left in the world. Oh, she could be called upon to produce great amounts of money, and she owned a wonderful house, but what really counts is the people we're closest to and the love they give us. It brought Marsha back to this undesirable place, day after day.

Although she'd stopped bringing people in to see America some months before, this time she led a young man directly into the semi-private room. Sarah and Bonnie looked at each other with a curiosity neither could satisfy. George Shrub followed behind Marsha, stumbling more from the bags he carried than from meekness or clumsiness.

Before the door clacked shut he began to lay things out in what appeared to be a particular pattern. He pinched green leaves and sprinkled the dust on her head. Nothing happened. Then he mixed something together and it made a liquid that more resembled skim milk than anything else. This he dipped his finger into and rubbed on her lips. Again there was no response.

Marsha didn't expect much. The number of peculiar ideas tried could not easily be counted. This new one, somehow she felt would work. She picked it. She had some kind of insightful power, granted by the powers-that-be, deities of night, Gods of illusion and magic. She knew this had to be the way. She just *knew* it.

George spent the next hour and a half with different herbs and potions, none creating a reaction from the sleeping girl but some crinkled the noses of those awake. Through the tiny door window, Sarah's curious young face watched in awe until her calves became tired from her standing on her toes and she had to fall back on her full feet allowing her heels to support her upper body. From that height she could not see in. She went to look for a chair or a stool.

Marsha watched in rapt dedication. Her heart longing to hear the young girl's laughter once again, her mind watching to make sure he didn't try to hurt her further, her soul praying with all its might that she be freed from this curse to live a normal young girl life once again.

As time wore on and George's potions began to run out, Marsha could see the resolve in his eyes wan. He knew what he had to do and yet reluctance hindered his very movements. He looked at Marsha with pleading all over his face. She chose no response; only the stern motherly look she knew would offer no other options.

"Are you sure this is what you want me to do?"

"I told you, I *felt* something when I looked over at that piece of paper, I saw something out of the corner of my eye. It means *something*. I can't explain it any better than that. You *must* proceed."

He looked at his palette of herbs and shook his head in a sad and dejected manner. With a wave of his hand he pushed it all aside and stepped closer to the bed. He looked again at the mother standing nearby, awaiting, hoping.

"None of these other things seem to be having even the slightest effect. I appear to have little choice."

"Get on with it, then," Marsha said, sounding like a woman who has accepted the inevitable, no matter how distasteful it may appear.

"Are you going to stay in here and watch?"

"She is such a beauty, isn't she?"

"Huh? Oh, yes. She definitely is."

"Now, you're sure you can...perform, can't you?"

"I can."

"Even if I stay?"

"It's not that, but somehow it just doesn't seem right. You want to...*watch*? I mean, she's your daughter."

"Look, I've done some things I'm not proud of. But for the sake of my daughter, I won't hedge. I want this ritual performed and I won't just turn my back and hope you don't mess it up. If that means I'll see things no mother should ever see, then so be it. But she deserves any chance I think might be genuine."

"You mean you've watched other people..."

"I've watched a great many disturbing things in the last ten years, Mr. Bush," she interrupted.

"Shrub."

"Whatever. Please proceed."

George looked despaired. He turned toward the sleeping beauty and slid his hands under her at the shoulder and the ass level. After burying his arms to the elbows, he grunted and pushed against gravity. The girl came away from the table...a little. Then with a heave, he tossed her over. She came to rest, face down on the bed, her gown hardly closed behind her, her nearly perfect buttocks mounded up from her muscular back and curved down to her athletic thighs. The view had an obvious effect on George. He pulled at his shirt collar with one finger as he had at Marsha's home while staring at her breasts.

Marsha put her hands on her hips. Something told her he was hesitating. She glared at him like a mother at a child with a broken cookie jar at his feet. One foot involuntarily tapped against the tiled floor making a surprisingly loud noise. She raised her eyebrows.

George began to undress. As soon as his shirt went, Marsha noticed he looked quite underdeveloped for a man in his thirties. *He should be built like a hunk. I should be drooling. But he's so...scrawny.* She looked to one side and tried to focus. When he dropped his pants she looked back.

Although his body lacked any real bulk, his penis was quite substantial. *Maybe his name should be Dick,* she thought hastily, fighting back any giggle that tried to escape her lips. She felt a pang of protectiveness. His girth might actually hurt her daughter. Perhaps she should look for someone smaller. Before she could allow for such a change in plans, he managed to climb on the bed, nearly falling off the other side, and straddled the girl. Then, with one clumsy movement, he began poking at the girl, missing, and basically being a clod.

This guy is nothing but a big dick.

Again she fought with a giggle. But this time it wasn't all humor. She felt sorry for him, and even sorrier for her daughter who would soon be skewered on that massive pole. *Perhaps,* she thought for the first time in a decade, *watching might not be such a good idea.* And yet she did not turn away.

After many tries, George found his target. Even unconscious, the girl's rectum clenched against the indelicate entry, gripping him, trying to hold him out. But his weight fell upon her and his manhood entered half way up the shaft. Marsha needed to be sure.

She approached the bed from behind George. She grabbed the girl's feet and spread her legs as far as they would go. She *had* to be sure. She looked at where the action took place. The man, George W. Shrub, did indeed have his penis inserted in America's anus. She nodded her approval.

"Go ahead. Get moving."

George turned slowly and had no control over the dejected look on his face. Nevertheless, his erection remained and to Marsha, that's all that mattered. After a moment she shot him a sharp look straight in the eye.

"I said, let's get this show on the road."

Without a word, George began to slide his non-lubricated penis in and out of the girl's tight butt hole. A look of pain showed on his face as beads of sweat formed on his forehead. He did not stop moving, in and out, in and out.

After a time, as such things go, the girl's anus relaxed and George began to move more freely, faster. The entire thing looked more like a porn movie than some sick, sadistic torture chamber horror as it first appeared.

"Faster, George. Harder. Bang her, good. Pound her."

George seemed lost in the feelings and hardly noticed the woman speaking to him. He looked up sharply when Marsha slapped him on the ass as he raised it up in the air. The red mark told the tale of how the slap had not been playful and had stung quite a bit. To his credit, George didn't stop moving, though he didn't exactly increase his speed as instructed, either.

Pretty soon, the friction and nerve endings took over and George fell completely into the moment, driving his manhood deeper and deeper into the beautifully round ass on the bed. He could no longer help how good it felt. Animal desires, age old, drove him to increase his speed as he pounded his pelvis against her ass cheeks, making a slapping noise.

"Oh, my God!" George exclaimed.

"Don't let up, George."

"But I'm about to..."

"Shoot inside her, for all I care. It's not like she

can get pregnant that way. But don't you dare pull away!"

George pounded hard into her, never minding being delicate or gentlemanly—if one could even be called a gentleman while performing such an act on a helpless young lady. Nevertheless he pumped away with wild abandon, driven not by any sense of helping the poor girl—at that moment he cared not for her. No, the driving force was a simple, base, animal lust and the need to reach his climax.

In some sick way, Marsha seemed caught up in the moment. Her voice raised in excited frenzy, she nearly shouted at him. George seemed unaware—his mind so occupied with the physical sensations he could hardly be called upon to say what time of day it was.

But Marsha, the excited onlooker, did not fixate on the gyrating nether regions, but on the face of the girl, now twitching in tiny spasms. Even though that's not a sign of independent life, it looked a far cry from the comatose girl she'd been looking at for the last ten years. At some point in time, Marsha could not precisely tell when, George finished pumping his hot seed into the girl's back door and fell on her. He nuzzled into the base of her neck just below the hair line.

"Stop that! You're not in love with her, you just had an orgasm," Marsha admonished. "Men have orgasms a couple times a day, even without a partner."

"I know, but it was the best I ever had."

"Phooey. I bet you've been with plenty of girls."

"Not really, ma'am."

Just then, America coughed.

"Get off her! Quickly!"

George did as instructed. He reluctantly stood near the bed, wiping the mess off his manhood and sorting out the front of his jeans. He began dressing but never took his eyes off the girl, now moving slightly, in jerky motions. First her arms and legs, then her head, each came up from the bed in turn, held for a moment, then fell back without grace of any kind.

"Is she..."

"I think she is, George." Marsha sounded choked, unable to form words with proper elocution. Her smile perpetuated across her face and wouldn't calm down. "I think we did it, George!" Then she ran out, nearly hitting Sarah with the door.

"I think..." Marsha began but ended by simply pointing over and over. She kissed the young nurse/lover and ran to the floor desk. Bonnie stood behind, waiting for some sense of the commotion. "America..."

"What about her, Mrs. Coutier?"

"She's...awake!"

Bonnie didn't wait for further explanation. She darted around the desk and headed for room 314. What she saw there brought tears to her eyes. With what appeared to be massive effort to control any further

222

outburst, Bonnie entered the room and began a preliminary examination of the girl.

Her eyes remained closed and she lay still on the bed, but the nurse saw movement and the monitors suggested something other than coma. "I think she may need some rest, Mrs. Coutier," Bonnie suggest, looking at George.

"I—I should go." George's earlier confidence had completely drained from him with his semen.

"Yes," said Barbara Omaba, who happened to walk in the room that very moment. "I think that would be a good idea. I can take over from here. You've done quite enough already."

"What are *you* doing here?"

"I'm here to make sure you leave."

"You think you can do a better job than me? I woke her up."

"You still don't get it, do you? You weren't great. You won't go down in history. You didn't accomplish anything Pulitzer-worthy. You were just a catalyst, nothing more."

"Well, more power to you, you old Gyp. These people are going to chew you up and spit you out just because of the color of your skin. And I'm going to laugh."

"You're the reason she was like this in the first place."

"You put her to sleep."

"And you would have rather she died. Get out."

223

He sheepishly pulled his over shirt tight around his chest and left the room. Mrs. Coutier hardly noticed. She spoke to the nurse.

"How can she need rest when she's slept for ten years?"

"The struggle."

"What struggle?"

"The struggle to come out of the coma. It's not an easy thing to do. It's such a comfortable place, your mind and body both want to stay. There's quite a lot to it."

"Really. I had no idea."

"I'm here to help," Barbara inserted.

Marsha turned. "Oh, hello there. Come on in. We've managed to wake her."

"At some cost, I hear."

"There's always a cost," Marsha Coutier confirmed.

"Well, maybe I can help now."

"Maybe you can." She turned back to Nurse Bonnie. "I still don't understand about this exhaustion. Is this common?"

"Yes it is. And that's not all. Since the muscles haven't been working for so long, they have a tendency to atrophy."

"Atrophy? Isn't that where they become non-functional?"

"Yes," Bonnie confirmed.

"I don't think she had that problem."

"Why not?"

"Let's just say I saw one of her muscles working just fine a few minutes ago."

"Which one?"

Marsha was taken aback. She stood aghast, wondering how to respond to such a direct question. She hadn't expected it and didn't know how to respond. She blinked a couple times, hoping a vision of something coherent would flash across her eyelids.

The nurse continued to work. She checked vital signs and readings on several machines. She hit the call button that would summon a doctor to the room. She shone a light into America's eyes behind lids lifted by the nurse's thumb. But at each space, every moment she didn't need to focus on what she was doing, she looked at Marsha Coutier, calling—pleading for the answer to her question.

Barbara Omaba looked on, dumbfounded, Not doing much in the way of helping. Things were a mess.

Marsha decided she couldn't deceive the nurse any further. "Her anus," she admitted.

"The sphincter muscle?" Bonnie asked, not entirely sure she'd heard properly.

"That's right."

"Why would you have noticed that?"

"That boy…" Marsha trailed off and refused to speak further. She waited anxiously for further responses from her daughter—proof that the darkness had been lifted and the nightmare was finally over.

***

No conclusive cause could be listed for the girl's coma, neither could there be anything on record for the cure. She simply woke up one evening, without any apparent reason. After a few days of observation, they had no rights to keep her any longer. They released her in her mother's care. She went home and grew stronger each day.

Soon independence took over and the girl struck out on her own. She coordinated a revolution movement against those who would assume power over someone so small as she and heralded in a new era of a country run by its people. Her name is revered by most everyone...except the Shrubs.

About a week after America's release from the hospital, Marsha wandered to the carnival in hopes of thanking the old gypsy woman for all her help. She also wanted to tell her that the girl had been awakened. She thought the old woman would like to know how much she'd helped.

However, she was unable to find the old woman. But the younger one, Gina, found Marsha. They exchanged a fiery look. Gina waved a finger, calling Marsha in the right direction. Soon Marsha found herself in Gina's wagon, naked, and in the throes of passion. Gina buried her face between Marsha's legs and her tongue moved relentlessly.

Gina explored and roamed as if searching for something buried inside Marsha. When she found nothing, she simply dug further. Marsha struggled to keep her wits, at least enough to return the favor. After three or four times, she wasn't sure she could.

After some rest, Marsha found out the truth about gypsy pussy. It tasted a lot like all the others. Although distinct, unique as any one person is from another, the girl was not abnormal in any way Marsha could tell. She tasted like a woman. Delicious.

However, something about the heady aroma and the dark gypsy mystique and Marsha lost herself in those gypsy folds, burying her face deeper, extending her tongue farther, searching for a buried treasure of her own. She enjoyed the young gypsy girl for hours. In the end, the sun rose and neither could properly walk. Nevertheless, it was time for Marsha to leave.

"I'd always been told white people don't care about anyone else but themselves. After last night I think not all white people are the same."

"You've shown me a great many things, too, Gina. Pity I can't stay."

"It's all for the best, I fear. The gypsy way of life is not for everyone."

"For many nights like that, I could get used to almost anything."

"At least you've discovered the price the Gods would extract from you."

Marsha stood, nonplussed. How could she have forgotten about that part of the deal? And what did the girl mean *now* she'd discovered? "What are you talking about?"

Gina reached out a hand to pat the older woman's head. She brushed down her hair to her shoulder as one might do to a beloved pet. When she pulled her hand back, a large portion of hair came with it. Marsha screamed.

***

Three years blurred by very quickly. One of the social reforms that came to pass under the new America regime allowed same-sex marriages. Although, no one could be sure why it was ever an issue in the first place, it seemed to be resolved with a simple signature.

Even though Marsha explored that single night with the young gypsy girl and had such an amazing time, she never again roamed and Sarah asked Marsha to marry her. A most beautiful ceremony, notable for its spectacular floral arrangements, took place in an open field of green alfalfa grass. Marsha wore her red wig—she'd managed to accumulate quite a collection— and America presided over the wedding.

Wedding nights can be bliss, a final resting of the taboos of pre-marital sex. But to a couple whose very relationship is considered a taboo, this never goes away. It can also be a night of discovery to those who abstain until then. Once again, no such magnificence came through for Marsha and Sarah since they'd already been together so many times. But on that night came something that shocked Marsha, a question Sarah had been afraid to ask before.

"How did that guy wake America? No one else could do it."

Marsha stopped. She looked at Sarah, wondering if the girl meant to sound sarcastic or just curious. Would the answer offend her? Would this be a good time to put such a dark knowledge on their newly-formed union? And what could the girl possibly gain by knowing? On the other hand, why would she be offended if she learned the truth? She did, after all, ask. And somehow, keeping things from her new mate seemed like the wrong foot to start out on.

"No one else could do it, that's true. But after I visited that old gypsy, I felt drawn to the answer, as if it were a part of me and I only had to ferret it out."

"A part of you?"

"I know that sounds corny. I can't explain it any better than that. It's like one of those undersea explorers that just *knows* there's a sunken ship down there and they keep diving deeper and deeper to find it despite everyone's contrary opinion."

"Deeper and deeper, huh? Sounds like fun," Sarah added, taking off her shirt.

Marsha chuckled. "I had this deep seated feeling. Something drew me to this piece of paper."

"What piece of paper?"

"The one that told me everything I needed to know about how to wake up America. There were several pieces at first. But this one grabbed my eye and wouldn't let go."

"What did you find out? What did it say?"

229

Marsha went to her night stand and withdrew a piece of paper. "I've kept this as a memento. By itself, it hardly means anything. But to me, it proved to be the key to unlock a most difficult door." She handed it to Sarah.

Sodomize the girl with great force.

"Wow! You mean if America got fucked up the ass hard enough by some guy named Bush, she would finally wake up?"

"Shrub, my dear," Marsha corrected. "His name was Shrub."

World of Pain

By:
Blue Canyon

The lone motorcyclist rode into town on the roar of his V-twin engine. He pulled up in front of a store and parked the bike, looking more like a cowboy tying his horse to the post outside a saloon.

He had a look about him. Not exactly handsome, but striking and intense. Angular, chiseled features made women swoon for him. He stood well over six foot and weighed-in at just about 220, maybe a little less. Muscular—yet on the slender side—his jeans fit snuggly to his legs and ass.

More than one pair of eyes watched as he lifted one of those legs up and over the motorcycle and swung it around to the ground. They were all trying *not* to watch. One such pair of eyes did not belong to a Miss Molly Gerkin, from the Gerkin ranch just east of town.

Molly, it seemed, had come into town simply to buy supplies. She was not looking for any 'male' involvement. She was already involved with a man, the owner of the hardware store. He was busy arguing with her about the things she wanted to buy.

"Molly, Molly. If it were up to me, you know I would let you buy the stuff. Your credit came back denied. There's nothing I can do."

"My credit is better than most people's around here and you know it, Mr. Barker. You are denying me because of that shit—Tanner."

"Molly, you know Mr. Tanner has nothing to do with the credit reporting agency."

"Mr. Barker, you are not a nice man. You would let my ranch go to ruin before you would sell me supplies?"

"I don't make the rules, Molly."

"No, Tanner does. You just follow him."

"Now that's a pretty strong accusation. You shouldn't say things like that. I'm not trying to treat you bad."

"It sure sounds like it from here."

They both turned to the odd, silky voice that spoke to them. The first thing Molly noticed was his dark blue shirt. It not only went well with his jeans, but contrasted perfectly with his well-tanned skin. She thought he looked gorgeous.

He carried the few things in his hands he'd come to purchase. He approached the counter and set them down next to Molly's and looked the man in the eye with a stare that could make a statue blink first.

"I'll take these."

The man behind the counter moved nervously. He began to obediently scan the items, but he never stopped staring at the stranger and making sure he didn't move too quickly. The first thought travelling through his mind was not the gun that fit so perfectly on the wall right next to the register just out of customer sight, but rather of how much hiding room he'd have underneath that counter should he need to duck.

"And these," he added, pulling Molly's things closer to his and the register.

"Mister, you don't want to get involved in that. You'd best leave it alone and ride out of town." It was the first sign of back bone the shopkeeper showed.

The stranger didn't intimidate easily. He leaned forward at the waist which just brought his face closer to Barker's. He said nothing, only staring deeper into the man as if that were enough. But it was enough. The shopkeeper sheepishly reached out and began scanning the items Molly Gerkin had put up there.

The stranger paid properly with cash, Mr. Barker looked at it as if he'd never seen money before. The stranger grabbed the things and left, leaving Molly to stand there, looking back and forth from his back to the shopkeeper. Finally, just about the time the front door closed behind the stranger, she managed to unglue her feet and made her way quickly to the door. Without so much as a wave or a glance backward, she went out.

"Hey, wait a minute."

"Which car is yours, Miss," he said, realizing she'd finally caught up. "I'll put these in it for you."

"Who are you?"

"I'm just a guy who's passing through."

"You got a name?"

"Clint."

"Clint? Sure, why not. Clint, what?" She had a sinking feeling she knew how he would answer.

He sighed.

"Clinton Theodore Sterling, Ma'am."

Not the answer she expected, at all. Backing up a bit to stare at him, Molly smiled but, to her credit, did not laugh, although she felt inclined to. Instead, her finger poked out in the direction of the El Camino parked right in front of the store. He walked over to it and set the bags with her things in the back.

"What brings you to this town, Mr. Sterling?"

"Please, call me Clint."

"Okay. Clint."

"I'm here to see a man."

"Oh?"

"Hank Tanner."

Molly backed up again and looked like she would run for her car and leave as quickly as she could. But she hesitated.

"What do you want him for?" The way she said *him* made it sound like a curse word.

"He's not a very nice man."

"And you want to see him. Does that mean you are not a very nice man?"

"I do not intend to be friends with him, Ma'am."

"Please, call me Molly," she added, her voice softer than before.

"Molly," he said, smiling. "That's nice."

She smiled more warmly.

"Thanks."

"As I said, I'm not here to make friends with the man, if you know what I mean, Molly. But as to whether or not I am a nice man…well, I may be, but then again, there are those who might dispute it. I can't really say."

Somehow, Molly felt more comforted by his words. He was not here to be friends with Tanner. Someone once said: *the enemy of my enemy is my friend.* To this day she cannot tell you why she said what she said next.

"Do you have a place to stay?"

"No, Ma'am. But the night will be clear," he said, looking up at the afternoon sky.

"There's no need of that. Stay at my place. I have room."

"I wouldn't want to intrude."

"I have lots of room and I live alone."

"Wouldn't you be afraid?"

"I already am, every day."

"Excuse me?" Clint looked surprised.

"What could you do to me Tanner hasn't already threatened?"

"I see." Then he thought about it for a moment. "Lead the way?"

She smiled again and sat down in her car while he mounted his motorcycle and kicked it in the balls until it roared with power. He followed her through some turns and down a dirt portion of road, finally reaching her ranch. It looked a lot like a ranch, a simple, though large house surrounded by fields for miles with fences dissecting throughout. Some horses grazed in the distance.

"Very nice, Miss."

"Molly."

"Yes, of course. I'm sorry."

As they walked in, she showed him briefly around.

"That is the bathroom if you need to freshen up. Also, if you like, you can take a hot bath and I can wash your clothes for you." She looked into his sparkling eyes.

He stared at her as he had the shop keeper, but it felt differently to her. Somehow he seemed not only to be looking into her soul, but he was communicating with her on that level. She felt overwhelmed with an urge to wrap her arms around him and...

She quickly pushed the idea out of her head. It had been too long since she'd been with a man and she was being just a little too eager for modesty's sake.

"That sounds wonderful, Molly. But, may I ask, what is that wonderful smell?"

"Oh, I'm so sorry. I've forgotten my manners. That's dinner. It'll be ready soon. Are you hungry?"

"Yes, I am. Thank you."

"Good. I've been told I'm a good cook. It will be nice to have someone else appreciate my food for a change."

"If you don't mind my asking," he spoke to her back as she retreated to the kitchen, "why aren't you married?"

She turned and looked at him with a stare that asked why he would want to know such a thing. She decided he was just being curious and neighborly. So she chose to answer honestly.

"He died."

"I never understood why, but people believe it appropriate at times like this to say 'I'm sorry'."

"It confuses me, too. But thanks for the sentiment. It was a long time ago. I'm over it…sort of."

"Is it something you prefer to not talk about?"

"Yes it is."

"Then we won't talk about it. You run this place by yourself?"

"I have a hired boy. He comes after school to take care of the horses. His family went on vacation to Florida so he won't be around until next week."

"Okay," he said as he sat down to eat. She placed a plate in front of him and he ate as if he hadn't in days. Afterward he sat back and rubbed his muscular chest and firm belly. "That was perhaps the best meal I've ever tasted."

"I wouldn't go that far, Clint."

"I would. I don't come from a long line of good cooks," he joked.

"I'm glad you liked it."

They stood and he stepped over to her. He raised his hand to her arm in a simple friendly gesture but she stiffened and held her breath. He mistook her action for fear.

"I won't hurt you, Molly."

"I know."

"Would you mind if I took that hot bath now?"

"Be my guest. I usually run out of hot water before it's full, so I'll just put the pan on the stove. It

239

gives me just enough to top it off and make it feel comfortable."

"Thank you very much," he smiled.

When she brought in the water, he had already gotten his shirt off and she could see the rippled muscles in his stomach. She tried not to stare. This was going to be a difficult night.

She poured in the water and left quickly as he wasn't stopping at the shirt. She didn't know if he would undress completely in front of her, but she knew she had to leave the room before he went any further.

After a while, as she walked through the house, she passed in front of the bathroom. The stranger hadn't bothered to close the door. He was out of the tub and beginning to dry off. He saw her and dropped the towel and stared at her. She could do nothing but stare...at his penis.

He invited her with his unabashed gaze. She stepped forward as if someone were manipulating her with a remote control. His eyes never left hers and hers never left his cock. He made no move to stop her or suggest he didn't want her. In fact, he was beginning to rise to the occasion.

She wasn't sure she believed it, but she thought he might be as interested in her as she was in him. Could that be? She felt like she'd gotten so much older since Frank died. No man called on her and she felt unattractive.

But she kept walking. When she got close enough, she reached out a hand. It came in contact with his leg just to the right of his testicles and she caught her breath again, like she had in the kitchen earlier.

It had been a long time since she was with a man. Emotion and lust overcame her. She made no effort at modesty as she touched him in intimate ways like a familiar lover. His body gave her feelings she wasn't sure she *ever* had even back when her husband lived.

He too, came willingly, placing his rough hands on the tender flesh of her breasts. She moaned with pleasure. The pain hurt and she wanted more. When his hands slid down her back she felt a shiver surround her body like another skin.

He seduced her completely, either because he had talent or because she desired it. She didn't really care which. She needed him inside her and she was going to have it, and he seemed willing.

Their lovemaking lasted well into the night and Molly deeply breathed in the scent of sex that filled her room. He didn't have the finesse as he pounded into her gracelessly, but her pleasure increased with each thrust.

They rolled together in sweat, seeking a solace which could be achieved no other way. A smile consumed her face and she lay peacefully, enjoying the memories playing over and over inside her head. But sadness overshadowed her bliss.

She looked deeply into his eyes and saw more lust within. But no matter how deep she looked or which way she searched, she could not see him staying with her for long.

After a time, she let go of the sensation that coursed through her and relaxed into sleep with her head resting in the crook of his armpit. The lingering odors of soap and sex wafted into her senses as consciousness fully escaped her.

The morning rose in the east and the sun broke through her eyelids disturbing her perfect slumber and dreams of clover and butterflies...and sex. She came back to consciousness reluctantly, fighting to remain in her fantasy realm and the bliss within.

But the sun had become unrelenting as it burned through her sleep, rising up to a perfect height to shine through her window and directly onto her face. She lazily pushed back the covers and exposed her naked form. She hadn't slept in the nude since she was married. She looked down at herself and, for the first time in a very long time, admired what she saw.

It was not vanity, but rather that he'd enjoyed her so well. He found her so attractive. He hadn't kept his hands off her. He desired her and devoured her. She felt like a queen.

Molly felt she could float on the fluffy clouds that danced around the blue sky. Then she looked over to the other side of her bed. Her *empty* bed. Had he left so soon? She *knew* he wouldn't stay, but why did he have to leave so soon? Something inside told her she would *never* know the answer.

†

He parked the motorcycle on the side of the road more than a mile away from the ranch. The noise would attract too much attention and stealth could still be on his side. He walked the rest of the way in the trees for cover, but no traffic rode by and he was not seen.

The edge of the trees lined the ranch in a smooth circle, but it looked like an acre of open land between that line and the main building which was his goal. He would wait until nightfall, even though it appeared abandoned.

✝

Darkness could be a double-edged weapon. While he could maneuver with less chance of being seen, the likelihood of him being surprised by a guard or an alarm greatly increased. He took great care to look out for traps and trip wires.

Once inside, there was a greater chance of setting off some alarm. However, that no longer concerned him. Inside was...well, inside. He surveyed the well-adorned home and decided which way would be most likely to hold his quarry.

Clint Sterling crouched behind a china cabinet as the man walked by. The bulge in his jacket under his arm was evident. As soon as the man went past and his back was turned, Clint jumped out from his hiding place.

The guard went down without a sound. Clint slid through a doorway and came face-to-face with the only other guard that seemed to be on the premises.

The man drew his gun, pointing it expertly at Clint's chest.

"Who are you?"

Sterling considered his many answer options. There would be no stopping his bullet and any answer would more likely aggravate the situation. So, he decided to carry on the great American tradition, he'd learned from some of history's greatest heroes.

He fainted.

The man with the gun approached quickly, abandoning any safe distance considerations. Clint Sterling moved quickly. His hand shot up and deflected the barrel of the gun enough for his other hand, equipped with a sharp object mostly resembling an ice pick, to find its mark. The man went down in a pool of his own blood.

Standing over the body but looking around the home, the stranger finally moved toward the stairs leading upward. The bedrooms would be up there. With any luck, the owner of the house would still be asleep. Clint had come to see that he slept for a *very* long time.

Walking up the stairs quietly, hands once again empty, he saw the man approach from a distance of several meters. There was no cover, no stealth, no way to avoid a direct confrontation.

"Who?"

"Sterling."

"I don't know you."

"No. No way you could."

"Then..." the man looked around, "...why?"

"Because it must be."

A moment of silence passed between them. The other man seemed to be trying to absorb what he'd heard. Or perhaps, Clint thought, he was just assessing his situation and creating a strategy. Maybe he just wanted to run.

"Well, my name is Tanner. I'm afraid, my friend, I am not as informidable as my so-called *guards*."

There were no more words to be said. The two warriors crouched and parlayed, evaluating each other, guessing strengths and, more importantly, weaknesses. Neither made an aggressive move...at first. Both chose to assess the other for a time.

Then, inevitably, a hand struck out, and it began. Both men trained in martial arts-like styles, simply grabbed each other, attempting to throw the other to the floor. This would certainly gain one the advantage, but both being more or less equally matched, accomplished very little by what they were doing.

Also inevitable, though, was a change. Tanner feigned a stumble to his right and brought his left hand up to strike, hoping his entire body weight would go into the punch. It did. However, Sterling managed to dodge by less than a quarter inch.

Swinging full around, Clint brought his open hand down onto the other man's shoulder. The chop had the desired effect. Tanner fell to one knee. He swung his arm up to block the expected blow, but it did not come.

Sterling, anticipating Tanner's anticipation, swung his knee up into Tanner's face. The man went down as blood dripped from his nose. He struggled to focus his eyes but the broken nose wouldn't allow it.

Suddenly Tanner became very calm as if finding his center. He found his way to his feet and turned warily toward even the slightest sound from Sterling's feet. The stranger made a move to test Tanner's focus. The man reacted quickly and accurately.

Once again the two men danced—one seeing and one sensing on another level. The loss of sight didn't slow Tanner down by much. He lunged forward to connect with the other man. The stranger spun like a ballerina and reached out, grabbing a sword from the wall in one graceful move.

Without losing his momentum or his near-perfect arc, he unsheathed the sword and buried it to the hilt in the chest of the homeowner. Tanner went down, gasping as if trying to maintain the life that waned from his damaged body. Sterling stared deeply into the dying man's eyes and watched as the life force drained away like a feather in a gale.

"So," Clinton Theodore Sterling spoke softly, intimately, "you're the man causing all the trouble in this town. A pleasure to meet you."

The other man fell in a heap at the stranger's feet.

†

The lone motorcyclist rode across the desert where no road had ever been, enjoying the roar of his V-twin engine between his muscular legs. He rubbed slightly at his neck and then flipped a switch on his motorcycle between his 'fat-bob' gas tanks.

"I have made first contact. There will be no problem making them think we are friendly."

He reached for his neck again and pulled. The synthetic mask came off his head easily, revealing his grotesque alien features. His smile would scare the skin off a grand master martial artist.

"The baby I gave her will look like one of them."

The Rock

By:
Blue Canyon

And suddenly darkness fell. I looked hard but could see nothing. When I took one tentative step forward, I finally saw something. Stars. My chin connected with something very hard and pain shot up my leg, jerking me to an instant stop. It must have been short because I'd put my hands out in front of me—waving them about maniacally—and never felt a warning.

The thunderous roar from moments ago had ceased, replaced by random coughs and some weak moaning. Somewhere in the distance a woman sobbed. To my right I saw a flash from an electrical short—perhaps a bare wire hanging down. I could hear and feel the electricity in the air as it buzzed against a table top. Then all went black again. With people milling about aimlessly, that electrical wire could be very dangerous.

A part of me wanted to laugh. Danger, it seems, had found us without our wandering around searching for it. Still unsure what happened, I squatted to my hands and knees and began to slowly make my way toward the nearest voice. It called out for help but had no strength—as if the life had been taken out of it already. Yet it called.

At one point the electricity shot through the air again and I saw the wire, now merely three feet away from me. I began to question my sanity. Moving around, even in a crouched position as I was, could prove dangerous—even fatal. But the voice called on. So did others.

In the complete darkness, I tried to keep the image of the wire to my right—hoping to move past. Then it crossed my mind there could be other wires hanging—waiting to give their deadly gift to anyone foolish enough to get near.

I found a wooden table leg and swept back and forth in front of me. This made crawling more difficult. I felt like a three-legged dog, trying to move and maintain my balance, all at once. A table bumped into me and I went down, injuring my left shoulder. I'd probably have a nasty bruise on my upper arm. Of course, in this light, who would notice.

I worked at this facility for six months and no one noticed me anyway. But getting noticed wasn't why I came to work here, nor was it the reason for my earning a degree in microbiotics. I specialized in micro-computerization because I wanted to build the first nano-bots. I'm not sure, but I don't think I need a man to do that.

And yet I've felt so isolated. No one has spoken to me. I'm not just the new kid on the block, I'm the new kid with pimples. Some days loneliness overwhelms me and I cry. Somehow I've always managed to keep it in until I get home.

I worked with some of the greatest minds in the country, and at least two or three sexy men. But because I'm a young woman in a man's world, it leaves me being the outcast. And at only twenty-two, there's still so far to travel.

But I got lucky and landed this job with a research facility with a reputation for being cutting edge. Although, looking around the room at what little I can see right now, I don't feel so lucky.

My best guess is a cave-in. I didn't know these places even had underground levels before I was hired on. But this place had been here for years. Why there should be such a disaster now—I didn't know. Although we weren't doing anything with the military, perhaps some radical group decided we're a threat and planted a bomb. Buried down here in complete darkness, blinded by bursts of electrical light, there's no way to know what's really happened.

Then my hand touched something with hair. I jerked as I heard another groan. A voice came to me, weakened and odd, somehow. Something I couldn't explain rode those sound waves to my ears. An emptiness, or a lack of energy, perhaps—something beyond my words to describe.

"Help me."

"I'm here," I replied, trying to sound confident.

"W-Who?"

"It's Arianna Long. I'm the new girl." Even after six months I remained the 'new' girl. I would probably be the new girl five years from now.

"Ah, the pretty one, with the great body."

He noticed? Someone—anyone noticed? I thought they were all just scoffing at me, laughing at the newbie. Someone once gave such people a pretty name to take away some of the hurt. Intern. That was my title. No matter my field of expertise or the lab they assigned me to, I was just 'the intern'. It sounded like some old television show. I tried not to chuckle. Under the circumstances, it didn't seem appropriate.

"Thank you," was all I could think of to say.

"Can you lean a little closer so I can see you?"

I leaned down but could see only a rough outline, the darkness made any real clarity impossible. I quickly noticed something to my right. Lights had begun to flicker. I thought the wire might be chasing me. Apparently the emergency backup generator had kicked in. Fluorescent tubes began winking on—one after another.

Soon the light overhead flashed on and I caught my breath short. A boulder the size of my car lay on the body of the man I'd been talking to, crushing him from the chest down. I looked at his face—pleasant and handsome, though weak and pallid—he smiled.

His rich blue eyes set under dark curly hair. His striking nose with just a hint of a slalom hump came to a tip that pointed at me—following me when I moved. I offered him a smile in return, churning it up from the depths of the manners I'd learned as a child. The man's life was over. No medical team could save him even if they arrived at that moment. All I could do was keep him comfortable and happy.

"I've seen you around. What's your name?"

"I'm Doctor Shetzer." I guess he saw my face fall just a bit. "Brian," he added.

I smiled. "Well Brian, I've seen you around. What do you do?"

"Microbiotics."

"Oh yeah? Me too. Too bad we didn't get to work together."

"That's not likely to happen now," he groaned.

"Oh, come on," I lied as best I could. "You're just going to need some time to recover."

"Listen, honey," pain twisted his voice into a raspy saw blade. "I know what the score is."

"You do? Who is winning?" I tried to sound jovial.

Brian sagged. I felt terrible. When he didn't speak, I tried to move our conversation forward.

"You…" I began strong but wasn't sure how to continue. "You should try to keep a positive attitude." I was surprised to hear my voice sound firmer than I felt.

"Listen, Arianna—is it? I know the end is near."

I couldn't find my voice. Even if I could stop choking, I didn't have the words. I sat back to ease the pain in my legs, staring into his sad and sexy eyes. Taking a couple deep breaths I leaned an arm against the same block of wood Brian's head lay on. I got real close to his face so he could talk softly and not strain so much to make his voice carry. I rested my head on my arm.

"What can I do to help, Brian?"

"I don't have much longer. I can feel it."

"I know," was all I could manage.

"I want…"

I held my breath. My breathing had become so loud in my head I didn't want to drown him out.

"Do you believe in granting a dying man's request?"

"If I can," I replied, looking at the huge rock and hoping he didn't ask for me to pull him out, or something impossible like that.

"I…I want to see your tits."

"I…" my voice trailed off as I tried to find the right response. I scanned the room to see how many people would be close enough to overhear. "Are you kidding?" I looked down at my chest. Small bumps dented my shirt and I wondered how he'd even noticed I had any.

"Please?"

I wanted to say no but my hands came up to my shirt like they'd already decided. I couldn't be sure how best to let them out and still cover myself quickly if someone noticed. My button-up shirt was no longer tucked into my pants and I figured just lifting it up would be easiest.

So I grabbed the shirt at the bottom cuff, snaked my hands up to get my fingers under the bra, and pulled both hands to my chin. Both Brian's hands were free and he moved one over with a jerky motion and touched me. My nipples were hard, either from a chill, an odd kind of excitement, his intimate touch, or the fear of getting caught.

256

I watched around the room, allowing him to continue touching me while I scanned for observers, until I felt his hand fall away. When I looked back, I saw his eyes had dropped a couple inches toward the floor and they looked a little glazed over. I slowly lowered my shirt back over my breasts.

I leaned over and kissed him on the forehead. "I hope it was good for you."

A Name by Any Other Rose

By:
Blue Canyon

'Twas merely lust filling her inside, like a dark hand of animal desire wrapped around her heart. Her black soul wanting only the satisfaction of the flesh, her eyes wandering from one male to the next, the wanton woman sank to depths no fallen angel would dare.

Her mind twisted by her constant need, she continually sought only the physical gratification that sated her for barely a moment and then she would, as so many times before, return to the hunt. And one man after another would willingly yield, succumbing to her wiles.

She was born, Rose Antonia Riley Ford, from a prosperous family with some standing in the small community from whence she sprang. But prosperity and affluence held little meaning for a girl led not by her head—nay, not even her heart could be a true guide when lust bloomed from the depths of her tender body.

The better part of her youthful life spent in the futile search for more gratifying moments, she had now come to an impasse. She took the time, on occasion between her hunts, to ponder the meaning. She derived many conclusions, but for lack of any true guidance, settled on none.

And so, over time, her heart grew heavy with confusion and longing. She searched high and low for a nobler purpose to life, nary missing an opportunity to stop and devour some unsuspecting, yet willing young man—more out of need for blind fulfillment now than any real desire to continue her whorish ways.

Despite the urges that welled within her and would oft times drive her to the brink of insanity, the still-young woman would sometimes be struck full on by the remorse that often accompanies such a lifestyle. And her heart would, once again be rent with the pain and regret brought about by a budding conscience.

Verily, a young maid such as she could torture herself into an asylum with such dire contradictions of thought. And she found herself, when not on the prowl for the next sampling of fleshly delights, seeking more a solace than an understanding which continually evaded. She clung to any unmovable object that would support her through these tribulations.

One such object was Wilford Denton Hemmingforth, an Earl by his own claim, though none could prove his lineage. People, it seemed, dared not question his self-proclaimed title. In less than a year after his peculiar arrival, he declared himself magistrate, in a town that, heretofore, had none. And naught but a fortnight passed when the town was christened with its new name:

Hemmingforth.

Rose met Wilford quite by happenstance one sunny afternoon when the sky was filled with spritely birdsong that soon faded beneath the more prominent music from a different source. She searched, more in the open than she should, for satiation and momentary bliss, once again. Many prospects strolled out on such a day and her eyes made attempt at every pair that passed. To her dismay, none willingly returned her gaze.

Wilford, quite to the contrary, set about in a more dutiful capacity. Madame Chatterwell's boarding house was known to accommodate discrete liaisons and he and two other gentlemen marched in that direction with official papers to cease and desist.

The impromptu town council voted to eradicate all such undesirable elements from their Christian community in an ill-fated effort to extricate the seductive lure of the evil one that still managed to live among them, despite the town's innocent Christian beginnings. This, apparently, would be the first step in ensuring the purity of growth among the town dwellers. And Wilford, quite intent on his quest, never met Rose's gaze, even at a passing glance.

Nevertheless, Rose found herself inexorably drawn to the stalwart figure. Her footing faltered as she continued to watch the man—not where she trod—and she nearly stumbled into the abattoir. Her lust suddenly abated for reasons she could not fathom, she strode for the safety of home with many a confusing thought mulling through her head, drowning out the song that had begun in her heart—too far away to hear, too deep-rooted to ignore.

The two of them were heterogeneous, to be sure, despite her heritage. She certainly could not approach such a man with her desire unchecked. Should he see her with lust unfettered, he would surely hand her directly to the Abbess, and Rose would forever be without the warmth of a man's touch.

However, her desire remained checked at that very moment—tethered by an invisible rein. After some pondering, she came to realize she desired this man on a more spiritual level, although she could hardly be called upon as knowledgeable about such matters. She sought his companionship, his *favor*, perhaps, but not to seduce him. Though surely she could not soon understand why—nor, perhaps, ever.

Yet she knew him not. And would not until she gained control of her urges. His office held him far too busy for socializing and her stature surely lay beneath him. Rose knew this without anyone telling. *A true and intelligent person knows who and what they are. And one should always stand in the appropriate company. The crossing of such social barriers is considered ill-mannered and morally unacceptable.*

But as her thoughts became more focused on the magistrate and less on her own needs, she knew she would eventually have to cross those lines or forever live in despair and emptiness. This, more than any other thought, gave her pause to consider the choices she had made throughout her nearly twenty years. She felt as an old maid, for her toils had been fruitless and trivial and weighed heavily on her soul. If only she could bury her past and become a lady once more.

Would that there could be a way to purge not only the desires but the stains left from past indiscretions. She would keep her head high as people pointed, saying: Behold! There passes the lady Rose, Duchess of Hemmingforth, heir to the Ford fortune, wife of the Magistrate. None would dare say such things in her current state.

The weeks that followed proved to be the most torturous for Rose. Her heart longed for the security of truly knowing a man and being with him in all senses. However, as time passed in the manner it often did, and she'd only caught glimpses of him around town during the course of his duties, she began to feel daunted.

Sadness would not pass through her unaccompanied. It haunted her along with many other feelings, all vying for her attentions, all crying to be dealt with first. A myriad of erratic thoughts and feelings bombarded her at any given moment, giving her pause. There was no study she could partake, no council she could seek, no trust to which she could cling. Rose had never felt so solitary.

On one particularly glorious day in early summer, Rose felt like dancing. Her gait bounced as if to invisible music and her smile—perpetual. Her feet tapped to the spirited rhythm of a heartbeat. Life felt like fresh spring.

However, on this most conspicuous day, Rose had deeper reasons for a joyous demeanor and a pert glow. For truly, on such an auspicious occasion, her feet strode not to the beat of her own heart, but of his.

The moment had come and it was to be today. She walked in a bee-line toward the office of the magistrate where her appointment would be met by the figure occupying all her dreams of late.

Although her joy may have been premature as she was not going to meet for any social reasons or even a precursor to courtship. Nay, this day she would become the new secretary for the office, thus giving her both a place of respect and a proximity to Wilford Denton Hemmingforth.

Wrong though it may have been for her to have such thoughts; her mind put their names together in whimsical images of marriage. Rose Riley Antonia Hemmingforth, many would think it sinful to speak those names aloud in this manner.

Even so, her mind sang the names. She could see them in writing, though she dare not put pen to paper for fear of being overseen. As her hand touched the door of the highest office in the township, the image of writing shattered away as might a tea cup dropped. Her heart felt as if it would burst with anticipation.

Public offices demanded no knock and she entered with only the slightest of hesitations. Once inside, she stood immobile as she absorbed her surroundings. Surroundings of the like she'd never beheld.

Ornate could be considered self-gratifying and sacrilegious and yet intricate carvings and delicate scroll-work decorated the majority of furnishings. The magistrate, himself, sat behind a desk larger than any Rose had ever laid eyes upon. She felt diminished, overshadowed by its enormity.

With light sparse and furnishings heavy, the room gave the appearance more of storage than function, though Rose found the fragrance much less distasteful. Being of small stature herself, she felt intimidation from every direction and cowered from imagined overbearing. But was it *entirely* imagined?

The magistrate stood and peered down at her with enigmatic eyes. For the moment she felt a pang of guilt, as if she were of criminal background and he the acting judge. His voice came as thunder yet she felt soothed in a way she could not easily put to words.

"Is there some service this office can perform for you, Miss...uh?"

Try as she might, Rose could keep the quiver from her voice only in the intent. The sound that came out, despite her best efforts to the contrary, shook delicately—meekly. It sounded like fear, though she should feel none. This disturbed her sereneness and faltered her resolve.

"I am Rose Antonia Riley Ford. I have been appointed to the post of secretary to the magistrate, good sir," she spoke as she curtseyed. "Be that the title given you?" she asked, though she knew it to be so. She struggled to keep her eyes from meeting his as so many men had done to her in the past. Hers was not humble obedience but fright. Fear of being caught with a lustful thought in her head. Although such urges were abated…mostly, she felt them close by—never far from her—and feared their sudden and unpredicted return

"I am he."

In all things, Rose knew she must remain lady-like and proper. She felt she should look chaste and mannered, knowing her place. She must present the *new* her, despite the *old* feelings that rose within to belie and unravel her resolve.

Rose decided the turmoil inside her young mind must be like unto the feeling of a child when approaching a new horse. The beauty of the majestic beast lured while the sinewy musculature frightened, telling of its strength, and only a narrow tether held it abay.

The magistrate must surely have seen the struggle taking place within her very eyes, for as he descended toward her, he too took on a new expression. His—one of concern, perhaps even pity, a little too fatherly, he hurried to her side.

"Truly, why have you come, my child?"

"'Twould please me greatly to work for the office of the magistrate, your honor."

"My dear, there is no need to address me in such form. I am not an officer of the high court. Nor am I royalty."

"I would be remiss to allow my manners to falter, sir. I've been taught well how to address my betters."

"My dear, the brilliance of the very sun shines from your lovely smile, whilst I am but a humble shadow," he said, bowing formally.

"Oh, sir," she fluttered. "You do me too much honor. I assure you, I am not worthy."

"My dear young maiden, have I not seen you noticing me as we passed in the street? Several have been the times when the smile glimpsed from the corner of my eye has turned an otherwise dreadful day into complete joy."

Rose's cheeks flared with shame even as the sweetest smile spread from the corners of her mouth. The syrupy sounds that flowed as he spake made her head swim in wonderful images of hope and happiness. With some effort she looked up and...met his gaze.

"What would be the appropriate manner to address you, my lord?" she mouthed in bold tones.

"I should think 'Mr. Hemmingforth' would be an acceptable method of address. And if not offended, I shall henceforth refer to you as 'Miss Ford'."

"It would be an honor, sir...I mean, Mr. Hemmingforth." Now she fluttered all over. Dark desires and wholesome happiness fought with each other—mortal enemies—a battle perhaps of the ages, and it took place in all corners of her heart.

"Then come, Miss Ford, attend me. This," he pointed at a prominent desk, smaller than his and yet larger still than any she'd ever seen, "shall be where you will carry out your daily tasks. And may I say this room could not be lovelier."

"Thank you, Mr. Hemmingforth. May I inquire about the ornature?"

"A bit too much, perhaps?" his question given the semblance of rudeness by the aversion of his eyes as he surveyed the room. "And myself, no antiquist."

"It does appear a trifle vain, if you don't mind my saying so, sir."

"The truth is," he spoke quieter now, "some years ago I worked for the office of taxation and supplication. There was a man of some prominence in town who had a stroke of ill fate.

"He'd been tilling the soil in preparation for the next planting season and he struck open a vein of crude. Needless to say, it laid waste his entire crop before it could ever be planted."

"Ooh, the poor man," Rose offered compassionately.

"Yes. To make matters worse, not six months later I per chance found myself to be strolling through the office of patents, as I had business there, and overheard a rather zealous young lad carrying on about how he'd come up with a use for the vile substance."

"Indeed?"

"Well the prominent man could not pay his taxes. The rules are very rigid, leaving no margin for sentiment. Foreclosure was imminent, but he was not to be beaten."

"He created this beautiful woodwork?" Rose asked.

"He most certainly did. He labored for months. With no crop there was naught for him to do otherwise. So you see, my dear Miss Ford, I do not keep them," he pointed at his furnishings as he spoke, "out of vanity. The pride of having known such a talented man is my only sin. Touching the hand of a man so blessed by God creates a value to me that no monies could purchase."

"That is a fascinating story, Mr. Hemmingforth. It was very generous of you to offer that pour soul another means by which to keep his home."

"Generosity had little to do with it. In my humble opinion, his work is worth far more than money owed."

"You could have returned them."

Hemmingforth seemed hurt, as if he'd been asked to hand off his favorite pipe to a passerby on the street.

"I don't know that I have the heart to part with them. It would be akin to giving away a family heirloom."

Rose remembered a time of lost innocence in her own life—a time she'd given away something precious—a family heirloom, of sorts, lost, never to be returned. A touch of sadness crept into her smile.

Rose lived and studied and played in that town as a child until the summer after passing her seventeenth birthday when she happened upon a scene of such surprise and distaste that she could not avert her eyes.

Strolling aimlessly toward the small river that provided drinking water for the town, Rose hardly noticed any particular detail. She sought only an afternoon unfettered by obligations—not to mention the sound of horses which she found unpleasant—and to enjoy the beauties of nature.

As the trees yielded and she passed back into the sunlight near the banks, she could hear the babbling water and smell the fish and mud—though less pleasant than the smell of horses, she always felt calm when near the river. She just stood and admired the area as she often did, but when she looked toward the North, she saw.

Blinking several times to wipe out the image, she was afforded a full view of them. A boy she knew but not by name lay on top of Cynthia Greenwold, a girl from Rose's class. Neither wore a stitch of clothing.

The most interesting things were happening and Rose studied intently. Driven by budding forces she did not understand, she lost track of time. Her eyes glazed as she became unaware of her surroundings. When she found her sight once again she discovered the two had gone and her hands were buried under her own ankle-length dress. She was exposed.

Embarrassment swept in quickly and she dropped the hem of her dress down appropriately, looking around for witnesses. Her maiden purity remained untarnished by any eyes she could see. Accepting her good fortune, Rose returned to her home and the innocence of her family.

But the day after the next, whilst walking to the general store with vegetables from her garden to trade, a boy approached. He spoke in mannered tones...at first.

"Good day," his voice almost sang.

"And a fine day it is," Rose replied with a slight curtsey.

"I've seen you about, Miss—"

"Ford," she answered curtly. "And I would say you have. After all, I live here."

"Do you often walk by the river?"

His words struck her as a hand and she started, blinking back the beginnings of tears. Would that she could be sure he hadn't seen her base act, but some intuition told her he was about to reveal he had. A flush came to her cheeks and she lowered her eyes.

In that moment, he knew. Perhaps he had before, but now he was assured, convinced further by her expressions of guilt before even being confronted.

She had spoken her words of confession without muttering a sound. No doubt the town leaders would be proud of her confessions.

"Perhaps we could walk together," he said with abominableness.

"But I know not even your name, good sir."

"Tim Henning, at your service. A pleasure to meet you." He bowed accordingly.

"'Twould be inappropriate for us to be seen."

"Then we shall not be seen."

And then, rather suddenly, some sparkle in his eyes became apparent to her. She recognized him as the boy from the river before. Rose chastised herself for not seeing it when he'd first approached her. He'd been with Cynthia Greenwold on that day. Now, she too was convinced this young man had seen her own sinful actions. Her face flushed further but her curiosity swelled.

Thoughts of abjuration swept through her mind and she trembled. Her vows to the church would be for naught and her soul would be cast out. Confused, driven both by morals and desires alike, her feet chose for her. She made way in a different direction, leaving the boy without so much as a by-your-leave, though it be away from her chosen path.

The young Mr. Henning, not so easily put aside, accosted her once again, on a later day—this time managing to find her near the river. She'd come to ponder the thoughts he had first planted within her that now raged like a wildfire.

Morality, a subject always so crisp and simple, confused the maiden and she muttered to none but herself as a feeble woman near death. She spoke to no one yet sound escaped her lips. One might have thought her possessed, had they happened upon her as Tim Henning did.

He did not think her possessed or feeble. He thought her beautiful and approached in quiet. His hands were on her before she was aware of his presence. She struggled in reaction but soon succumbed to the touch of his manly strength. He touched her in ways not appropriate—sinful. And Rose found herself enjoying the warmth he ignited within her.

Time became as a blur, much the same way it had the day she'd seen him with Cynthia. Only glimpses of consciousness washed through her mind. They came in waves. At one point, her clothes had been removed. She became completely seduced by black desires and he amorally led her to further depths with the touch of his fingers—and his lips.

His weight on her gave her a feeling of safety, and even the pain of him stabbing her in that manner offered some strange comfort. Deep inside she longed for the moment not to end. This, more than any other thing, convinced her what they were doing was evil. And she definitely would not stop.

It took little time for Rose to master the simple skills required of her. At the end of three months, the Magistrate granted her charge over the entire office leaving him to matters of greater import as his position demanded.

Any person or home with so much as a rumor of un-Godliness would be called before him to answer charges of heresy or worse. And while Rose felt uneasy about the heavy sweep of righteousness that rolled over the town and risked washing away all remnants thereof, it had gone well into removing all evidence of evil as it intended.

She remembered her and poor Tim had coupled several times before the unfortunate accident with the new stallion his father bought. He'd not been an evil boy and Rose felt something akin to love for his show of intimacy. She later found that most girls fell in love with their first, only most waited until marriage before engaging in such physical couplings.

Sometimes tears would come, but they would be short lived as a boy walked by and drew her attention away from the painful memories. She would concern over a lack of conscience, and then a new boy would be on her—and in her. In those younger days, it happened often.

In Rose's life, distractions came easily. Despite her deep concern for the survival of the town, one late summer day Rose found reason to put aside her thoughts for sake of new ones. Wilford offered her thoughts that would occupy her mind for many nights to come.

"Miss Ford?" Wilford called on an early Friday afternoon.

"Mr. Hemmingforth, you startled me. I did not hear you enter."

"Forgive me. I..."

For the first time since she laid eyes on him, Wilford faltered. He seemed not to know how to proceed.

"Is there anything wrong, sir?"

"Wrong?"

"Has my work dissatisfied you in some way?"

"No. Certainly not. However, I wonder if you would be so kind as to attend Sunday meeting with me."

Rose's heart did a summersault. She fought to suppress her joy so her answer would sound calm. She felt no need to consider the offer, she knew her answer, and yet she hesitated. At times like these, control could be so elusive. Finally, she turned.

"I would be honored, Mr. Hemmingforth."

"Good." He too breathed a sigh of relief. 'Then it's settled."

Rose enjoyed the way her life began to unfold. First came the Sunday meeting. After which she accepted every opportunity to spend time with him. *Perhaps before long*, she hoped, *he will brave an announcement of our courtship.* It would come as no surprise to the townspeople who all had eyes.

Within her heart Rose could still, on occasion, hear the call of black desire sweeping over her soul like a cloud blocking the sun. Sometimes these moments were quite overwhelming. However, fortune had graced her—she'd endured most of these in private. After a time, and some embarrassment, she'd learned several methods of self-satisfaction. These would abate the call, if only for a short time. And although the scent that remained on her fingers allured, it did little to keep hidden her true nature.

The strongest power to help overcome that call was her proximity with Wilford. His strength, his heart, his voice—all were strong medicines in fighting the disease that churned within her most distant recesses. And she longed to eradicate it, to rid herself of its vile presence. She listened to the melody of his words at every opportunity.

No doctor could help but perhaps God had shown her a path to salvation. She felt compelled to walk it as narrowly as possible for surely there would be no alternate route. All other roads led away and she would forever be damned. Eternity did not frighten Rose but eternal damnation should not be sought by anyone believing of God, not as long as she still had the will to choose and the strength to govern her emotions—if only a little.

Rose felt assured, as days became cooler and were called weeks, there would be no evil dare set roots in Hemmingforth. As it surely had become a town where the sun shone always and God Himself came to rest from fighting the evils that lay elsewhere.

Let it not be said there is no evil one but only blackness within a person's heart. For verily, on that day late in November as everyone prepared for their feast of giving thanks, an evil greater than any known in the little town had taken notice of the war waged against it and the losses incurred.

On a dark night, as temperatures dropped in foretelling of a strong winter, the evil one sent a messenger to the unwary town. Not one to be known outright, he sent a messenger not of savagery but of subterfuge.

His messenger arrived only two nights after the feast had passed and people still hid from the gluttony of which they'd partaken. The messenger, as with all sent by the dark lord, did not announce itself, rather taking quiet root, seeking out the softer soil to push through.

It could smell the weakness, the desire, in a person's heart, even from great distance. Drawn to it as a moth, it gradually swept through the town, searching each person one by one until that bitter-cold night a week before the celebration of the birth of Christ, when it discovered the heart of Rose Riley Antonia Ford and the darkness that lay buried deep—yet remained.

The beast's messenger drew to it, swam in it, savored the taste as one might a fine wine. The messenger wrapped one soft, warm hand around Rose's heart and massaged lovingly. The other hand swept to her pudendum. The messenger rubbed vigorously but with great focus. Rose hugged her pillow tightly remaining asleep yet disturbed out of any *real* rest. When she awoke between dampened sheets she felt irritable and knew not why. Nocturnal emissions were an embarrassment and she scorned the hands that betrayed her steadfast effort to remain on the path.

Somewhere in the bowels of the earth the messenger sat in darkness, smiling. The heart it found that night would make a wonderful home. It could dwell there for eternity and not find unhappiness or boredom.

Something inside that heart said a great many conquests lay ahead and, properly tempted, the whole of the town would sway and in time, falter. The evil one would be pleased and reward the messenger. But this town would offer its own rewards.

The grey haze of temptation swept over the land and lay ankle deep and—for the lack of sight into the supernatural—could be seen by none. Verily, no sign of evil would be foreseen or even felt until the messenger made ready to allow it.

That dark and ominous day didst arrive for any to witness on three days past the celebration of the New

Year. It came in the guise of innocence, announcing its presence from within a girl—a mere teen.

It took over her body as easily as one dons a suit. It bade her make evil where no man would look yet many would dare go—with proper persuasion. As the girl seduced each new man to sin, the messenger grew stronger, it would need that strength to control someone strong willed. Someone like Rose Antonia Riley Ford. Into her, the messenger thought, every man in town would come. And it would have say over all lest it smite them with its power. Power it would soon have. Power it would soon wield.

But not yet.

Winter blew in with a bitter tooth to gnaw at the mortal flesh of the good people of Hemmingforth. Wind, borne of the north, could not be stopped by something as trivial as a wall. And the fires stoked against it did little to bring about true warmth to any souls nearby.

Yet walls were constructed to force its direction in hopes of protecting that mortal flesh. And fires were stoked to head off the burn of the icy north winds. Oft times these very walls were put so deeply upon by that wind they wouldst sway with the rhythm of the music brought about by the gales themselves. And the people huddled together against the threat put to them, pulling ever closer to the fire.

The danger lived and fell upon them as a blanket against the cold whistling outside the flimsy walls. But the truth of its being and purpose was surely lost on the people. For true evil did not reside within the winds. Thus, the people were blinded by their innocence and genuine dependence on a man they called Magistrate.

He, as any other mortal soul, could not save them from the evil, be it the cold, pounding of winter's fist or the messenger sent from the dark lord. The solitude of winter so struck the tiny town even that messenger would not dare come forth and present itself, should it ever have chosen to do so.

Cold is not the way of the evil one. He hath chosen the fires deep in the belly of the Earth for reasons. And, indeed, come spring thaw, many would begrave loved ones taken by the dropping temperatures. This served no purpose nor was it analogous to the messenger's goal.

The young girl's cajoling postponed, and the messenger's strength waning, time slid by as a snail in tree sap and the evil one grew impatient. Hope for an early thaw faded as the cold battered on through February and March. In the end there would be many dead, including some who might succumb to the wiles of a girl who lacked the grace of age to resist.

Any number of weak-spirited men would fall into her web of jasmine and musk, the scents of womanhood she'd not yet achieved. The pools of her eyes would devour them and seduce them. Her body, not yet fully blossomed would become as a receptacle for their seed. All thoughts of decency would be cast aside while in her. And a tiny flame of desire for her would continue to burn within them even after they managed to get away. The evil living among them had taught her well how to use these weapons and others.

Good men of moral standing would seldom take notice of such a girl but the messenger lent her the power to so confuse and entice, few had the fortitude to say, *away!* And many would lay with her as the spring came upon them and the air became warm enough for such fornications to take place outside.

For such as a teen-aged girl would have no home of her own in which to make private her true purpose. So, behind a barn, inside a stable, where the forest became thick, even inside the church as the pastor was about, these became her boudoir. And her tender young body offered release from the lust she, herself placed in their hearts to draw them closer into her. And she collected the seed so craved, though she knew not from whence such cravings sprang.

Her given name, she could hardly remember, Elisabeth...*something*. The strength to retain her true self grew faint with each moment passing even as the thoughts of another became like unto her own. She felt

283

a growing want for the men who entered and knew not how to stop the evil that had overtaken her morality.

At just barely over seventeen, she knew only of chores and mischief. She would shy away from boys because...they were boys. Her and the other girls would giggle and talk about them. Then—homework and chores. But never would they touch one, for truly their immortal souls would be lost. The pastor had said as much in his sermon.

Elisabeth felt her soul slipping away as water from a cup with holes. Even as this, the ninth man, came into her and she felt the pleasure of his warmth, she knew her soul journeyed away and would be kept from her forever. It would languish in the fires of hell as she, all the while, led one man after another away from the cross of his own salvation.

Was such meant to be the whole of her life? Would there be no other place for her to lie but beneath the hardness of a man, all men. Some part of what was left of Elisabeth wept. She made a last noble effort to take back that which had been hers, but she had not the strength and her efforts availed her naught. She slumped beneath this man even as he became mortal inside her, as was the way with each and all of them.

Knowing the deed to be done and be there no turning back, the man left hurriedly, taking his chagrin with him. Elisabeth lay for a moment; still, floating on her thoughts, then gathered her garmenture and slithered into the brightness of an otherwise innocent day.

As she set about the task of imitating a person walking on the street, she saw the face of the man who had so recently been inside her. Without conscience, no reason to evade, she strode ahead with no sign of remorse. The man, to the contrary, studied the small patches of grass that still grew in the street with earnest. His head bobbed from side to side as if in search of retreat.

"Fine day, good sir," Elisabeth spoke, as if naught were out of ordinary.

"F-Fine day, young m-miss," he stammered. Fortune favored him and no one observed his discomfort. He walked on, temporarily extricated, though his desire mounted and he would seek out her immature pleasures again soon, and a smile of devious proportions encroached upon Elisabeth's face.

The hint of a scent brought on by her actions didst not cause her embarrassment but urged her to further debauchery. She studied the path ahead for another tasty treat to explore the stables with. The shadows there appealed to her and cessated her uneasiness.

But empty streets met her eyes and sadness— her heart. She knew despair and solitude before womanhood. In many ways, her young life began similar to Rose's, manipulated by a pull stronger than any control. Elisabeth had as much power to resist as any child.

The beast lay happy within the bosom of the young girl. But its true goal and ultimate fruition would come from occupying the older and ever-more experienced Rose Antonia Riley Ford. She would be the tool with which it would conquer this town and then—the world, perhaps?

The demon lay upon bedrock; resting, plotting, as the girl, Elisabeth, slept. The time had come to exercise the power it had, test its bounds. Its time in the girl—nearly over, it looked upon the heart of Rose once again.

Many a night it visited her bosom, feeling the rise of her chest and the rhythm of her heart. The demon would touch her in that special place; a place no other could touch, or see. A place inside.

She would writhe to the pleasures she thought derived from her own hand and would often wake with embarrassment from such actions. At times she didst pursue such fleeting delights, but always at a time of her choosing and within her control. If she acted out in her sleep, what manner of control did she truly have? Surely even *her* demons had to rest, did they not? Still the creature of darkness had not the strength to dominate such a woman.

A sound! Strong, as though next to its ear, but clearly faraway, drew its attention away. It started. Searching its own feelings to discover those of another, it sought only to know. But truth be told, it feared what it might find, and with good reason. Elisabeth had gone to her father's tool shed. Her intentions...

The demon had to move quickly to interfere. Prevention was imperative; it had to stop her. What she planned...couldn't be allowed. It was not ready.

With an unholy link, established over many months, it could see through her eyes as its own. The rope looked to be three-quarters braid, very durable. The beast moved faster.

The images within its mind altered. It now gazed into the grain of a six-by-six wooden beam—just as the rope slipped over. The images became jumbled, perhaps because it *knew* where they led.

Once inside the shed, the beast stilled. Quiet came to its ears as darkness encroached upon its eyes. When it settled its sight on her body swaying in the air as the reeds of a willow, it stumbled.

With Elisabeth gone, it hadn't yet the power to take Rose; it would have to rely on her *weakness* for aid. The lust within Rose's heart would be that which allowed it access to the deepest regions of her soul. Perhaps it could persuade her with offers of the satisfaction she'd craved even so recently.

The beast had gathered some strength; the rest would be up to Rose.

A warm spring night, Rose wrestled with sheets that did not attack. Sweat beaded on her skin, smooth but toughened from hard work. Her mouth moved but nondescript sounds were all that escaped. Even though her lids stayed closed, it would have been easy for anyone to see her eyes darting from one side to another, up and down, in circles, completely out of control.

In frenzy her hands sought to hide between her legs, although their true purpose became clear within minutes as they found their own way to the tender folds of flesh that lay there—folds that moistened in anticipation of her touch. A reeling mind fought for control but base urges became deviant and proceeded in their own purpose, and at their own pace.

With wild images crashing through her mind and hands frantically jerking to an unheard rhythm, Rose drove herself to spasms that served only one need. Distressed as she slept, the nightmare fed further on by her physical exertions and twisted into something she could not possibly have dreamed up from her own Earthly experiences. She sat up quickly, disoriented, a struggled to breathe.

After realization dawned, she sobbed in despair. She worked at untying the sheets holding her fast and considered that she'd now been forced to become a morning shower person. The sheet knots resisted and she tugged harder, finally falling to the floor in complete disarray. Hysterical laughter dribbled from her lips.

"Can I have no control over these urges? Must I forever succumb to the temptation of the devil? Am I so damned?"

Rose had dreamed before, intense images and feelings, leading to physical interactions. This night had been different. This night something drew her, compelled her, she could feel its lure—its seduction. Something changed and she could decipher none of the images remaining in her early morning mind.

Living alone—perhaps the only good fortune she could tout—she rose without dressing, prepared the morning coffee to brew, and set about the necessity of that shower. She felt a new feeling of warmth inside— warmer than normal. Perhaps she'd fevered during the night. Most times when night fever struck, she bore the mark for many days—usually on the lip. But a healthy body was nothing to be ashamed of, even in a town as prudish as Hemmingforth.

However, no mark appeared and her skin didst feel dry and smooth as always. No sign of fever or other sickness could she find—and so it was that she went about her daily business as if nothing had fallen out of proper place.

Her first official duty was, as always, to the office of the magistrate. On this day, upon entering, she met with silence and dust. Had not the place been occupied as yet this day, and she being late? An eerie foreboding fell over her as she began to look about. She saw no signs to the contrary of order and yet the clouds of bad omens remained.

A singular piece of paper stuck out of the top drawer of Wilford's massive desk. Her curiosity would not allow her to consider looking away as her disobedient hand withdrew the missive. Her heart fluttered and her eyes darted around in search of another presence—any presence—from which she might take leave. Finding none, she moved toward the light and began reading the document.

Be it known that, on this the 28th day of November, in the year of Our Lord, 1807, Wilford Denton Hemmingforth didst willfully and knowingly cheat on an exam, causing disgrace to himself and this institution. His unconscionable act has left a black mark on the school and its faculty that will be difficult to remove.

At the behest of the headmaster, the typical punishment of expulsion has been commuted. While I am not privy to the wisdom behind such a decision, I will abide by it until I can see a way to overturn the decree. The immutable proof of young Mr. Hemmingforth's guilt is on file. I saw myself as his hand swayed toward another student and his eye turned to examine the other's answers.

Conduct of this caliber is unacceptable.
An honorable school such as this must not be
allowed to tarnish itself by overlooking such
actions even for the most exemplary reasons.
To my knowledge this is the first time this
facility has been witness to such an abomination
of the Code of Conduct, written so long ago by
those great scholars that founded the school.

I have more than enough proof to take
this higher, to the Magistrate himself, if need be.
But I write this more as a dedication. If by
chance, I am not conciliated in this venture, I
shall immediately and forthwith tender
my resignation with as much haste as I can
muster.

For I will not remain bedfellow to a
criminal mind—not he who would commit the
crime, nor he who wouldst cover it up.

I do declare on this day, my intention.

Marcus Danforth Brody
Professor of Practical Law
Walton University

When she'd finished, her teared eyes glanced toward the door—still undisturbed by the passage of even one soul, save her own. The parchment would not return to its original hiding place willingly and Rose pulled at the drawer. It came freely. Inside were any number of papers, all of which appeared as official and ominous as the first. She dared not read further—not only for fear of exposure, but of what she might learn.

Wilford had cheated. This alone brought a chill to Rose's heart. The stalwart man, God-fearing, upstanding, community leader, and Magistrate, possessed dark clouds in his past. Although Rose preferred not to judge another lest she be judged for her own less-than-proper life, she could not help but conclude that those who have a dark cloud often have several—perhaps many.

If she could be with such a man, she would know the truth—all truths. These truths, to which she had right, could only show her the man inside, bringing her deeper love through understanding. She would view his darkest secrets and then forgive him. Then a thought ran through her mind.

Would she be willing to give up all her darker secrets for his judgment? If so, would he be so quick to forgive? Rose shuddered to think of the calamity that would ensue should Wilford ever find the truth about her own past. She vowed that he would never be privy to such knowledge as long as she drew breath.

Without warning a tingle slithered through her body. This kind of tingle she knew from experience. Her promiscuous days gave her knowledge average, proper women would never know. The desires, dark and strong, welled up and tugged at the very core of her womanhood. While this was common on many days before, those times were passed and Rose had managed control over them for quite some time. That they should suddenly reappear surprised her more than if someone had walked in and caught her rifling through Wilford's desk.

The few memories that came to mind as she reminded of her past should not have been sufficient to bring about such strong urges. And yet, here she stood, in the magistrate's office, inappropriately going through private mailings, and being overwhelmed by deviant needs. Could the knowledge of Wilford's unclean past have provoked her own in such a manner?

She thought not. However, the urge to drop her hands and rub the desire away became too much. Knowing she would read them later, Rose returned the letters to the desk drawer and made her way to the shadows of the office behind her own desk. Once there, out of sight of anyone that might enter, but where she could clearly see the door, she began a ritual she'd not partaken of in several weeks.

Dousing the fires that burned within took an act scorned by God, but the alternative would be even less accepted. She'd thought herself well past being under the influence of such feelings and counted herself far better off for it—knowing her return to salvation would include abstention from such thoughts. *Where is the strong voice of Wilford when I need him so?*

Once finished she found herself still so overcome with need that she began again almost instantly. A second brief peak took her and she felt little better. Once the third came and went she began to concern for her health—hardly noticing if anyone had entered the office. She knew something was very wrong, as she could not withdraw her hands without feeling nauseous for a moment, then her hands would fall quickly back to her lap.

Slumped back in her creaking wooden chair, she pushed for another pleasure moment and then another, hoping each would bring the great release that would allow her to remove the devilish hands and focus on things proper. Several moments felt quite intense and yet her need continued. *Is there no satisfying this need? Can I not withdraw my hands from their fiendish work and set them to rights again?*

Rose struggled to make her hands obey her will. They'd gone about their own business far long enough and she would begin the work of her station. To do this, she needed her hands to be free of their self-chosen obligation. Time and again she raised them, thinking this time she could free herself from this devil's grip, then they would plummet back to their dark work that felt so good at first but now became quite painful. She knew not what drew them back—only that the urge was not of her own design.

The fight ensued. In her favor, Rose fought valiantly to bring about an end to the debacle. Try as she might she could not gain control over her wanton hands—if indeed she ever had such power. Losing count and most all coherence, she started upright at the sound of the front door being swung back with fury and banging against the storage cabinets that stood two-high behind it.

A burly man with dirty clothes entered, sporting an unkempt beard and scraggly hair. He paused to look around as his eyes adjusted to the shadow's contrast from the bright sun that filled the street outside. His recovery seemed to come quickly by Rose's measure. After hardly a moment he noticed her and approached. Two other men came in and stood behind the first. She managed to sit upright and appear proper, although one hand remained beneath the desk, continuing on its evil mission even as he spoke to her.

"There a man here named Hemmingforth?" His poor English and uneducated manner came through in loud tones and terrible breath.

"I-I..." Rose stammered beneath the man's stern voice and the unrelenting stroke of her fingers. "No," she managed.

"Damn, missed him again." The man looked around, then snapped back to Rose. "What is that peculiar smell?"

"Smell? I smell nothing, good sir."

The man offered a grunt in response. "When did you see him last?"

"Yesterday," she squeaked.

"So he's still in town?"

Rose chirped a bit but made no comprehendible noise. Obviously the man understood the noise to mean 'yes'. He stepped back. Perhaps he realized that he frightened the young girl.

"I'll be back."

As quickly as he'd entered, the door closed behind him and the other two with a loud slam, shaking dust from the rafters. He may have been overzealous but Rose considered it might be more. She thought perhaps he could be angry at Wilford. She feared he might intend harm and considered how to warn the man she loved. But she knew not whence he'd gone or how to find him.

At the very least, her worry, in the end, had distracted her wayward hands.

The man slithered in from behind, causing little noise but making his presence known. The evil snake—Rose knew it to be the same from the Garden of Eden—entered her with the gentleness of a man intent on causing pain. Delirious, she fought to recognize the surroundings, and perhaps the man that violated her in such a manner.

Although Sodom had been destroyed and she knew her act warranted damnation, yet she thrust herself back against his lustful advances in desire. Unable to resist the call of the flesh, she not only participated, but—*God save me*—enjoyed. The pressure asserted inside her caused pain and still she called for it to continue with every ounce of her being. She could not have asked for more if she begged out loud, which she dared not do for fear of being caught in such an act.

Again she made effort to turn and know the man who certainly knew her. With her dress thrown up her back and her petticoat around her ankles, she felt much more exposed than just her body. Somehow her soul lay out for all to see—the urges that grew within her had now come out for sunshine and she stood vulnerable.

Wicked thoughts ran through her head. She drew images of each and every man in town taking turns in her as she leaned against the fence and waited—exposed and offering. More than simple images, she *wanted* them in her, fighting for a turn, coming around for seconds, following her home, unable to resist.

Bile rose in her throat juxtaposing the joy she felt in her nether region. As the man finished and left traces of himself behind, she turned to catch a last chance look at his face, to know, at least, who she'd lain with. If she were to risk the budding love she had with Wilford, let it not be for some passing moment with a man she hardly knew.

Though turning away, his face offered enough for her to see. One of the two men who had visited the Magistrate's office on that very morn, now shuffled away carrying with him a confused look. She could see

297

his despair. He knew not why he'd come. Rose could find no memory of the experience, either—save the ending. Had she lured him? Did he force her? Would anyone in town have noticed?

But in Rose's deepest consciousness remained one paramount question, rising above all others, drawing her focus from all others. She focused on it, turning it over in her mind to see it from all sides. The question shown clear, but the answer eluded her as much as any other she'd encountered in her life.

Why have I taken up my old ways once again?

The demon lay in the soft folds at the bottom of Rose's heart, warm and cozy. It found tugging the right strings easy with a woman half way to hell already. She took the journey with so little provocation; the demon hardly had to work at all. Life would only get easier from this point forward and the town was as good as handed over to the evil one.

Looking out through the eyes of the woman, it desired a further test of her obedience and devotion—if not to him, at least to the desires that burned between her legs, desires of the past never fully quenched. It watched as she walked through town trying to avoid others, hoping to take back control.

"Nay, control is mine," it scratched at her, even though she could not truly hear.

But the demon knew it'd won the battle, even though it did not understand her unorthodox method of coupling. It could see inside her heart and knew her desires had been rekindled and, with a little of its help, would burn hotter than the fires of hell itself.

The seed had been planted. It would grow.

Rose walked awkwardly as the pain kept her from proper gait. She struggled to portray a lady-like image while intentionally avoiding populated areas for fear of having to address questions for which she had no answers. She wanted only to go home. Once there she would pray for forgiveness and strength to overcome the urges welling within.

As she turned north toward the part of town where her small ranch stood, she spotted Jimmy Waller. A man in his own right, but just barely, he looked somehow more enticing than Rose could ever remember. Her mouth became dry as she turned her step slightly in his direction. Life became fuzzy.

When her mind cleared enough for coherent thought, she discovered herself lying on her back in the hay with Jimmy on top, pounding into her like a rabbit. His youth drew him to finish in a very short time. His seed shooting into her, she wondered why she didn't feel disappointment as she would have in the past.

As soon as the deed was done and she found herself back on her way home, Rose pondered. Something had surely changed in her. In the past, her urges were for her own satisfaction and yet she enjoyed pain from one man, and brevity from another. Neither of which would satisfy the needs of a woman like her.

Nevertheless, she felt satisfied. Nay, euphoric, complete, as if her day could not have concluded without her dangerous liaison along the way. Never had feelings such as these entered her mind. Had the devil completely taken over her soul and she no longer walked the path of salvation she'd sought so long?

Once inside the privacy of her own home, she knelt at her bedside, sobbing, calling upon the name of the Lord to come into her life and bring His salvation. *Wield Your mighty sword, just and true, and cut away the evilness that dwells within my very body. Bring me the strength to stand against the call of animal lust overflowing in my soul. Wash away the blackness that hast befallen me, Oh Lord, that I may, once again follow in Your footsteps. Lead me…away…*

The words became difficult as she felt pain inside.

…from…the evil…that would…dwell…inside…

Rose took deep breaths, forcing each word out, focusing on her lips to form each syllable properly. She would not allow her grammar to slip while she spoke to God.

...the...body...of...a...girl...who...would...be...your...

Rose collapsed to the floor. Unconscious before her head hit the wood, she fell instantly to a dream state that had her tossing about like someone demon possessed. Her dark dream images flashed into her mind with increasing speed.

When she woke in the middle of the night she felt surprise at how many of the images remained. At first she could see the parade of men, lined up, trousers down, taking turns in her as she held tightly to the fence—the only thing around solid enough to offer support. For hours she collected each seed and waited for the next, only having to wait for the briefest of seconds. Then another man would enter her. Some even sodomized her.

Afterward, she saw images of women, gripping her breasts, twisting her nipples, as another man gave up his mortality inside her from behind. The women watched in glee as each took his turn. Sometimes they too were without clothes, most only from waist up but many completely—even old Mrs Whippel, whom Rose regretted seeing naked more than anything else. Rose felt like she'd been shackled in the square and each of the townspeople could walk by and throw vegetables at her or whip her at whim.

But she wore not shackles. Her hands remained free to move. Yet move she did not. She waited, longing for the next and the next, moaning under the pinching pressure of the women who also took turns at her chest. Pain and pleasure mixed together so well, like an onion soup with just the right amount of beef flavor. She yearned for each and every diabolical moment as she sank further into depravity.

And the images became darker, more exotic and deviant.

In the dream she closed her eyes. Not in embarrassment, but waiting—yearning for the next entry which took longer. In her delirium she felt a tap on her head. When she opened her mouth to speak she discovered a man there, as well. A thing to do she'd never imagined and could barely tolerate—and still she wanted it.

In time, perhaps minutes, three men entered her at once. Although she could not, heretofore, have imagined how it would be possible, it nevertheless happened. She could not fathom how all could fit, but she wanted it. She wanted it desperately. If she'd known she could have asked for such a thing she would have begged. She thought she had sunk to the deepest depths possible. But darkness had not fully fallen on her dream state as yet.

She felt the stinging sensation across her buttocks—sending shivers of delight up her spine. Rose had felt pain before, even from childhood when she'd earned a stern beating from her father. But nothing had given her body such a surge of joy as this had. Perhaps, she thought as she dreamed, it is because the men are using me and it feels so good.

She turned at the second strike of pain and noticed a man behind her—inside her—using a switch across her bare skin. In her dream the man's face became her father's. But her father had never touched her inappropriately like this man was doing. The pain and pleasure mixed to send her somewhere past delirium and into the twilight world where shadows came to life and your head could spin and you lose your way in a moment.

She felt another stripped tree branch slap across her back and still another striking her underneath— striping her belly and breasts with red welts of pain. The pain continued, as did the penetrations. Her mouth filled with one man after another, she could hardly scream for the torture to stop. And she wasn't sure she wanted it to stop. A deep seated, nymphomaniacal force drove her to willingly accept and even crave the continued degradation.

At some point, long after she'd lost track of time and count, everything stopped. Two women stayed near her head, on either side. They focused on something of interest Rose could not quite see. Something to do with her hands on the fence. *Oh, they're tying my hands to the rail. That's nice.*

Her delirious mind swung through each image as if it simply watched a play and someone else occupied the stage. Rose couldn't have resisted even if she wanted to. And she definitely did not want to. If she could have spoken, she would have asked for more.

Her mouth, suddenly devoid of manhood, now filled again with a ball and a cloth tied around her head holding it in. So her hands were tied and her mouth was tied. She looked to her feet. Sure enough, two men drove tent stakes into the ground next to her feet and two more women were tightly knotting rope around them and to her ankles. Rose felt powerless against the onslaught of what she felt sure was coming. A part of her feared, but another longed.

The woman on her right caught a string tossed from behind where Rose could see. She pulled it closer. The woman on Rose's left had one just like it. They walked their strings forward to where Rose's hands were tethered to the fence. They held tightly against something that jerked and tugged.

Confused, Rose tried to turn her head but was held fast by something or someone she could not see. But she knew something was back there, closing in, breathing on her in forceful snorts. She heard the bray of a horse at the same time she felt the splitting pain between her legs. She screamed against the ball in her mouth but very little sound came out. Pulling against the ties cut her skin and tiny droplets of blood dripped to the grass beneath.

She tried desperately to emancipate herself and soothe the pain wrought by some unseen demon man. After a moment she began to relax. The feeling became quite tolerable almost a pleasure. Her needs began to rise once again and she could feel release approaching. When she felt large amounts of something washing inside her, she went over the edge, succumbing to the ecstasy of peaking in such pain.

Her body collapsed, falling off the skewer that held her moments before. Exhausted, she simply fell to the ground and lay in a bath of sweat and other fluids. Her mind, sated and unable to focus, forced her eyes to glance up. The stallion stood proud: unaware of his indecent exposure. His large genital swung, dripping, glistening with juices from Rose.

She could not believe. The vomit she felt earlier rose and did not stop. Tears streamed from her eyes. No sobs could be heard even as her bonds were released and the ball fell from her mouth. Finally free she pulled herself into a fetal position at the base of the fence and once again looked at the stallion. It was no longer a stallion, but a demon. It stood as a man, although bent and twisted with evil. It had not skin.

The demon's penis, larger than any she'd ever seen, larger even than the stallion's, began to rise and enlarge. As it came to full glory, reaching near to the demon's neck and chin, Rose shuddered knowing that, as the demon was a horse, it entered her as a horse. This, much larger instrument, would surely rend her womanly parts perhaps completely in two.

The demon began to laugh a sharp, raspy sound that hurt Rose's ears and its penis bounced with the laughter. She looked around and saw everyone standing near her. They all laughed with the demon.

Most remained unclothed as though modesty had been abandoned for sake of the demon's will. She forced her sore hand to make the sign of the cross and the laughter grew.

Then the demon drew near and the laughter abated. Rose could already see the moisture dripping from its excited manhood. The men and women each grabbed her limbs, pulling her apart, spread, ready, inviting the demon inside. Her pudendum called for the penetration, but her mind didst tremble. The evil thing mounted her, poised for maximum insertion. Rose held her breath as the demon lifted its hips, like cocking a musket. Terror, beyond insanity, rent her unconscious in her dream, even as she awakened in reality.

Now sitting at her table she shivered in abject fear. Though only a dream, its vividness stabbed at her soul with all the pain of a real experience. And she could not shake the feeling that more than just dreams happened this night. Of course that would be absurd. She knew no one would treat her so and no demons existed in Hemmingforth.

Then she noticed her wrists were sore and on her right one—a small laceration.

When next she saw Wilford she ran to him for protection against something she neither could see nor explain. She'd done nothing. *Haven't you?* But even telling such a story could prove destructive. Dimorphic demons that seduced her and made the whole town partake? Even as she said it within the safety of her own mind it sounded preposterous. And completely unbelievable. When he asked her what's wrong, she could not possibly say. Only that she needed him.

"Where hast thou travelled, Mr. Hemmingforth?"

"Across the plains to the east. I had to conduct a matter of urgent business there. News came of a child possessed by a demon."

"Is that not a task best left to clergy?"

"Sometimes it takes more than one man to move a mountain, Miss Ford."

"Forgive me, sir. I meant no disrespect. But a man has come to town. He seeks you. He calls you by name."

"And did he offer his?"

"He did not." Somehow, Rose felt embarrassed by her ineptitude. In all truth, the burly man would probably not have given his name even if asked.

"Perhaps he will come by again today," Wilford said.

"He will, sir. He seemed most persistent."

"Did he, now? Did this urgency, by chance, have anything to do with another demon possession?"

"Not to my knowledge, but he spoke not of his mission. Only that he would engage with you. I think very little will deter him."

Wilford smiled. "You have done well, Miss Ford. Return to your duties. I shall be along in due time."

"As you wish, Mr. Hemmingforth." She couldn't be sure how to accept his compliment. But returning to work brought her some ease of mind as she now had focus. That is, until she passed through the doorway and spied her own chair; the memories of her uncontrollable hands came flooding back with fervor.

Apprehension flooded her body as she approached her position, knowing the evil must surely reside there, perhaps under the chair. Of course her Sunday school teachings told her that evil could live anywhere and only needed a catalyst. *Is that what I've become? A catalyst for evil? And what of the day Wilford discovers?*

Rose pushed such thoughts from her head as she set about her daily duties. This time, apparently, she had no reason to fear, though that strong emotion had overwhelmed her only moments before. But this time her hands did as she bade and no desires came to call.

Shadows grew long and her eyes tired when she next looked up from her work. Duty had kept Wilford away the rest of the day. She would have to close the office by herself. Although she closed many times and could accomplish the feat without needing to double check, eeriness befell her. She half expected some dark urge to pull at her hands or carry her feet to the barnyard. Perhaps the gruff stranger would reappear, frightening her more than before.

But once again her fears were in vain. No one called on the Magistrate's office and her hands minded their master. *Which master is that?* She meandered home, hoping Wilford would be seated at his desk on the morrow.

"Ah, Miss Ford. A pleasant morning to you."

"And to you, sir." She half expected him to not be there and yet she longed for his presence with every nerve in her body.

"A report came in this morning, to the sheriff's office."

"Oh, nothing too terrible, I hope."

"Three men were found dead just south of town."

"Dear God! How dreadful. Anyone we know?"

"I don't think so. Strangers, according to Sheriff Cornell."

"And the sheriff saw fit to inform you of such unpleasant news?"

"Being the Magistrate, I am privy to such dealings. He often consults me in legal issues. I am, after all, trained in these matters."

"Ah yes. That you are," Rose finished, turning toward her desk.

"Is there something wrong, Miss Ford?"

"Oh, no. Not at all, sir. I just wondered who those three men might be."

"And did anything come to mind?"

"I thought of the men who sought you and thought perhaps it might be them."

"Yes." Wilford seemed to accept her suggestion and mulled it deeply. "Perhaps they came for me and I was not here. Then, as they waited for the next day when they could return and address their business, some tragedy overtook them."

Rose found her desk and sat safely behind it as Wilford began to pace, speaking to himself maniacally. She'd never seen him like this before. Though much was mumbling, she could understand snippets—not quite every other word.

"If they...why didn't...could I be...how can I help?"

And so he rambled on, incoherent and disjointed, Rose allowed him room to explore whatever turmoil rampaged through his mind. When his eyes cleared and he spoke to Rose again, his mind seemed as focused as ever. But what he said took her aback more than her dream the night before.

"Miss Ford."

"Yes, Mr. Hemmingforth?"

"I thought perhaps…that is, the annual town picnic is coming soon and I thought—if no one has already asked—you might agree to accompany me."

"Mr. Hemmingforth! We've known each other little more than six months. It is a bit too soon to be courting, is it not?"

"I have been in town for nearly two years. Who is to decide at what time we first met."

"Is that not deceitful?"

"Perhaps you are right. Forgive me, Miss Ford. I overstepped my proper place."

Rose discovered victory wasn't so sweet after all. "I think I would like to go to the picnic with you, Mr. Hemmingforth."

His demeanor brightened visibly. He stood taller and his smile radiated his joy. She could not help but return it. "Do you not care about the proper way for us to conduct ourselves in public, then?"

Rose stood and approached him. She made one last glance around the room for assurance, despite knowing they were alone.

"I think an observant man like yourself already knows I have feelings for you—I have had since I first laid eyes on you. I care little for the whisperings of the townspeople. I've never been concerned with such drivel."

"So I have heard."

Rose became suspicious, stiffening. "What have you heard?"

"Nothing that would prevent me from asking you to the picnic."

She smiled. A true gentleman to the last. How could she do anything but accept?

The impromptu band, made mostly of homemade instruments, could not have sounded much more dissonant. Local farmers, she knew all their names, sat at one end of the field and did their best. Rose, who'd experienced the finer compositions of great masters like Mozart and Dvorák, knew the difference. To the contrary, many of the people living in Hemmingforth could not tell, or chose not to care. They danced spritely and laughed loudly.

Rose thought they could adapt the same attitude toward her and Wilford. It may not sit well on their palate, but they could just keep their cares to themselves. She had wanted to be with Wilford since the beginning and she wouldn't allow a budding relationship to turn sour on the count of the inability of other people to keep their condescending mouths shut. She needed no acceptance from them. She never had in the past.

A brief shudder ran through her as she thought about what stories Wilford might have been told. Her only comfort came from the fact he still asked her and he walked proudly next to her as they entered the town square in full view of everyone else. Rose caught a few unfriendly stares but Wilford seemed not to notice.

Rose knew he did not have a blind eye and therefore probably saw all, but rather chose to ignore such condescencions in favor of the more Christian attitude of forgiveness. Something that resembled real love bloomed in her heart and she looked up at the eyes of the man standing next to her. He caught glimpse of her stare.

"Are you uncomfortable? Would you like to leave?"

"I feel wonderful. I do not wish to leave, but if we must, let us be together."

"A few upturned noses do not bother me. From that angle, I see directly up their nostrils at how tiny their brains are."

Rose could not suppress her laughter. She reached over to grip his arm which elicited more glares. To Rose, it could become a game. The more brazen she became, the more open their mouths would fall. She imagined their jaws would reach the limit before her daring. An image she could not squelch flashed into her mind.

She saw herself against the horse post, bent over as in her dream, dress thrown up her back. Wilton took advantage without shame. She could imagine people running, covering the eyes of their children, even some who stayed and watched—feigning disgust and horror while delighting in the immoral show.

She pushed the image out of her mind with some effort. She felt no sense indulging in such fantasies; they would only lead to troubles she could not undo. If she began to feel those urges and could not control her hands, the square offered no privacy of which she could partake and no excuse for an early exit came to mind. In all, it would look far too suspicious and she would have no answers to the inevitable questions everyone would throw later.

All this and how bad it would make Wilford look. Perhaps some would think he had mistreated or insulted her. And worst is how he would feel. She thought he would be diminished and embarrassed, even though he'd done nothing inappropriate. She could not allow it. She pushed the effort harder, burying the erotic images floating around her mind.

As a distraction, Rose asked Wilford if he could dance. His twisted face suggested he would refuse, but he must have recanted the thought at seeing her joy. She grabbed his hand as casually as possible and skipped to the tiny area where everyone else who dared, danced. Her happiness culminated in her grace and well executed dance moves. Wilford, quite to her surprise, matched her technique precisely. They looked like a well-practiced stage act.

While many sat in awe, there still remained an undertone of judgment in the faces of people Rose had known most of her life. Some of them called themselves friend. She'd been to many of their homes, brought food, helped with the young when their mother was sick, and acted like a proper neighbor. However, now they didst not act so.

"It would seem, when I'm needed, I'm accepted. Otherwise, I am to be ostracized. For what, I do not know."

"Worry not, fair maiden, for I shall bear you succor and you shall not want for love."

She looked at Wilford as if he'd spoken in jest. But his face betrayed none. Try as she might, she could not fathom the depth of his mind nor the truth of his spirit. Once again she remembered the writing from his desk. He'd been cast out, a common criminal. And then men came looking, seeking his presence with urgency. And those men were now dead. Could Wilford have had something to do with that? Could he kill?

She looked into his eyes once again and saw no anger, no malice, no evil. She sought the comfort he offered, leaning just a bit closer, feeling the warmth of his body, though the summer solstice had just passed. His heat cast out the chill she felt from the eyes of others.

She'd not mentioned leaving and yet she did feel a need to be away from prying gazes. But she thought remaining would be more appropriate for her station—and, indeed, if she and Wilford would begin courting, there would be many such opportunities for people to judge or judge not. They would simply have to get over it.

"I could not be more grateful for your words of promise. I sought no reward, only to be accepted as equal. If this is not to be, among these people—my neighbors and friends, then I shall live without it. Jesus was persecuted as well. I am no better than He. The time has come for me to be with you and they shall see the happiness you bring me. Understanding, if it not be given now, will have to come later. I promise you, only *their* sleep will be disturbed, not mine."

Wilford laughed. "Child, you say the most uncanny things. I do believe Mrs. Cowen has made some punch. I've overheard several people exclaiming how marvelous it tastes. Would you care for some refreshment?"

"Oh, do fetch us some, good sir," she mocked, batting her eyelashes. "I would rather enjoy a cool drink."

Wilford went. He returned quickly with two tall cups of pink liquid and handed one to Rose, smiling handsomely. Chivalrous and mannered, he bowed slightly as she took the cup and brought it to her lips.

Oddly, Rose thought the elixir quite bland, offering only the savor of sweetness perhaps from honey. But the sun shone high and after drinking she did feel refreshed. She concluded that all she'd needed might have been some sugar. In the end, with an empty glass, she just felt much better about the day in all.

"Quite good," she lied as she handed the beaker back to Wilford. He took it and his own empty and returned them to the table from whence he first took them. Mrs. Cowen nodded her head to him in thanks. Rose assumed he'd paid her a compliment on the pallid liquid. If she'd returned the cups herself, she might not have been so gracious. The liquid was drank, the cups emptied, that should be sign enough of the delight it offered. Beyond that, compliments became lies.

When Wilford returned to the seat he'd left Rose on, and finding it empty, his eyes searched the horizon but discovered no sign of her. Confused he began walking about, but not asking anyone for sure they would scoff and tell him he'd be better off without her. He felt no such relief and continued his search in silence.

But no one even bothered to ask if they could help. No one noticed that he searched, or they did but chose to look away. *Would they turn their backs on me so quickly, and because of my association with Rose? Could they be so small-minded? They do not deserve one such as she.* Frustrated with their apathy, he strode on through the small crowd searching, sniffing for her perfume, looking for any—even the slightest—sign of his Rose.

Once away from the main group, all chattering about daily events which everyone already knew, he managed to hear other sounds. Sounds that came from different directions. Animals brayed about, creating their own special music, perhaps speaking to one another. But one noise Wilford could not so easily identify. He sought it out.

Behind a barn, as the afternoon sun set heavy, he saw the sight of his life. He watched in abject horror as the vision unfolded its devious tale, shaking him to his roots. His mouth fell open but no sound would come, though he knew not what to say at such a sight.

Wilford watched as a man—pants around his knees—pounded into some willing beauty beneath him, lying in tall grass. Her legs raised high and her voice a low growl, she drew the man into her, calling for each thrust, begging for no end to come. Female legs curled and her feet pushed at his back, forcing him deeper. Her wanton willingness accosted Wilford's soul more so than seeing such an act out in the open.

The man's eyes crossed and lips twisted as he squirmed his last into the maiden. Then he rose and adjusted himself. When the man turned to return to the picnic, Wilford saw his face clearly. Though he knew not the man's name, the look shone through clear. He was bewildered and contrite. He continued adjusting until he appeared normal and made his way back without seeing Wilford.

Then the woman rose. Her guttural chantings disturbed Wilford in a way he could not understand. She stood, fully nude, and bent for her clothing. When she again became upright, Wilford could see her face—the face of his beloved. Rose.

A sharp pain struck his chest and he fell to his knees. The image of beauty he saw in her body did little to alleviate the despair in his heart. He looked again, through the rungs of the fence and watched. She'd managed to get on her petticoat and worked mindlessly to finish—but not in any hurry Wilford could detect.

Her undergarment buttoned in the front, leaving small openings all the way down. She stopped a moment and examined the lowest of these, fingering her nether region. She withdrew the finger and brought it to her nose, breathing deeply the aroma that he felt certain remained there. He turned quickly, not wanting to see what he thought she would do next with that same finger.

When he looked back, she stood in the same place and in the same state of dress. But she looked directly at him, even though he could not be seen by mortal eye. But her eyes didst not spring from mortality. She glared in a way that spoke evil. Her eyes drew Wilford's energy right from his very body. He felt sure Rose's eyes glowed, with a red hue. Fear took over—far stronger than disgust, cutting deeper than betrayal. He took to his feet and made way back to his sanctorum.

Although the Magistrate Office was not the place of his dwelling, he spent much more time there than any other place. He felt safety amongst the furnishings and flotsam of a different life. All his focus, his idealism, his hold on reality came crashing down about his head and shoulders. He physically ducked, even though nothing substantial came close to hurting him.

But the desk supported him, protected him, comforted him. He gripped its edges and worked to control his breathing. He'd heard the stories loose lips cared to impart, but believed little. No one said anything about her eyes. This incident might not be borne of the same rumors spoken before, if such rumors could at all be trusted.

Something evil had taken hold of his beloved Rose. She would not have looked at him—or anyone else, for that matter—in such a way. And the act, how could she sink to such depths so casually and in open view of the public? Had she not decency? What if someone had seen? Perhaps even a child might have innocently wandered around that barn, and she cared not?

As he thought through the pain, he realized the act might be forgivable. The red eyes and demonic growling were unholy and truly evil. Those things, whatever caused her to do them, would have to be exorcised. She needed his help and he determined not to disappoint her. He sat up straighter, knowing his path, his duty—his only hope. For true love dwelled on the other side of those eyes—the unpossessed eyes, the blue eyes.

He longed to see her smile, once again innocent and fresh, looking at him with what he could only interpret as budding love. He could not repay all the wrongs he'd done, but somehow God blessed him with such honest love. Rose needed his help and he would give his very life if need be. Surely with a past as unclean as Wilford's, God would ask for penance. He would accept that penance, embrace it, satisfy it. He must find a way to keep her close. He knew a way. Perhaps the only way.

Wilford, lost in his own deep thoughts, jumped as the door swung open and late day gloom washed in, bringing dust with it. He looked up and saw the raw face of Rose, searching, fearful. When she spotted him, she relaxed and smiled, slouching slightly—a motion Wilford told her on several occasions he thought very uncomely.

"Wilford. I mean, Mr. Hemmingforth. There you are. When I lost you at the picnic I thought you'd abandoned me because of what the others were saying. I could not find you. I searched. Why did you not return to where I waited?"

"Why?" Wilford hesitated. Her eyes betrayed no untruth. She spoke as she felt. Somehow she knew not what she had done. He did not pretend to understand, only to care. And he needed no pretense for that. Stepping down from his desk platform, he approached her. "While it does not displease me to

321

hear my name upon your lips, it would be inappropriate for you to utter such a thing in front of others. At least wait until we can be wed."

"W-Wed?" Rose stepped back.

"Darling," Wilford continued, unsure what spurred him on and what end he sought. "Is it not what you want, as well?"

"I've thought of little else since I first saw you arrive in town."

"Then why can we not speak of it? We are alone."

"I-I just, how could I have been prepared?"

"You feel even as I," he said.

But she gathered not his true meaning. "I would try and make you a wonderful wife, Wilford. But I must speak with you about a matter of utmost urgency."

"You are troubled. Come and sit. Tell me what troubles you, my dear."

"I have such visions, I see things I could hardly describe."

"Dreams, you mean. Tell me of your dreams."

"I think they are more than mere dreams. I do not know, but something frightens me about them."

"Sit," he bade her.

When he sat next to her, he noticed something that shook him deeply. He could smell the intimacy on her. The act from barely ten minutes ago, still lingered on her as perfume. Though completely distracting, he struggled to focus on the matter at hand. A demon had possessed his beloved. In her normal state, she professed her love for him. When taken from him, she sought comfort in other ways—ways he could not accept or ignore.

"Can you describe these visions?"

"You do not believe. I can see in your eyes. Wilford, how can you say you love me and not believe?"

"Darling, didst thou not say these were visions? I believe you see, but I do not fear they will harm you. If I seem cavalier, do not take offense. I am here. I will help you. I promise. Now tell me of your visions."

"First you must promise to remember these are only visions. I would not become unlike the women you see about town. I've had a past, Wilford. I past of which I am not proud. But what I see is not the same. It is evil. I can feel it. I fear it dwells within me and I know not how to remove it."

"I promise I will not have you ostracized for simply telling me stories. For the sake of my title of Magistrate, what you tell me shall remain nothing more. Therefore, no action will be necessary—whether legal or moral. For they are only stories."

Rose smiled. "I believe you."

"So, your visions? How many have you had?"

"Many. I've lost count. They come day or night. I have no control and when they pass I find myself disoriented and frightened. However, I clearly remember details about them. They are of me— partaking of unspeakable acts. Lewd and lascivious behavior unbecoming of a lady. In fact, I dare say they would be considered unbecoming of a lowly dog. And yet I am there, each and every time, participating, enjoying, longing for more. It's more than just recurring; I believe I am calling it back."

"The vision?"

"Indeed."

"One cannot call upon a dream. Don't you see how foolish this all is? Surely you don't believe you leave your home or place of employment and perform intimate liaisons with strange gentlemen? Even saying it sounds absurd."

Rose sat back, unprepared she was for his revelation. How could he have known of the details of her visions? Did he know more? And how much could he see? How much would he understand and forgive? But if she didst only dream them, was forgiveness necessary? So many questions for which she had no answers.

"How did you know?"

"Know what?"

"What my dreams were about?"

Now it was Wilford's turn to sit back. In his mandatory French classes he'd learned a term they use. *Faux pas.* Had he committed such a bumbling act? He searched his memory, examining his words…and hers. She had not mentioned the truth about her dreams. He'd said it himself. *Perhaps it is time for all truths to come out.*

Rose contemplated the juxtaposition of her lusty calls brought forth from within and those from some, as yet unknown source without. Although her life before may have been spiraling toward an eternity of hellfire, she believed it to be hers to squander. Now she felt as another woman. Fear mingled with the scents of a life of promiscuity.

Someone or something else pulled against her resolve and she drew ever closer to the fiery afterlife. According to the word of God, works alone do not a path to Heaven make. But by works, and truly with no intervention—divine or otherwise—may we enter the gates of eternal damnation

Every ounce of her fortitude backed up and stood for morals even as her hand lowered toward the object of her lust. He waited, exposed, stiff, frightened. The man's eyes twitched in all directions, settling on nothing, even as his anticipation brought him to the brink of ecstasy.

Her hand made intimate contact and his breath caught sharp in his chest. The tension building to the moment or the sultry beauty deep in her eyes, or perhaps both, cursed him with a quick response, quicker than normal. He was over before Rose could mount the steed projecting from his hips.

She looked at the mess in her hand and the muscle relaxing beside it. She felt as though something valuable had been stolen from her. Anger coursed through her and she looked into the sheepish face of the man, satisfied by a mere touch. Fire spewed forth from her eyes, the fire of true hell, and the flesh peeled from the bones of the man almost as sudden as the moment of satisfaction he'd stolen from her.

A kind of horror slapped at Rose's mind as she gazed speechlessly upon the result of her temper. She knew not from whence the fire had come and she froze to the spot, watching the steam of her breath dancing in the brisk air and mingling with the smolder from the body.

Truly there was a power within her. A power of evil, great it was. But she controlled it, not. It indeed stood in power over her and she—its helpless, willing subject. Rose knew not how to rid herself of whatever possession had befallen her. And at stake, nothing less than her immortal soul.

She waited as if for someone to apprehend her and yet none came. Confused, she found a lone thought floating inside. She grasped at it and recoiled. A passage she knew well, but the antithesis of appropriate for what had just happened, what *she* had just done.

Moses quoth: "*...and God looked upon what he had done. And it was good.*"

Rose felt as if bile would surely rise up from her feet, through her entire body and out her mouth. Running seemed the only answer. She willed her feet to make haste. They began their way to the safety of her own home.

Once there, Rose laid in bed, fighting back the tears—her only companion. An evil *had* taken her over. She did not envision her unholy liaisons, she *lived* them. She really did those terrible things. And Wilford had seen. Worst of all things, he had witnessed her deviant, casual, sexual depravity. More tears came, flowing freely, soaking her pillow.

She prayed—what to do, what to do. If God could not show her a solution, from where would she find such a thing? No one—no man could fight a demon. Oh, the pastor spoke of fire and brimstone, but he stood short of stature and wide of belly. Were he to face a true demon he would likely defecate himself. And the red of his nose suggested he spoke more to a bottle of whiskey than to God.

She could not live as she did. A tragedy approached. She could see Wilford quickly being forced to stand for righteousness and forsaking her to the judgment of the town tribunal. They would, of course, be forced to burn her at the stake in the name of the one true God, though he would infer forgiveness.

"What do you want of me?" she cried.

No voice came back. Or did it? Had she heard an answer, or did she just *wish* she had? Did she want an answer so strongly that her mind constructed one?

Wrapped it up in a bow, just for her, and spake it from an imagined mouth? *Perhaps I've gone insane.*

"Speak up," she tried again. "If you dare, answer me."

"*I dare*," whispered.

Rose recoiled at the voice, but upon searching saw no one. "Then speak, and be it the truth, for nothing else will serve either of us."

"*I thought my purpose clear.*"

"Well it is not. Make it so."

"*I wish to prevail myself upon thee, to fornicate with every man. My need has now become thine own.*"

"To what end?"

"*I crave the seed of man. It is my sustenance. I cannot survive without it.*"

"And I should care for your wellbeing?"

"*Thy concern is overwhelming, I'm sure. But my need is now thy need...OUR need. It is already too late.*"

"And if I resist you?"

"*Thou cannot!*" it answered, forcefully.

At that moment, Rose felt something pull within her. A physical tug on her mind that drove her to delirium, she could not help but thrust her hands between her legs as she had behind her own desk only days before. She focused on the spot that would quickly satisfy her need. But the urge continued. She could not stop, as had been the case before.

"No!" She willed her hands away. They swooned back. She buried them beneath the pillow.

Again they returned to their lustful duty. She locked them behind her back and laid her body on top. They wiggled and squirmed their way out and went back to work. Finally she rose and began her chores, neglected for days. For a moment she had won.

"There, I told you."

If she expected a response, it disappointed her. For a few minutes she managed to scrub dishes. But as soon as she turned to her next duty, her hands returned to theirs. Soon she fell to the floor and rolled into the wonderful feelings her fingers created, knowing rawness and pain would follow soon enough. The beast had won.

"What must I do to make this stop?"

"*Thou can do nothing. Our need is strong. Have I not told thou it is too late?*"

Rose believed. At that moment she knew not the path of salvation.

"You want what?"

"Can you do it?"

"Of course. But such a thing, what could it possibly be used for?"

"For that which it is intended."

"But why? Surely in Hemmingforth, such a thing would serve no purpose. It would be obsolete."

"I have the money to pay. I work for the office of the Magistrate. I say there is a need for a metal chastity belt that can be locked. I'd prefer you did not question further, as the Magistrate has said this thing is to be kept secret. No one is to know."

Rose thought hard about how she wanted the man to simply believe her words. She focused, hoping the determination in her eyes would convince him further than mere words. When she saw his head lift, a new look had taken over his face.

"You say you want it when?"

"How soon can you…" She paused. "Is there something wrong?" Then she felt the tug, once again. Not the same as she had at home, but similar enough for her to recognize its origins. The thing wanted more. She turned to leave.

"Wait."

She turned back.

"What about my payment?"

Perhaps because she recognized her possession, or for some other reason, but she knew her opportunity to retreat had passed. Her urge, combined with whatever power she'd exerted on the blacksmith, mingled to make an irresistible drive. She would resist no longer. Until she had everything ready, she remained at the mercy of the demon inside her.

She walked with the man to the back of the building where shadows lay like thick blankets on the ground. She dropped her dress and began the task of untying only enough knots to allow her petticoat to fall. Rose couldn't remember ever having bothered, but she now thought about how she'd have to clean her undergarment once again.

As the smith's eyes roamed over her nude form, she felt admired and adored. But she wished he would dispense with the pleasantries and get to work. She needed him inside her, offering his seed. She stepped forward.

With his pants around his ankles, trying to step backwards, he fell over, banging his head hard on the floorboards. He shook it several times but didn't appear to clear it. Rose, exasperated, pushed his head all the way back down against the floor once again. She looked at his manhood, ready for her, waving in the wind like a flagpole.

She had no time to waste while he found his sight. She straddled him and sat, taking him inside and closing her eyes. She moved like she was churning butter. Up and down, up and down, her legs grew tired and still she moved, pumping at him, pulling all the juice from him. But he had stamina and she continued.

Grabbing a post nearby, she kept her balance and moved herself faster. She knew he could hold out only so long and then she would receive that which it wanted. *She* wanted. She could hardly wait to feel it wash inside her, spraying deeper than any man could reach on his own—adding to the warmth of her already smoldering nether pot.

Now the man moved to compliment her efforts. His hips, made powerful by his constant work movement and carrying heavy objects, pounded against her, driving her off balance, bringing ecstasy. She finished and he still hadn't. Weakness entered her legs and they began to quiver with the exertion.

The man, seeing and understanding her plight, tossed her aside. She rolled over and lay on her back, exposed. He jumped on her, mounting like he would a steed, and rode her until she could feel pain in her back from the rough floor. Still he continued.

He rested his entire body on her, his powerful arms enwrapped her and squeezed tightly. Unable to get air, she began to swoon. When she felt consciousness slip away, she also felt him empty his wanton desire into her. She couldn't control another outburst of her own need before passing out.

When she woke, the smith had returned to work at the front of his shop. She dressed and walked out. His eyes refused to meet hers, even though she stared at him sharply. She watched his arms for a moment as he worked the red-hot metal into whatever shape he desired. She admired his work…and his arms.

"My piece?"

"What?"

"The work I asked for?"

"Oh, that. I can have it for you by tomorrow." He glanced around to make sure no one overheard. "Have you got a way to get it home?"

"I have not. Can you deliver it? Then I can pay you."

He whispered. "I think you paid me enough. Something like that at Madame Chatterwell's would have cost twice as much as the piece you require."

Again Rose's dark nature took over. "I'm sure there's a little more where that came from, just to make it worth your while. Call it a *delivery fee*."

The smith coughed and wiped his mouth with the back of a gloved hand. Not all his sweat came from the heat of the coal urn, she surmised. Although she would be rid of this demon, she could not help but admire the power she still wielded over a man. She strode out under a warm sun.

The smith came as he promised, and as the demon within Rose demanded. This time the man had little trouble mounting her. She led him to the bedroom and never even turned on her charm. The simplicity of not resisting seemed enough. The man's animal drives took over and she found herself falling onto her bed.

He dove in with fury and lust—two of Rose's favorite things. He kissed her, in several places. She did not resist. He touched things she'd never touched.

She did not resist. He tried to enter her in all her openings. She did not resist. He reached more than one peak and wanted more. Still, she did not resist.

Rose moved for him, into him, with him, dancing the whore dance. She cared not for lady status, as long as the men kept coming—coming back for more. The demon had spoken the truth. She needed it. The seed, the juice, the essence of man, the elixir of procreation, she wanted it all to fill her. At that moment, while this lone man wildly tossed her about and used her so roughly, she wished for the dream where more than one man slipped inside her at the same time.

If he read her mind, she hadn't been aware of it. And yet he rolled her over and took her in a different opening. Face down; she felt his pelvis against her buttocks, pounding her into the mattress. She felt pain and pleasure and buried her scream into the bed beneath. Her eyes crossed as another special moment erupted from her body and the spots he touched.

Finally exhausted and spent, he fell off her and rolled away. Whether embarrassed or simply finished and returning to work, she knew not—and cared not. He'd treated her to some incredible feelings, and he'd brought the object of her desire. Of all things, this one man, this smith, had been like a going away present, given to the demon by Rose. It knew not her plan...yet. But she offered it one last Harrah.

The smith left and she realized she did not even know his name. A laugh escaped her lips as she stood and examined the device. It looked perfect and she donned it with ease, locking it after she placed it proper. The ping of the lock bolt snapping into place made her heart jump.

Wearing only metal underpants, she put on a pot of water to boil and searched for a dress—just the right dress, one that would hide her new undergarment. When the water boiled she picked up the pot, took several deep breaths, and poured the liquid down the front of the chastity belt—scalding the tender flesh of her womanhood.

Rose screamed. When the pain subsided, she dressed and left to find Wilford.

Behind his desk, Wilford looked more like a judge than ever. Rose had been two days without showing up to work. She thought he might be cross but found him in complete disarray from concern for her wellbeing.

"I thought something might have happened to you. Something, terrible."

"I am all right. Would you keep something for me?"

"What is it?"

She handed him a solitary key. The lonely object fell into his outstretched hand with a nearly silent thud. He cupped it reverently, examined it curiously, and then clutched it affectionately. His eyes, full of questions, rose to meet hers.

"And what is this?"

"A key."

"As I can see. To what, may I ask?"

"Shall we just say it is a key to my heart? Sufficient answer under the circumstances, I should think."

"Please don't be so short with me, darling. I only care what happens to you. Would that we could be married this very day."

"A pleasant thought, my dear. Please hold it close to your heart even as you would hold this key. Both may soon unlock a love stronger than any other."

"But will you not stay and speak with me?"

"I cannot. I must go."

"For how long?" Wilford sounded quite desperate.

"I shall only need a couple days, I think."

"After that?"

"I shall return. I promise."

"And what of the time in between? How shall I ever contain myself?"

"Please believe in my love for you. One way or another, I shall return." She stood.

"Must you go this instant?"

"I...left a pot of water boiling on the stove."

With that she stepped out the door and did not look back.

The afternoon bore on and the water boiled. She could hardly stand the metal touching against her scorched flesh. She could not sit. She could not stand. She could definitely not walk. All things hurt. And yet she persisted, pouring one pot of scalding water after another down her front. Each time she screamed. Each time the pain subsided…a little. Each time she composed herself, she felt the urge to laugh.

She would laugh at the demon. Sooner or later, she *would* laugh at it. With the protection of the belt and the scarred skin, no one would have need to touch her ever again. Wilford would understand. *He has to.* She could not allow this to go further. The demon must go. No exorcism would be enough. No priest or judge would understand her despair.

"*Thou mustn't.*"

"Be silent. Your time is nearly over. I'm sure you know I can't be dissuaded. I've already scalded myself to disfigurement. No man will ever again find me attractive down there. I may no longer be able to bear children. I may not even find pleasure in my own hands from this day forth. But here and forever more, shall be of my choosing. I choose." She poured yet another pot of water down, bringing her screams as she fell to her knees. When it passed, she lifted her head proudly. "Ha!"

"I am beaten. How can this be? Thou art but human. And the desire already existed within thine heart. I had but to touch the right places."

"You did and I served you. If you had asked for but a short time I would have been what you need. But you ask forever and I shall have my own life returned. I cannot follow your path, no matter how tempting, or how pleasurable."

"But I loved thee, Rose."

"Love? You don't know what the word means. You think that little game men and women play is love? It is simply an expression of love. So who is this superior being? You are a *mere* demon—beneath me. One such as you could never understand the complexities of love."

She checked the water which had nearly reached boil once again. After the first couple times of throwing water on her floor, she discovered a quicker, cleaner way. She took a second pot and placed it beneath her on the floor. It caught most of the water poured and retained some of the heated temperature. After hours, this became quite efficient.

"Perhaps I could not understand human *love. But I offered something greater. I could have offered thee—."*

"Do not presume to be so magnanimous. You are not a savior. You are not God. You have no magnificence to offer. There is no salvation in your words, only sorrow. You could bring me nothing but eternal damnation. One wanton sexual encounter after another, deeper into depravity, perhaps with women or children, multiple partners, animals, to what depths you would not sink I am uncertain, and in the end you would be stronger and I would be burning for an eternity in Hell. We have no future together. I give you leave to depart at any time."

Again the water heralded its arrival to temperature. She poured, she screamed, she returned the pot to the stove. For a time her mind remained quiet. It could have been gone, but she knew it wasn't. She could feel it nearby, breathing heavily as if injured and dying. She maintained her vigil as long as she could past nightfall, then fell to her bed—exhausted. She didn't even mind the scent of the act she'd performed with the smith, clinging to her comforter and sheets. She knew she might never smell it again. Rose passed out and did not dream.

Upon waking, she began her pattern once again. Water boiled, water poured. Scream, knees, repeat. The demon's heartbeat, if indeed it had a heart, resounded in her ears, keeping her wary of its presence. She knew it was not far away.

Her vigil lasted all that day and into the next night, where again she fell into a dreamless sleep. Stopping seemed pointless. When she awoke, she began again, continuing for a third day. Her screams abated as the skin became desensitized. Then she would pour more water and realized it might still be more sensitive than she thought. She screamed again.

By that night she began to falter. Her resolve faded and she wondered how long the demon could hold out. She could certainly not maintain this for weeks, if it took that long. Even a couple more days seemed more than she could endure. She decided a confrontation might best resolve the problem once and for all.

"Show yourself," she said with a weak voice.

Nothing came back to her. She doubted her senses.

"I know you're still there."

Nothing.

Could she possibly have gotten rid of it and not noticed? Her aloneness struck her. Solitude—not exactly a lifestyle chosen by most women—had once offered her solace. Now it seemed more antagonizing, taunting, teasing her about the pathetic life she now led.

Perhaps the beast had left her, too. But this time she would choose not to remain alone.

"Rose! Are you well?" Wilford's concern showed all over his morning face. Stubble from a forgotten morning ritual sparkled with the beams of sun that shone through the wall boards. Dust fairies floated about, dancing when anyone walked through them. Her gait, pained and distorted, gave him cause for concern, but she pooh-poohed it away with a wave of her hand.

"I am perhaps not so terrible as I might appear. Are you well?" she asked, sliding one weak palm across his unshaven cheek.

"Sleep has evaded me. I have waking dreams of some terror devouring you, bite by bite, and casting your bones aside with nothing left on them but spittle. I hear your voice in the night, but it does not offer words of love, it cries out for help. Finally, unable to bear it further, I trod to your house in the dark and fell back on the front porch, awaiting your emergence. When the time came and the sun persistently stabbed at my eyes, I rose and came here, hoping this is the one place you would go when ready. And here you are."

"Here I am, my love. I have returned as promised."

"And so you have. I am so sorry that I should have ever doubted you."

"I can understand your concerns, and your doubts. But lay them to rest now."

"You are such an angel. How have I lived so long without you?"

"I have no answer for that, my love. But I assure you, there is no reason to live any longer without me. Nor I, without you. I care not for opinion; I will wed you as soon as you see fit to have me."

"Even if that were today?"

"Even so. I've known of my love for quite some time. Hiding it behind lies and denial cannot possibly be more Christian than a hasty wedding. Such a desire, filling my heart, taking my every thought, is that not lust? I would take that away, cast it out."

"What of your...demon."

"It is gone."

"Gone?"

"I have eliminated its hold over me, therefore it is powerless. I am free of it."

"Can you be sure it will never return?"

"Can any of us?"

"True," he said, glancing toward his desk. "There is a past of which I am embarrassed and would bury. Would that anyone could accept it and forgive."

"I can."

"But you know not."

"Perhaps I do."

"But how?"

"As you knew of my antics. I oversaw something I should not have. And yet, here we both are, together, professing our love. Perhaps it is all for the best. Now we can go forward without secrets."

Wilford smiled. Her words struck him true, and warmed him.

Rose felt relief knowing he knew about her past. She didn't know how much he knew, but she, of course, did not know all there was to know about his past, either. When time had passed and they grew ever more comfortable with each other, they could speak further— if they chose to do so. For now, enough was known. Except...

"There is one further thing I must confess, even now at the infancy of our relationship."

"You needn't bother, my love."

"I must."

"Why must you?"

"It cannot wait, I assure you. Would that I could put it off, but your decision may hinge on this truth as much as many others—perhaps more so. Once known, you may choose to abandon me."

He slid his arms around her and she felt so safe and comforted. "There could never be anything that would make me turn from you."

"Perhaps." She stood and paced a bit, unable to find the strength to continue. She feared his retribution. She feared he would leave. But to hide it until after a ceremony that tied him to her until death—that would be dishonorable and downright mean. She could not. She sought to explain, but could not find the words. She would have to show all.

"My love, I will need the key I asked you to hold."

"Is your heart no longer to be mine?"

"Perish the thought. My heart beats for naught but you. The need for my own life pales."

"It does not...to me." He pulled at his neck, producing a chain. Hanging from it she saw the key that had helped her rid herself of the demon. He'd kept it close to his own heart for safe keeping.

He held out the key now but she did not take it right away. She tried to raise her dress but its bulk kept falling back. She struggled for a moment and gave up. Reaching behind, Rose began untying the draw strings that held the garment in place.

"What are you doing?"

"Patience, my love."

"But you cannot undress in here. What if someone were to walk in?"

"I have locked the door behind me. No one will enter." Then the dress fell to the floor. Unable to fit a petticoat over the chastity belt, Rose stood naked except for it. Wilford stared. To his credit, he did not but casually glance at her bare breasts. However his curiosity drew his gaze to the metallic object attached to her hips.

"What is that?"

"A chastity belt."

"Chastity? But you..." He trailed off.

"I know what you saw. No matter the desire in my heart or the past of my life, this was a demon."

"I know. I saw your eyes."

"My eyes?" She thought about it and decided she did not want to know. "Never mind. The demon seemed to work through my womanhood, so I locked it out."

"Indeed? Such a wise solution." His voice carried genuine admiration.

"But there is more. A lock will not a demon keep out, of itself. I needed to further deter the beast that sought to control me—to bar its return. I needed to act swiftly before my will was lost forever."

"Again your wisdom is impressive. I am so lucky to have fallen in love with such an intelligent girl."

"Perhaps you will not think so when you see." As she spoke she struggled with the temperamental lock. Finally it fell away and the belt slipped easily off. Wilford got his first glimpse of her tortured nether area, as did Rose.

The rotting flesh, red with anger and blistered, stared at them both. No hair remained and all of her could be seen. The flesh down there could not withstand the torture she'd put it through. Had she chosen a place with toughened skin, as on her hands, it might not have looked so. Wilford turned away.

"It will heal."

"I know." His weakened answer struck her as a hand on her face.

"It seemed the only way."

"You may be right," he said, turning back, "for I have never heard of anyone removing their own demon before. You may very well be the first. And I promise you, when you have healed, I will learn to overlook the scars you have. For do we not all have scars from battle? The deepest of which are from those fought with ourselves." He moved close to her.

"Indeed they are."

"How did you manage?"

"Boiling water."

"Ah," he offered. "It could have been so much worse."

"I see not how."

He placed his hand gently on the tortured flesh between her legs. She winced, but did not withdraw. "This is a place of hiding—only I shall see from this day forth." He looked into her eyes. "That is true, is it not?"

"Only you, my love."

He relaxed and allowed a smile to lift one corner of his mouth. "Worse would have been on your face or somewhere everyone could see. No one ever need know of this."

"Should we lie?"

"A lie of omission. Surely no decent person would ask such a question."

"That is a truth I had not thought of," she answered with a tilt of her head. "But the question of marriage remains. What if I cannot bear you children?"

"In my many years of training, I was required to study the human body. From what I know, most of what you need to bring forth a child is inside. Unless you stood on your head and poured scalding water directly inside, I think children are not out of the question. The only question is how soon you will have

346

healed enough for us to act as man and wife in this manner."

Now it was Rose's turn to smile. If only he could be telling the truth. But then, why would he not? Nothing could be gained by his falsehood. And only he would lose if she could not bear children. Yet he persisted.

"Then we shall proceed with the plans for a wedding. I shall announce it today."

"Shall we go right now, Wilford? Shall we?" Her childlike excitement could hardly be contained and she turned toward the door.

"I think…" he began. She frowned at his hesitation. "…we could wait for you to dress first."

She looked down and giggled. It wouldn't do her already tarnished reputation any good to go out in such an array. "I'll have to go without anything underneath. I brought nothing and I cannot don that terrible thing again."

Wilford kicked the metal bucket to the side. "Pray God you never again have to wear this device. We shall place it on our mantle as a reminder."

"But it is not proper for me to walk about freely with nothing under my dress."

"Yes, people might think you've become promiscuous…on your way to announce plans for matrimony."

They both laughed.

Few people attended the wedding. Though held in church, the pastor could find no comfort sanctioning such a union. God, he said, did not approve of unholy joinings. Her past and his uncertain beginnings would be exposed someday. God would not allow such things to remain hidden from the eyes of the righteous for long.

Rose laughed at the 'eyes of the righteous' comment. She knew many of the people in town. She felt little concern for the tainting of righteousness. Men lured by the demon's lust could easily be discounted, and perhaps forgiven, but many men had visited Rose when she led that life—without a demon's influence—having no remorse for their lustful acts. Why should she be the only one to bear the burden of sin? Had they not sinned as well?

Despite all the judgment against her, and the poor gathering of people to celebrate her special day, Rose stood tall and proud, enjoying the moment as much as any woman ever did. More, perhaps. And she would not let the foolish minds of the 'righteous' darken the few bright clouds that floated in the sky above her.

To her, all was as it should be. She went to her home with Wilford and began a life she knew would be happy for eternity. Though her scars faded in the weeks that followed, Wilford would not have relations with her unless the room was totally darkened. Rose needed no lights and, although it pained her heart, considered it a small price to pay.

The first time he tried to enter her, the pain kept her from fulfilling his needs. She could have nothing touch her there and often slept in the nude without covers. But she soon grew tolerant and could accept him as she had any man. After a time she even began to enjoy his advances and thought she might someday return to her old self, finding pleasure and release in the act. She longed for that.

In the meantime, she allowed Wilford his own pleasures and shared in his satisfaction. Each time he gave his seed, she felt more like the lady she sought to be. She was still wanton, but only with him. And under God, this was not a sin since they were married proper.

And every night Rose prayed for herself and for Wilford, that they might have a long and Christian life together, under the watchful eye of God. She prayed they be accepted by the town. And she prayed for healing—both physical and emotional. She also prayed that Wilford find true happiness in her—both physically and emotionally. And she prayed for children.

The world became a wonder for Rose. Her wanton urges subdued, the growing relationship with

Wilford, a job to produce money, all these lent way to a level of happiness she'd not known. Though pride be one of the seven deadly sins, she could not keep it from her heart. She felt it about her marriage and home. She felt it about her victory over evil. And now she could feel it for the budding life growing within her. Wilford had been right. She could still bear children.

She walked with a bounce, unaware of the evil that still watched her every move, stalking each step, waiting for strength and opportunity. Rose trod as a lady but the evil messenger knew her true nature as being one of a lust that flowed through her as much as the seed of man. With ease she held at bay the desire to taste each one as they passed. And even though such desires were not entirely purged, she fought with the natural feelings of turmoil within her. The doctor told her that womanly urges sometimes became greater during pregnancy. She would have to live with it—and resist.

The beast knew this would move to weaken her even as it grew stronger. As it planned its own return, the hellspawn lay casually in the undeveloped bosom of another younger girl, seeking, desiring, collecting. Wanting, needing only the seed; rich and vitalizing, to quench its need and produce offspring.

But Rose, despite her darkened past, was innocent. She knew not the world and nature, nor of things unnatural and other-worldly. The Sunday sermons told her all she knew of the afterlife, be it dark or light; fire or sunshine. And the first time the demon appeared in her mirror, she dismissed the image as dark fancy—frightening, to be sure, but nothing more than smoke.

She spoke not of it to neighbors for fear of retribution. But inside, she knew it had been there and remembered what it looked like. If only she could know why it appeared to her. By mid-fall, she had caught glimpses of the image all of eleven times. The latter ones becoming longer and more difficult to so easily deny. One day in early October she spoke to Wilford about it through trembling lips.

"I've seen it several times, my lord."

Wilford knew when she spoke so formally, she feared his reaction. This he'd learned in a short time as her tone often told of her true feelings. This moment, he could tell by the quiver in her voice, would have to be handled in a most delicate fashion.

"Do you recognize it? What did it look like?"

"A horrible creature. Like nothing I've ever seen or heard tell of."

"Did it hurt you?"

"No, but I was terribly frightened."

"Indeed, as well you should have been. It does not sound holy."

"You think me mad, or possessed."

"Be still," he spoke softly, touching her gently. "Hush. I think no such thing. But it is difficult to believe without having seen it with mine own true eyes."

"Knowing is not the same as hearing, but you must believe. Hear with your heart. I speak the truth. And I know not what to do," she broke into a sob.

"There," he coddled her.

Rose gathered her mettle and stood fast against Wilford's doubt.

"What must I do?"

"Without knowing what it wants, we may have no recourse. May it be that you could find out?"

"How would I accomplish such a feat?"

"This from the woman who eradicated it all by herself the last time it dared approach.

"You think it the same demon, then?"

"What other?"

"So how do I set about discovering its purpose?"

"You might…ask."

"Just come out and inquire about its intention? I hardly think that's an appropriate method of addressing a true demon."

"Perhaps it simply wants to reenter you."

"As do many men, I'm sure," she said, not without sarcasm. "But that time has passed."

"A time will come when its true goals shall be known. For us to bend to its eventual will dictates we must know."

"I do not understand, my husband."

"For any slave to obey his master, he must be made aware of the rule of law. What will make his master happy? What makes him cross? And what are the punishments for disobedience?"

"So you believe it will *want* to tell me?"

"Perhaps. Subterfuge can be difficult to see through. We must remain hopeful."

"Somehow it seemed much easier to stand against when inside me."

"Probably because you could not lay eyes on its evil form. Fright has taken some of your strength. You must regain it. Remember this is a demon you already bested."

Rose slumped, an unattractive gesture to be sure. Nevertheless, the weight of burden pressed down upon her and she sought refuge. Something within told her she could stand and face the creature and yet fear overwhelmed. She could not remember life being so difficult when she lived it as she had. Hunting for men to offer that which they secretly sought was no burden at all. All she need do was maintain an attractiveness that could still lure.

The time would come in her future, as with any woman, when appearances would fail and the body— falter. She knew such things to be inevitable. But one so young as Rose did not fully believe in the inevitability of aging, even as her body began to grow with child.

Life, however, had taken an unexpected turn and she wanted to be with Wilford. This concept left no room for promiscuity. She'd mended her ways only to discover newer, taller obstacles to overcome. Rose felt sadness because she knew other adults would rather turn tail and run than face such terror. She envied them.

Somewhere within, she must locate a deep strength. She drew so much from Wilford, but knew this battle had to be won by her and her alone. She must call upon the desire to be rid of the demon. She must find it if she were to live.

Winter had fallen and an evil pursued her. Rose ran toward home, toward Wilford—for he would surely be there. *But perhaps it would be unwise to lead it to him and have him share my fate.* She sought to change direction. *The stables would smell of comfort,* she thought without knowing why. To her dismay her feet had not done as she'd commanded of them. She still ran full speed toward home, and him.

She recited the Lord's Prayer over and over again through puffed breathes.

Her feet slowed, not at all, but her mouth came to an abrupt halt. Rose had the feeling of not being alone yet no one stood near. The sparse trees accented by white snow would go far to expose any who might skulk as a thief. Such a barren landscape could hide naught but the winter-white rabbit even as twilight fell heavy upon her.

However, the feeling of a companion persisted, haunted. She turned to and fro in search but her eye caught nothing. Her foot, oppositely, caught very good hold of a strong and still-green pine root that jutted up in a most inconvenient manner.

Rose went down, her mouth poised to scream, quickly filled with fresh, dusty snow. Her body heat, raised by the exertion of the run, melted the snow in her mouth almost instantly. She drank as she assessed herself for injury.

"Thou art unharmed."

The voice sang in Rose's ear and she looked around, focusing into the depths of darkness hiding behind every tree, growing deeper as the sun sank further beneath the horizon. Her stomach fluttered from the fear—renewed. Her voice, when she spoke, quivered with uncertainty.

"Who's there?"

The wind answered with a low growl that sounded quite out of natural and Rose shivered against more than just cold. She gathered back to her feet and stopped still, as in shock, when the voice danced through her head, once again.

"Thou should hurry home, child."

Rose listened close to the voice within her ears that seemed to come from nowhere and yet lingered as the scent from a stew pot.

"Make haste, thy husband awaits."

Rose set out again at full gallop, this time watching closely as her feet pounded the earth—propelling her at a speed she'd never experienced. As she ran she wished herself to greater speed though she knew the futility. Her legs began to ache and she knew her time of running would soon come to an end.

Then, she saw the light splash against the snow from the windows of her own home. The figure. It stood fast in puddles of melted snow beneath its feet. Heat from the body created steam, floating like an early-morning mist that gathered about it as if by choice. It stood between her and the door.

At first, believing it to be Wilford, Rose pushed her way forward. Now, as her eye approached and vision cleared to see the truth, she faltered. Although arreptitious, she stood to ponder and examine.

The apparition before her stood as she did. Arms protruded from its shoulders and the body turned almost as if in pain. The scream which sprung from it would confirm that. But the horrible noise turned into a sound to frighten even more. One might call it a laugh. Rose shivered.

Before her eyes the thing faded and she saw her own doorstep become visible through it. When it fully dissipated she made her way through the door, slamming it behind her. She found the house, however, devoid of life save her own. Wilford must have stepped out for some reason.

Feeling the fear grow she made her way to the bedroom. An ache stung at her and she made way to examine. Some pains came from areas she could not easily see and she made her way to her large mirror, but her reflection faded even as the demon had moments ago. What took its place stole her breath.

Its misshapen head turned to her and it glared with fire-filled eyes. Arms with a half dozen joints each, jiggled and twisted—legs with no knees hobbled with weight first on one then the other—the beast looked as though it were trying to dance through fire and agony.

At some point—Rose had lost any real sense of time—the thing peeled back its mucous lips in a hideous mock smile—though the rotted stubs protruding inside that mouth could hardly be called teeth.

Swollen areas on the chest (could those be breasts?) raised as it sucked in air. A viscous fluid— the color of watered-down milk—dripped from each one. Finally, it spoke and the voice grated like the bay of a horse with a broken leg. It said only one word.

"*Rose!*"

Rose cringed from it as if its breath came putrid and she could smell through the glass. Digging from deep within she found the fortitude to reply.

"What art thou?"

"*I am called* Beelzertft. *I am a succubus.*"

"What would that be?" Rose spoke with uncertain austerity.

"*I come for the babies.*" Something about the voice seemed confrontational, daring her to inquire further. She glanced down at her slightly protruding belly.

"No babies have been born here for many months. You attempt to deceive."

"*I do not. The babies have been provided.*"

Confused, Rose looked about; searching for the strength she counted on, the name of her power. Wilford. But he would not be found. She could not fathom where he'd gotten to when she needed him so.

"*Worry not for him, child. But mourn over thine own self for truly thy soul be lost.*"

"You will not have me or my baby."

"*I need not thy baby. The seed thou hast drawn from the men of this town hast given me many babies. Thou art their mother.*"

"No!"

"*Thou art the new Eve. Together we could bring forth a whole new world.*"

"I will not give in to your temptations. I have a life now."

"*What life? As a mere woman? Thou hast the same life as any mortal. Is that all thou aspires to?*"

"I will not be drawn in!" she shouted.

The creature in the mirror withdrew slightly.

The arrival of Wilford heralded a lifting. 'Twere as if a knife had been withdrawn from her back or shackles removed from her limbs. Rose stood tall and strong against the power she faced.

"'Tis said no weapon of God's Earth can destroy the beast but spiritual purity wilt surely cast it out!" Wilford's voice carried above the din.

"I am not pure," Rose confessed. "Thou knowest."

"True, perhaps, but thy God is. He is there to take on the fight in your behalf, if you only let Him."

"What of our baby?"

"God will nurture the innocents. You need not fear."

"I know so little of such things, Wilford." Yet her feet didst move forward again, but human strength alone could not stand against the supernatural.

"You must have faith, my darling." Wilford spoke softly yet his voice still carried. His words, nay his *one* word; *darling*, caressed her ears.

Rose felt more powerful than ever. Her heart sang and she *knew* if she survived, she and Wilford would be together for eternity. The joy of first seeing him on the street that day came into her that moment, creating a renewed purity. The pureness of dawning love, true love, untainted by anger or lust, as she felt it that morning.

God moved through her as she thrust out her hands. No force seen of the eye flowed from her yet the beast withdrew as if in pain. With her heart light and her mind focused only on the task, she never so much as diverted her eyes. All was for *Beelzertft*.

Blood flowed from its eyes even as the screech came out of its hideous mouth. The claw-like hands spasmed, trying to grasp at salvation. Naught would help. The power of Rose became more than it could stand against.

With a final scream that turned into a cackle, the apparition faded into the mists of dimming memory, leaving Wilford unsure of its demise. Rose slumped and he rushed to catch her. She managed to reach her destination on the floor before he could encompass her with his arms and lift. He picked her up to rest on one squatted knee. Stroking her hair from her face, Wilford softly called to her.

Moments stretched in Wilford's mind as thoughts of the worst came to him. Yet she stirred with pained effort and managed, after some coaxing, to open her eyes. As she beheld the object of her love, a smile crept weakly to her lips. She opened her mouth to speak but *Beelzertft's* voice came.

"Beware. Evil may be abated but ever shall it return. My time is nigh as this visit has foretold. Be thou prepared if thy wishes. But I say unto thee, I shall have my due, be ye prepared or otherwise. And no amount of sweetness will force me hence."

Wilford stared.

"My love, why dost thou look at me so?" came Rose's innocent query.

"Didst you not hear? The beast spake from your very mouth," he added, touching her lips with his fingers.

Shocked, she inquired further. "What didst thou hear, my beloved?"

"It foretold of its return and warned we would not be able to sto—."

Susann's fingers gripped at the tender flesh beneath Wilford's chin. She lifted him even as she stood. He looked at her in puzzlement. She returned his gaze with the eyes of the underworld. A fire burnt deep within those eyes. Wilford recognized the demon look from the day of the picnic and feared.

She held him with only one hand, his feet unable to touch the floor, as she called upon the strength of the unnatural one. Evil, in its own right, didst have strength over mortal man. It could not easily be denied. Her other hand slid intimately down the front of him. She reached the object which she sought and freed it.

Stroking him in such a manner made him recoil. Arousal, though, seemed involuntary. A smile fell upon Rose's face when the beast within saw his reaction. Even as Wilford's life ebbed—her one hand continuing to keep pressure on his throat—myriad thoughts ran through his head, but he drew only one to the front. *How will I live without her?*

361

The short-bladed sword he always carried—
although hidden not to cause undo fear—came easily
from its sheath. A family heirloom, the blade swung in
a perfect, almost beautiful arc, contacted the neck of the
woman Wilford loved. An eternity in the moment, he
considered that he would never cry into that neck, nor
find any comfort there from a gentle embrace. Their
children would never nuzzle as they burped, freshly
taken from her breast. He would never hang a necklace
from that neck—bought perhaps for her birthday. And
he would never kiss her there as they made love in their
bed—in their home.

The finely-honed blade hesitated for naught.
Through the neck, it slowed little and the swing carried
it over and pulled it from Wilford's hands. The blade
dug firmly into the wall on the far side of the room.

Wilford wanted to hold the woman he'd loved
so completely. Yet he feared. The hands clutched in
death spasms, gripping at his arms, squeezing and
releasing—squeezing and releasing. Rose's chest
heaved with unholy breaths. And a horrible sound
emerged from the neck as if the imperishable beast
continued to throw curses at him.

And so he dropped the headless body to the
floor with a tear—it continued taunting him without the
ability to form true words. Hardened by the tragedy the
beast brought upon his home, he retrieved the sword
then turned and left without uttering a word at her
departure. No words spoken over the body would allow

her into Heaven, or him. Mounting his horse, he rode toward town.

Was this to be my penance all along? God, thou hast truly forsaken me. Hers was the purest love, the bravest soul. Did she deserve to die? She carried my child. Was that the reason? She needed to die because she carried a child born of my seed? Am I evil so dark? God! Answer me! Was there no other way?

No answer came. His horse knew the way to town and stopped for nothing along the way. When soon the buildings appeared to him, he wondered how he could explain what he'd seen. The pastor would believe. He believed in evil. That was his job. Surely the Sheriff would be compassionate. They'd worked together and he knew Wilford to be a man of honor.

The horse carried him into town, but he didst not stop. No life there remained, not for him. With nary a backward glance, Wilford Denton Hemmingforth left the town and would not be heard of again in the village named after him.

In time, people chose a new name.

PRIDE AND PERDU

By:
Blue Canyon

The warm liquid shot into her. This sensation created more fear than anything else had so far— anything she could remember in her whole life. She had no protection. She didn't think she needed any. The evening should have been quiet and alone, she made no plans to be intimate with a man.

Darla couldn't explain a thing. Obviously a man, a man with a face that couldn't be seen, had found his way in—inside her apartment, inside her bedroom, inside her vagina.

He must have been there the whole time, since she got home from work. He would have seen her undress. He'd probably watched her shower, too. She masturbated in the shower. Further embarrassment washed over her.

He must have been there while she ate dinner and read the latest novel, *Steel Mill Mafia* by Al Musitano. Darla got quite engrossed in the gangster story that didn't read like a gangster story. She laughed and cried and cheered for the underdog. She couldn't be sure, but she thought she might have cheered out loud, once or twice.

Then, when she got up to slip into bed and try to sleep, she felt his strong hands grabbing her, pushing her robe off with ease. Exposed, she felt so much weaker and instantly forgot everything she'd been taught at the martial arts classes she'd taken almost a year before.

When he first grabbed her, she couldn't understand how she'd missed him for hours. But now, as he shot his sperm into her (like a fireman, he just keeps coming!), she knew the answer. She could see the ceiling above her bed. She could see right through him, as if he had no head. When she looked down she saw no body either. No arms held her tight. No ass bounced in the air above her. No penis that pumped gallons of baby batter into her aching pussy. An amusing thought tickled her brain. *Is his semen invisible, too?*

Despite seeing nothing, her legs were forced wide open. She could feel that penis, rubbing against the inside walls of her womanhood. She could feel his eruption inside. The weight of his body lay on top of her. Something she couldn't see—some *man* she couldn't see—raped her, came inside her, and quite probably impregnated her. *Pregnancy. That would be the worst.* Fear washed over her like an ocean wave.

His throbbing *something* slid in and out of her, rubbing her, mixing her fear and disgust with desire and ecstasy. Her heightened emotions and his continued movement had her nearly at a peak, but the splash of his fluid inside sent her into an unexpected orgasm.

Her nipples tightened painfully. She thrust her head back and squeezed her eyes shut, hoping she looked to be in pain. She didn't want to give the impression she enjoyed any part of this, despite her body's reaction. Darla noticed her inner muscles gripping him—milking him—and she felt as transparent as her attacker. Then suddenly, silence. She could feel his weight still on her, but he'd stopped moving—stopped gushing into her.

When he got up, a part of her felt empty. She never saw him leave. She never saw anything—as if he was the invisible man. If she got caught by his seed, would she give birth to an invisible child?

He went away but Darla just lay there sobbing, her hands quivering, sweat and bodily fluids dripping down—following the crack of her ass to the mattress, tears flowing out of her eyes.

I can barely find my car keys, when I need them. How will I ever keep track of an invisible child?

Girls

By:
Blue Canyon

The moment came and so did I
When I saw the twinkling in her eye
I hadn't so much as removed my pants
Yet my breath came in short pants.

I stood behind to feel her breasts
As we hid in the closet, full of zest
Her zeal and pleasure were matched by none
As my hands explored her nipples, having fun.

Her back so soft and muscles fine
From my lips escaped a whine
Her little lace panty clung to her ass
My hands shook, I didn't want to move too fast.

The girl had curves that wouldn't quit
We made some noise, I frankly didn't give a shit
My penis rose hard, so I let it out.
When she saw she gasped, nearly a shout.

I knelt behind, kissing her derriere so sweet
As I dropped her panties to her feet
She tasted fine from the back side
And I spread her cheeks really wide.

Then I stood again, preparing to thrust
To enter the girl, fulfilling my lust
When I reached around in front to my shock
As I gripped the girl's full erect—and larger than
mine—cock!

CYCLE OF

THE MOON

By:
Blue Canyon

The new moon, shadowed by Earth, watched over the hordes like a closed eye. The noise and lights of the carnival assured that no one would notice, so the moon hung in lonely silence above.

Howard Payne sat at the half podium, waiting for the lines of curious and morbid to pay their eight bits and enter the macabre trailer. The view inside—one of horror unseen in normal life—drew in the mundane who searched for a thrill to awaken the miserable adventurer within.

Denied such pleasures in his own life, Payne stole excitement vicariously from those partaking of the festivities. The thrill of a clown juggling fiery baseball bats, the fright of a distorted reflection in a bent mirror, a breathtaking drop from a roller coaster peak, all these gave the illusion of life to the otherwise lifeless.

He turned, examining once again, the words painted on the side of the trailer.

SEE THE HEADLESS WOMAN WHO STILL LIVES!

Beneath that, the image of a woman—a beautiful, voluptuous woman—in a red dress, laying on the ground, writhing in pain, her head removed and her neck bleeding her life away, and yet, somehow, not.

Payne thought the woman sexy, although he preferred his women taller. He hadn't been with a woman in a very long time. He travelled, wandered mostly, no job or town holding his interest for very long. Relationships took time, time he wouldn't waste on anyone or anything. With so much life waiting just around the next corner, he could not resist the call.

377

Still his loins, rooted in the weakness of man since time began, called for coupling—mating; the release of mortal urges to procreate. He felt *urge-ent* at that moment as he looked up and saw her standing—waiting.

Susan Sharpe stood nearly six-feet-tall. Looking down on other people had not been only in condescension for her. She offered Payne a fiery look, one that spoke to his urges—or was that just his imagination?

"May I help you?" he asked with a manly squeak.

She reached down and lifted the 'Help Wanted' sign, showing it to him. Payne, he abhorred being called 'Howie', looked at her incredulously.

"*You* want to work *here*?"

Susan said nothing, tipping the sign forward to draw his attention back to it.

"You *can* talk, can't you?"

"Of course."

Her syrupy voice poured over him, warm and clinging to his skin like liquid silk, nourishing the lust through his pores. He could feel tingling in his nether region. Discomfort grew inside and he squirmed in his chair. Under the podium lay a small stack of paper. From the bottom he withdrew one and handed it to the woman.

"This is a pre-app. Just fill it in and the owner," he cocked his thumb over his shoulder, "will call you."

She finished in seconds, coming around behind to hand it to him intimately. She leaned close and put her lips to his ear. Payne could hear her draw in a breath to speak.

"I'll be in...touch." Her finger slid down the side of his arm, stopping at his elbow, falling short of his lap where he hoped her hand would go.

Unable to calm his breathing, he responded with a simple grunt. He tried not to stare as she sashayed away, but no one would witness—no one could see—no one cared if he ogled. Several others eyed her movements as she walked.

Though it wouldn't be any of his concern, he studied her app, her handwriting, her signature. Susan Sharpe, a poetic name that rolled off the tongue like 'chocolate cake' or 'mint julep'. He savored the sound and longed for a taste.

He didn't have to wait long. That night, as he closed up, a hand touched him. He tried not to jump in fear. Still, he turned quickly.

"Susan! I mean, Ms. Sharpe. What brings you back here?"

She tilted her head to one side and ran her finger down his arm again. This time, she picked up his hand. Payne thought things couldn't get any better. Then she placed his hand on her C-cup breast.

He smiled. "Would you like to go back to my place?" He struggled not to stammer as he spoke.

She responded with a simple nod of her head. Her silky hair bounced gently with the movement. *A woman of few words. I could get used to that.*

Closing took too long, but fortunately his apartment wasn't far. She didn't stand on ceremony and immediately, upon entering his place, began to disrobe. After locking the door, Payne followed suit. Like most guys, he only wanted to wait because he thought that's what women wanted.

This woman, Susan Sharpe, didn't seem interested in typical social graces. She had a get-down-to-business attitude that Payne found quite refreshing.

Now, both nude, he embraced her, kissing passionately and exploring with his hands. She responded in kind. She wiggle-walked him toward the couch—not letting go of him—and fell, pulling him on top of her. She definitely didn't want to waste any time.

Entering her almost felt painful. He never considered himself well-hung, but this felt so tight he had trouble getting in. *She must not have been with many men.*

She wrapped him up tight in her arms and legs, not allowing him any more movement than was needed for the act they performed. She didn't want him taking his time, or changing positions, or doing anything other than pleasing her vagina.

So that's what he did. He held his orgasm off for as long as he could, hoping the extended motion would make up for all the other play he would have done but she hadn't given him the opportunity. Still, the entire incident lasted a very short time.

He remained on top of her, inside her, after everything had finished—draining, dripping. She appeared satisfied, but Payne couldn't be sure. Still, he felt a real attraction for this woman. He hated to think of love so soon, especially when a man felt love easily while in the throes of passion. Or right after.

She smelled so good and her comfortable smile suggested she had no plans to leave. He rolled next to her, his penis falling out of her pussy and laying against his leg, but never lost physical contact. Her skin electrified his entire body.

Before he fell asleep, he hoped he'd given her even half as much pleasure as she'd given him. Then the lights went out.

He woke alone, disappointed and a bit hurt, but not entirely surprised. She was an enigma. Work didn't start for several hours so he looked around for a note from her, just a sign that he hadn't dreamed it all, and that the feelings growing inside him weren't all one-way. By the time he had to leave, he'd found none.

Payne sat quietly at the podium, hoping she would show. The day passed with no sign of her. He looked forward to seeing her again with earnest, but a fortnight passed before she returned, apparently at the beckon of the owner. The smile embedded on her face told that she'd been hired. Payne tried looking into her eyes, hoping to find an explanation for her absence. She seemed to not notice him at all. His heart sank.

She disappeared into the motor home parked behind the trailer, Payne assumed for an interview. The hours passed, some people straggled in to see the anomaly in the trailer, but the girl never came back out.

The time arrived for Payne to close up, which the owners often left him to do on his own. He folded up shop, put away any paperwork and signs, and walked away, taking one last look back at the motor home.

His eye, drawn to the image on the side of the trailer, saw only sadness. He'd hoped to make a date with her when she exited. The image on the trailer he saw in his mind moved as if to draw him closer, he shook it off like dust in an attic.

Payne had only gone inside the trailer once when first hired. The headless body moved as if filled with life, trying to escape the terrible bonds that held it. He never wanted to see it again after that. It disturbed him and he hadn't slept for two nights following.

Sadness accompanied him home to his small apartment this night, haunting him with dreams of a night he could have had with Susan Sharpe, a night of unspeakable ecstasy. Perhaps the time for him to stay put for a while had finally arrived.

However, the next day saw no trace of her and Payne began to wonder if the opportunity for him to plant his root had truly come or if he should seek out other goals, and other potential mates.

As the day wore on, he tossed between wanting to forget and wanting to find the truth. He felt an interest in her and she'd obviously reciprocated. Somehow, he couldn't just leave another day without knowing what happened to her.

Hours progressed slowly and Payne felt a kind of madness temporarily sweep over him and he longed for the end of the day. His plan—search for her; find where the desire of his heart had gone. He wanted to know for sure he hadn't imagined her touch, or her scent.

Darkness fell and the crowds continued to fill the area. But the time to close arrived and people began leaving. Payne knew this process could take another hour, so he waited.

The time had come. He folded the doors and windows, bolting down the show, making it secure. During the day he'd been confused but knew one thing for sure. He decided where he'd begin his search.

The motor home parked out back.

He approached the run-down conversion truck with a touch of fear. The creepy, too-short couple that hired him made his stomach turn. And something inside made him sure they held truth in little regard.

Rather than face them even once more, Payne decided on a more clandestine approach. He peeked in one of the windows. He met with curtains and dim light, leaving him without any real proof of anything.

He climbed to a different window. A bit of light streamed out from a crack in the curtain and through this Payne forced his eye. He struggled but found if he turned just the right way, he could see almost the entire room.

On the floor, leather straps bolted through the metal bottom, held tight the woman Payne searched for. She lay nude, struggling. The man, Owen Scragg, knelt beside her, fondled her, his dirty smile made even uglier by the lust in his eyes.

Into the room waddled Polly Scragg, wearing a dirty house dress and wiping a large kitchen knife against her filthy apron. Her enormous tits hung to her waist, no bra hampered them.

From the look, the knife had been cleaner than the apron when she started. Payne hoped they didn't use that on food. He felt bile in his throat.

"Quit foolin' 'round with 'er, Ow. You 'ad your fun last night. S'time to get down to business," she slurred with an almost British accent.

Owen Scragg removed his hands from Susan Sharpe's breasts and moved up toward her head. She gasped but Payne could not see her face.

"Don't worry, Honey," he said to Susan. "The drug is working. You won't feel nuthin'."

The troll of a man moved around to kneel above Susan's head, putting his back to the window Payne saw through, blocking his view. Scragg took the knife from his wife's hand and began to work against the gurgled sounds coming from Susan. All the while Payne could see nothing. But his heart tossed in his chest, knowing whatever was happening just a few feet away could not possibly be good.

When Scragg finally moved out of the way, Payne could see the horrible continuity, the fatal circle that completed the story and answered all the open ended questions but still left Payne chilled to his soul. Speechless, motionless, he stood there, watching, waiting…gasping.

Scragg had removed Susan's head with the butcher knife. Now, with a poor imitation of a doctor's precision, he injected something into the neck with large hypos. The body writhed and shuddered but failed to stop moving altogether.

Mrs. Scragg, who had stepped out of the room for the moment, re-entered with a camera in hand. She looked at the image with shock. Sucking in her breath, she spoke condescendingly to her betrothed.

"What the 'ell are you doin'?"

For a moment Payne thought she might run and call the police, even as he should be doing.

"You know you're s'posed to put those in diffrent places. If you inject in the same spot twice it'll turn black. People don't pay for no black spots, makes it look all fake," she said with a sneer and a little dance.

Mr. Scragg looked up at her then down at his masterpiece of macabre and shrugged like a child who had just been caught painting his school project the wrong color.

"This can be such a pain in the ass sometimes," he growled.

"Yeah," she agreed. "Too bad we can't keep 'em squirmin' for more'n a month."

When thy closes thine eyes against the darkness, keepest thy thoughts pure, for evil lurks ever near.

Closer...closer...

Keep the faith, my friends. If that doesn't work, at least keep a flashlight.

Blue Canyon

"Collect the BackSides"

Be sure to check out the fine asses on the back covers.
Each edition has a different ass. Collect them all.

www.songsinthekeyofgoth.webs.com